Whatever else I would do with my life, whatever else I would become, inside me there was a bright, burning core that whispered, witch. My desire for an existence that breathed more was like a kidney or a lung – a vital part of my whole. Without it, I just wouldn't work. I wouldn't be me.

Before I'd ever even known what to call it, I'd been seeking my own enakelgh. Had I found it last year, standing right in front of me the whole time in her faded, frayed clothes, with that careful, guarded expression painted across her face?

Gwydion had written in his notebook that enakelgh covens tended to end badly. It was too much of a risk. She was too much of a risk.

Wasn't that kind of power worth the risk, though?

~ Summer

Praise for

The Graces

'Fabulously dark and addictive.'
Bookseller

'The ending will make readers want to read the entire novel
again ... Though the facts may be slippery, the prose
never is; it's precise, vivid, and immediate. Powerful.'
Kirkus

'Mysterious, beautiful and unnerving, *The Graces*, like its titular
family, will keep you enthralled from beginning to end.'
Samantha Shannon, NYT bestselling author of *The Bone Season*

'As intricate and deadly as a spider's web. *The Graces* will draw
you in, with no guarantee of letting you go. It's powerful,
deadly, chilling and compelling. It is a masterpiece.'
Melinda Salisbury, author of *The Sin Eater's Daughter*

'Laure Eve breathes new life into witches. Thrilling,
dark and atmospheric *The Graces* will hold you
spellbound from start to finish.'
Jess Hearts Books

'Appropriately for a book about a family said to be witches,
The Graces is absolutely spellbinding!'
YA Yeah Yeah

'*The Graces* is one of those books that you finish and think,
damn, I wish I'd written that. Without a doubt, this is
one of my favourite books of 2016.'
The Mile Long Bookshelf

The Curses

LAURE EVE

90 YEARS OF EXCELLENCE
FABER & FABER

First published in 2019
by Faber and Faber Limited
Bloomsbury House, 74–77 Great Russell Street,
London WC1B 3DA

Typeset by MRules
Printed by CPI Group (UK) Ltd, Croydon CR0 4YY

A CIP record for this book
is available from the British Library

ISBN 978-0-571-32804-8

2 4 6 8 10 9 7 5 3 1

CHAPTER 1

Wolf had been back from the dead for almost three weeks when we had our first midnight picnic of the year.

Some childhood moments have a way of sinking deep into your bones, lingering on, casting their long shadows into your future. The midnight picnics were something my siblings and I had created between us as kids. They began as the kind of rebellion that ignited darkly addictive sparks in our bellies and that gradually, with repetition and the unofficial sanction of our parents, had become a spontaneous ritual.

We'd sneak out, laden with goods lifted from the pantry and fridge, and ramble into the darkness to find a place and a time and a moment that came together. We liked to allow our secret selves out of their everyday cages, just for a little while.

This was how I came to find myself in the hallway of our house, shivering in the late-night bite, eyeing my brother with bleary agreeableness as he stood in front of me and pulled my favourite scarf snug around my neck. I'd gone to bed early and he had shaken me awake, looming over me in the dark of my bedroom like a pretty, tousle-haired ghost.

It was early January and it had been a sharp and bitter month so far. Snow was promised but hadn't yet delivered. I had always seen snow as a purifying substance that offers a clean slate – until it melts, exposing the dirt hidden underneath all along.

'What are we doing?' I said, still stupid from sleep.

My forgot-to-be-a-whisper carried clean across the hallway, and Fenrin shushed me softly. Cold air wound around our legs from the open back door.

'It is veritably *shocking* that you haven't figured it out yet,' he murmured, and gave me his naughtiest smile.

I pulled my gloves out of the pocket of my leather jacket and wrestled my fingers into them. Fenrin took my gloved hand in his and led me outside, moving across the lawn's frozen, crackling grass towards the fruit grove at the bottom of the garden, heading straight for the guard dog.

The guard dog was the ancient oak tree that squatted at the start of the grove, and family legend said that it had been here before the house, which had been deliberately built within its shadow. It was a sprawling, knotted old thing with a mind of its own, known for swaying its branches on a still day, as if it felt a wind no one else could. In the spring, tiny star-shaped flowers grew haphazardly on its trunk, which Esther would pick and use in small batches of face-cream formulas that her customers swore made them look younger overnight. Her back orders for that cream often extended into the previous year. One anonymous customer paid handsomely to have a guaranteed annual order, with a stipulation that it be made from the very first flowers of the season as, according to Esther, they were the most potent.

Right now, though, it was too early in the year for the star flowers and the guard dog's trunk was bare, but its base was ringed in light. Tiny flames clawed up towards the tree from their candle plinths, turning the bark bright, sending orange-gold sparks against the dark. Higher up, the tree had been strung with fairy lights that glittered against the winter-sparse branches, illuminating the sky. Electric magic.

Spread out on the ground underneath the guard dog and its ring of candlelight was a blanket covered in plates and trays. Two dark figures crouched at its edges. They paused as we arrived, faces lit from below with candlelight.

I gave an entirely un-Summer-like gasp of delight.

'Midnight picnic,' I whispered gleefully, and Fenrin gave me a wink.

My sister, Thalia, balancing easily on her haunches, looked up at me. She was swaddled in a white woollen scarf that hung in huge mushrooming folds around her neck, her caramel hair spreading across the wool in soft waves. She had on her heaviest winter skirt, the colour of deep burgundy wine, and it swirled around her ankles, just long enough to flirt with the ground when she walked. I'd once borrowed it without asking. I was shorter than she was and had accidentally ripped the hem by repeatedly treading on it. Thalia hardly ever lost her temper, but when she did it was spectacular – almost worth provoking her just to see it.

Next to her was Wolf, his wasted frame buried under layers of muted pebble tones. With his black eyes and pale skin warmed underneath the fairy-light glow, he almost looked whole again – closer to the lean, lanky creature of the past, that distant country where we had all taken things like life and health for granted.

I arched a brow at him. 'Aren't you supposed to be swimming with the fishes?'

He grinned. 'Came back just to torture you all.'

We'd been making variations on this joke with

appalling regularity. It wasn't actually funny, but we pretended it was.

There was a time I would have thrown myself on top of Wolf and teased him relentlessly until he shoved me off, but that had been a different him, a different us. Now we were all so afraid to touch him, as if he would shatter like glass and break the illusion that he was really back.

Wolf might have been brought back to life, but it was obvious that he wasn't exactly at full health. A hospital visit had produced a cautious pronouncement of pneumonia, plus a bonus vague catchall of 'with complications'. The hospital had sent him off to convalesce armed with an impressive array of drugs, half of which sounded like they had been included just because the doctors wanted to cover all their bases.

I couldn't really blame them. It must be tough trying to diagnose a severe case of resurrection.

I sank to my knees. Down here we were sheltered from any wind by the guard dog's sturdy, craggy branches, and all was calm and still. The winter air took a mild bite out of my exposed cheeks, but my leathers kept the rest of me warm.

It was perfect.

Balanced on the blanketed ground before me was a tray of four mugs that held mounds of tiny marshmallows nestled in their depths, waiting to be filled with the cinnamon-laced hot cocoa that sat beside them in a giant, wool-swaddled pot, its spout curdling steam into the air. A stone serving plate was piled high with Thalia's signature chocolate brownies. Sugar-rimmed molasses cookies were stacked in a row next to them.

'Whose magnificent idea was this?' I asked.

'Mine,' said Wolf.

Fenrin scoffed. 'Not quite. He kept moaning about being bored and said he couldn't sleep, so I suggested it.'

'You know what we should do?' I said, inspired. 'We should have a late Yule party.'

'Erm, I think that ship has sailed,' Fenrin said. 'The point of the Yule party is to have it at, you know, *Yule*, and we didn't.'

'Why didn't you?' Wolf asked.

Silence descended, a silence so awkward that I felt my toes curling in my boots.

Because you were dead, and no one felt like celebrating.

'We should ask if we can have a party now,' I said doggedly, leaning back into the tree trunk and digging my spine comfortably against its rough bark.

Thalia sighed. 'Sure. And put in a request for a holiday to Atlantis while you're at it.'

Fenrin's mouth twitched. 'Slices of the moon in a pie.'

'Made of unicorn-butter puff pastry,' I said. Suddenly hungry, I reached forward and picked up a thick slab of chocolate brownie. Thalia had made them earlier that day. The fresh ginger she had used in the batter bit my tongue, and I savoured the sting.

'Oh god, it's freezing,' Fenrin moaned. 'Why didn't we do this inside the house like normal people?'

'It's bracing,' Thalia said. 'Wake-up weather.'

Thalia was a creature of nature. Being out energised her. I knew some people thought it was all a show that she only put on in public, but I'd watched her run out barefoot into fresh snow, late at night when she thought no one would see her. Later I'd found my beloved idiot sister desperately pressing her pinched, blue feet against her radiator.

Normally we ventured further afield than just the bottom of our garden, but this felt far enough right now. We had hardly left the house over the Christmas holidays, what with Wolf's condition and the adults hovering over us all like a particularly annoying combination of hawks and bees. But it hadn't felt suffocating. It had felt safe.

Wolf leaned forward and took two brownies. Each was thicker than my hand and almost as big as my palm. I watched, impressed, as he chomped through the first in two bites and immediately started on the second. Just how had he fitted that entire thing in his mouth so quickly?

One thing resurrection had *not* wasted away was his appetite. Recent mealtimes were quite a thing to behold. He ate everything in sight, with a relish that bordered on orgasmic. This was an entirely new thing; the Wolf of before had always tackled food fastidiously and almost never finished everything on his plate. The rest of the family had begun to tease him for his newfound gluttony, but I thought I understood it. Pleasure was a very real, obvious way of feeling alive, and Wolf needed to feel alive right now.

I grumbled through mouthfuls of brownie. 'Who the hell wants to wake up? It's winter. We should be hibernating like all the best mammals.'

'Don't be a cliché, Summer,' Thalia declared. 'Just because you have the name doesn't mean you're supposed to embody the season.'

'Names are important,' I rebuffed her. 'Names mould us. We fit into our names, our names don't fit into us. For example, as I recall, Fenrin's is based on a Norse name that translates as "asshole".'

Wolf burst out laughing in his rich chocolate voice. Absent so long from us, it was a glorious sound. Fenrin swallowed a sudden, happy grin and tried his best to look unimpressed.

'Well, what about Wolf?' he said. 'Are we really saying that his name means he's a hairy predator because . . .' He paused. 'Damn it.'

'You see?' I crowed. 'It's destiny.'

'Thalia was named for the muse of poetry,' Fenrin retorted, 'and when was the last time you saw her reading any?'

'The original Greek etymology of *Thalia*, brother mine, means *luxuriant. Verdant.*' Thalia stretched her arms upward and tipped her head back, exposing her throat. '*To blossom.*'

'And she does make things blossom,' I offered reasonably. 'Herbs. Flowers. The groinal regions of schoolboys.'

Thalia brought her arms down and shoved me. 'You always have to lower the tone.'

'Give me some of that cocoa, then, before it goes cold,' Fenrin said, surreptitiously moving closer to Wolf. I had begun to wonder if Wolf's newfound love of indulgence yet extended to my brother. Having the boy you were in love with come back from the dead must be *quite* the relationship minefield.

'Pour it yourself, lazy ass,' Thalia said comfortably, but she did it for him anyway because she was Thalia. I tipped my head back, feeling for the first time in a long time an ache of happiness.

Wolf spoke into the silence, punctuated by the soft soughing of the wind above us.

'I have something to say.'

My stomach clenched, and I wasn't sure why. Wolf was pressing a hand to his own chest, palm cupped over his heart.

'What you all did for me, bringing me to life . . .' he began with an earnestness that made me profoundly uncomfortable. 'Someday, I promise, I'll find a way to repay you for it.'

This was so unlike the sullen Wolf I knew that I was struck dumb.

'If you think about it, you're like my gods,' Wolf continued over our shock in a musing tone. His eyebrows rose. 'I should worship you.' He turned and placed his palms flat on the blanket-covered ground in front of a wide-eyed Fenrin. 'I should get on my knees and praise your names,' he declared soulfully, his voice climbing in proclamation.

I began to laugh while Thalia made shushing noises and Fenrin did nothing but gape stupidly.

'Summer, I thank thee,' Wolf howled up into the sky. 'Thaliaaa, thou art my *saviour*. Fenrin, I *worship* thee . . .'

'Hush, you'll wake the parentals,' Thalia hissed frantically.

'Oh please, as if they don't already know we're out here,' I sniffed. They usually tolerated whatever we might get up to as long as we were doing it on home ground where we were 'safe'.

Fenrin had the world's sweetest blush creeping across his face. A mischievous part of me wanted so badly to point it out, but I held my tongue. Wolf sat back and flashed me a highly enjoyable grin.

'I'm alive because of you,' he said, and my heart gave a lurch.

I knew now why Wolf had wanted this midnight picnic, why all of us did. It was a rare and precious snatched moment between us all. We were only back home for the weekend – tomorrow we'd be going back to the boarding school our parents had, in one of their regular fits of protective madness, transferred us to last term.

We would once again be cut off from the boy who had only just come back into our lives after leaving an awful, ragged hole behind in his absence. The hole still hurt. The wound still gaped. It felt like he could disappear on us again at any moment. It was a horrible feeling, like falling down forever and never hitting the ground.

There came a dull-sounding crack from out of the darkness beyond, cutting the moment in two.

'Badger,' Thalia whispered, eyes wide and glittering in the candlelight.

'Are badgers that clumsy?' I hissed back.

'They have those giant claws. It's probably hard to maintain your balance—'

'Guys,' Fenrin said.

A figure emerged from the murky trunk shapes of the grove beyond our circle of light. The grove backed onto the dunes, which led out and away to the beach and the coast, a wide expanse capable of throwing up any kind of creature it was possible to imagine – and imagination tended to be fuelled by the dark. In my head I saw a serpentine sea monster that had dragged itself out of the waves and slithered its way up to us from the cove. I saw a werewolf with bared and saliva-glistened jaws, shivering in a knotted-muscle crouch.

Sadly, it was more mundane than anything like that, though perhaps no less dangerous.

It was Marcus.

Marcus Dagda, our ex-best friend and Thalia's ex-love. He was banned from our house. He was banned from our lives. He was not supposed to be here.

He took a long look at us all, his face pale and waxy in the grey dim beyond our candlelight.

Then he collapsed to the ground.

CHAPTER 2

'They'll hear the engine,' Fenrin said.

I turned the key in the ignition and felt the car kick into life beneath my thighs.

'Just tell them I went to the all-night garage for ice cream because we're such crazy kids, so young and carefree, thinking nothing of the reckless abandonment it takes to eat freezing food in the middle of the freezing cold,' I replied.

Fenrin sighed. 'Just ... don't take too long.' His eyes lingered briefly on the huddled form of Marcus, curled up like a miserable beetle on the front seat beside me. 'Make sure he gets home.'

I wasn't too sure if that was out of concern for Marcus or a desire to know that he was far away from us. Probably, knowing Fenrin, a little of both.

They had been best friends once. I remembered them binge-watching old classic cartoons that no one had ever heard of, hunched over Marcus's secondhand laptop for hours, singing the theme of each cartoon on every single episode, and never skipping over it. (One of their absolute favourites was *Pinky and the Brain*, a weird cartoon about two laboratory mice plotting to take over the world.) They would make each other cry with laughter over obscure references that the rest of us never got. Best friends stuff, the stuff that binds hearts together.

It must have hurt both of them to lose that.

I eased us out of the driveway and up the lane, every crunch of loose stone underneath the tyres sounding like a twenty-one-gun salute, shattering the quiet night. In the rearview mirror I could see my brother, his arms folded around him as he watched us pull away. Thalia had stayed back in the garden with Wolf, who busily hoovered up the remaining cookies at her side.

She wasn't too good at being near Marcus these days.

I glanced at the object of our collective tension. He was staring at me oddly.

'What?' I asked. 'Something on my face? Chocolate? Blood? Invisible alien monster?'

'You're just so . . . bright,' he said.

I had to ask. 'Marcus, are you high right now?'

He sighed. 'No, nothing like that. Look, I'm sorry.'

'You said that already, several times. Are you sure you're okay?'

He didn't look okay. He looked stretched and faded, as if some of the colour had been washed out of him. The hair on his forehead had rolled into limp strings from the sweat damp on his skin, and his pale eyes were stark and luminous in the car's dashboard glow.

It had not been a pleasant experience, seeing him faint. He had recovered pretty quickly, but for a while there I'd been freaking out about a possible concussion, even though he didn't seem to have hit his head.

'I'm fine,' he muttered. 'It goes away after a moment. It only started recently. I get all light-headed, and colours get really bright around some people.' He paused. 'I hadn't fainted before, but there's a first time for everything, right? They said it might be migraines.'

Concern kicked in, making me feel bad about the 'high' comment. 'Have you been to a doctor?'

'Yeah. They've run a load of tests. Poked and prodded. They can't find anything.'

That sounded better than discovering some terrifying shadow on a scan, I supposed, but it was almost worse not to know.

'I'm really sorry,' I said. 'I hope it goes away.' No matter what had happened between us all, I wouldn't wish that on anyone.

Marcus sounded tired. 'Doubt it.'

'Why?' I asked.

But he wouldn't reply, and I wouldn't pry. I didn't get to mine him for secrets any more, now that we were no longer friends.

'Marcus,' I tried, swinging the car towards town, 'you've got to stop this.'

'Stop what?' he asked.

'Turning up at our house. I know you showed up in the garden at the twins' birthday. Thalia told me. If our parents had caught you here tonight, you'd be in deep shit.' I risked a glance. He was staring out the passenger window, watching the landscape slide past.

'I know that,' he said at last. 'But you guys are back at that boarding school, so you're never around. I haven't seen any of you in weeks and I can't exactly call you on the phone … I didn't know how else to talk to you.'

'What about?'

Silence.

It didn't matter. I knew what this was about. In recent times, with Marcus, it was only ever about one thing.

'Look,' I said, trying to be kind, 'it truly sucks, but she can't be with you, okay? It's just too risky. She's moved on and I really think you should too.'

In fact I had no real evidence that Thalia had ever moved on from Marcus, but here I was saying it anyway, hoping it did the trick, expecting the standard, hurt retorts from him. *She was my girlfriend. I'm still in love with her. It isn't fair. Just because I'm an outsider.*

Your stupid family curse has wrecked my life.

So I was utterly astonished when he said, with high irritation lacing his voice, 'What? No. That's all over, okay? It was over ages ago. Don't you think I know that? This isn't about Thalia.'

'Then what is it about?'

'River.'

I felt my hands grip tight around the steering wheel.

It was the first time I had heard the sound of her name out loud since the night Wolf had come back. We did not talk about who was responsible for his death and who was responsible for bringing him back to us. We did not talk about how it felt like there was a void in the middle of our coven, an empty space that should be occupied by another girl.

We did not talk about River.

'She told me what she did,' he continued. I felt him stealing an appraising glance at me.

I forced myself to remain calm. 'Did she?'

'She told me about Wolf.'

'And what did she say about that?'

'She told me about conjuring the wave that took him into the sea and drowned him. And then how she brought him back from the dead. *Jesus*, Summer!'

'Sorry,' I said, straightening the car with a hammering heart. In shock at his bluntness, I had jerked the steering wheel too hard to the left and sent us swinging across the road. 'Just . . . run that past me again. She really told you all that?'

'I didn't believe her. Not at first. The rumour going round is that Wolf fell in with a bad crowd, did a load of drugs, went off the rails and disappeared for six months to detox. It's easier, right? In the absence of any other evidence, it fits.'

It did, and I was relieved to hear that it had caught on.

Fenrin, Thalia and I had made a pact. We would not turn Wolf's life into a nightmare circus by admitting to anyone what had really happened. Now that we had him back it was our duty to protect him any way we could.

So we lied.

We lied to our parents and we lied to his. I normally hated lying but it was the only thing we could do. Wolf had once confessed that the first time he had been sent to spend the entire summer with us, aged fourteen, was because his parents had wanted to get him away from what they deemed a bad crowd of friends – the kind of friends who had enjoyed getting their teenage kicks from petty crime and some moderately serious drug use.

Wolf had been embarrassed by the admission, claiming that he had never participated, but it seemed like a plausible fit to suggest that the same kind of thing had happened again on a grander scale. It wasn't hard to see why the adults believed that drugs were involved, considering Wolf's thin and hollow appearance, and we couldn't afford to disabuse anyone of the idea.

Wolf wasn't a Grace, or not exactly. He lived in the city with his parents, who were long-time friends of the family, but he'd spend summers with us, visit for Yule and Beltane and Imbolc, for my birthday and the twins'. He was part of our family circle, so naturally that made him ripe fodder for gossip. We knew word would get around about his return – how could it not in a small town, with small-town minds? So all we needed to do was make sure we were controlling the story.

Resurrection – it was utterly unprecedented. It went against all the laws of nature. I didn't think anyone would even believe us. The crash-and-burn scenario seemed easier all round.

'It fits,' I echoed, 'because it's what happened.'

'No, it isn't,' Marcus said. He sounded so sure that I found myself snatching glances at his profile as I drove, looking for clues about what he thought he had seen tonight.

'Why the hell would you believe a crazy story like that from someone like River?' I asked.

'Because of what else she can do.'

'What are you talking about?'

He rubbed his face, discomforted. 'I think … she's the reason I've started getting sick.'

I pulled the car over to a lay-by, stopping next to one of the walking paths in the woods that ran parallel to the road, and cut the engine.

'Well, this categorically does *not* feel like the start of a serial-killer film,' Marcus said, nerves making his voice bubble.

'I just want to make sure I don't crash the car,' I said firmly. 'And now I want to make sure I understand what you're telling me, which is that River is responsible for your illness.'

Marcus thought for a moment. 'I wanted to

believe her about Wolf,' he said, 'but I couldn't, quite. So I tested her. God, it was a stupid thing to do.' He drew in a papery thin breath. 'She asked me to give her a desire. Something I really wanted, something other people wouldn't necessarily know about. A secret desire.'

'What did you ask for?' I said softly.

'I told her I wanted to be a witch.'

My heart spiked and then sank. 'Because of Thalia.'

I understood Marcus's reasoning all too well. It was all about the Grace curse. Our precious, savage family legacy. The curse always reared its murky head around the age we began to fall in love, running its awful course until one of us ended up dead. Either us, or the lover we had chosen. Accidental death or intentional – it was always the same result. Someone died because we dared to love. It was impressively specific, too – it only seemed to bloom when a Grace fell for an outsider, not another witch.

If Marcus somehow became a witch, he could theoretically circumnavigate the pitfalls of the curse in order to be with Thalia again, couldn't he? But he was shaking his head.

'No,' he insisted, and then amended, 'at least, not just that. I wanted to ... be able to *feel* magic, the way you do. I used to watch you all, you know, and envy you. You don't understand what it's like being on the edge of that. It's as if your outlines are somehow richer and brighter than everything else around you. The witch bit of you – that intuition, that power, that *moreness* of you all – it's there all the time, inside you, like an innate part of you. I want to be able to feel what you feel. I want to be able to feel magic, down in my blood.'

His brain seemed to catch up with his mouth and process what was coming out of it. He fidgeted, quieted, looked away from me.

Last year, I had discovered the existence of a website called 'The Truth about the Graces'. It was an info dump dedicated entirely to my family that anonymously detailed every scrap of rumour, insight, and downright made-up bullshit the town we lived in had conjured up about us over the years.

Anonymous it might officially be, but to me it was plain as day that the author of the website was Marcus.

I was furious for a while, but though it might have started off as an invasive, petty revenge tactic for being caught *in flagrante* with my sister and unceremoniously kicked out of our lives, it wasn't really about that at all. Marcus was an avid researcher with a giant brain, a thirsty curiosity that might even outweigh mine, and a deep, unrelenting fascination with magic. It had been our favourite way to tease him, back when we were all the best of friends. He craved it the way some people crave sunlight. His website had grown from a cheap little rumour mill to a sprawling thesis about magic and power, rite and ritual, folklore and religion.

'So what did River do?' I asked him.

He gave a bitter laugh. 'I asked her to make me feel magic, didn't I? Well, I feel it, all right. I feel it so much that it makes me sick.'

Slow horror burned its way down me like cheap alcohol. 'What? No. How do you know that's what it is?'

'There's a pattern. The only time I feel like this is when I'm around her.' He fidgeted. 'And now ... all of you.'

The pieces fell into place.

'That was why you fainted?' I asked. 'Because of us?'

'Look, I didn't know for sure,' he said. 'I came to your house because I needed to test out my theory.'

'Some way to test out a theory, Marcus.'

He just shrugged. I knew he was determined to the point of recklessness in pursuit of his theories.

'That's a horrible thing for her to do to someone,' I said slowly.

'I don't think she means it, not like that. She told me about all the other things she's responsible for. She just wants someone to shut up, or go away, and then it happens, but it *really* happens, in a way that's totally out of control. It's like . . . with her, a wish can become a curse.'

Wishes as curses.

Last year, an ex-fling of mine, Jase Worthington, had spent a good deal of his precious time on this earth starting many a nasty rumour about me. While we were together, I'd felt like nothing more than his dirty little secret. Everyone knew you didn't get properly tangled with a Grace, so to him I could only be a novelty, a shiny, exotic toy to take out and use and fascinate himself with. He had a far more passionate and intimate relationship with surfing than with me because the sport asked nothing of him.

While out indulging in his passion, Jase had broken his leg. This happened not long after we had split, and everyone at school decided that I'd cursed him in revenge – but I hadn't, even though I'd been tempted. I didn't bind him, hurt him, or otherwise shut him up by any magical means other than my own cutting mouth.

I knew what living under a curse felt like. I did not curse people lightly.

I had thought about Jase breaking his leg, though. I had *wanted* it to happen. I remembered the thought so clearly. If he loved surfing so much, wouldn't it just be too bad if something happened to take that away from him, even temporarily?

It was a mean, dark, fleeting little thought. What I didn't know back then was that mean, dark, fleeting thoughts tended to come to life around River. Later, much later, she admitted to me that she had broken his leg with a thought of her own as she'd watched him surfing. She had wanted to punish him.

For me.

'What is it like, having Wolf back?' Marcus asked. 'Is he okay?'

I blew out a breath. 'For the most part.'

'Does he seem different?'

'He's been through a lot. That's got to change you. I'm not sure he's totally dealt with it all yet, to be honest, but that's okay. We'll help him and he'll be fine, and he'll be the old Wolf again, laughing and japing his way through life.'

The last had been intended to lighten the mood. Marcus had met Wolf a few times over the years, and he knew enough of him to get that if there was one description that did not fit our Bulgarian brooder, it was 'laughing and japing'.

I started up the car. I felt as if Marcus could see through my words to the doubt that lay beyond them. No, actually, I didn't know whether Wolf would ever be the way he was before, but we were going to make damn sure that life for him from this moment on was as good as we could make it.

The rest of the short journey was conducted in silence. We reached the quiet residential street where Marcus lived, and I parked a few doors down from his house.

He just sat there.

I tried. 'Do you want me to walk you to the door . . . ?'

'I can walk,' he responded quietly. 'It's fine.'

I gave a gusty sigh. 'This is ridiculous. How can you know for sure that it's River who's responsible for making you sick? Especially if she doesn't even realise it herself?'

'You're right,' he said, and so agreeably that I was taken aback. 'We need more evidence.'

'We? We're a team now, are we?'

Marcus shrugged. 'I can look into it on my own. But while I'm doing that, you'd better come up with a contingency plan because, if I'm right, this isn't going to stop. It's only going to get worse.'

'What makes you say that?'

He opened the door. Paused.

'You think I'm the only one who has asked her for something?' he said. 'There are more of us.'

With that, he walked off down his road, hunched against the cold. I sat in the car watching him, my heart fluttering anxiously in my chest.

There are more of us.

'River,' I said into the dark. 'What the hell are you playing at?'

CHAPTER 3

It wasn't snooping, I told myself, as I stood in front of the door to my father's study.

It was a contingency plan.

I opened the door as gingerly as I could and slipped inside, surveying the room's cushioned, velvet silence. I had spent a lot of time in this room over the years, slipping in to curl up beside the darkness of the walnut-wood desk with a book, or flopping into the plum-coloured, high-backed armchair over by the windows, earphones in and listening to music. But I normally neither entered nor touched anything inside without permission.

As a child I had been allowed, under supervision, to open the sturdy, glass-fronted cabinets that lined the back wall and examine all the tantalising things that Gwydion kept locked up in them. His study cabinets housed all manner of divination tools – obscure, odd and beautiful objects collected from around the world. The giant golden ball with the complicated mechanics inside its hollow shell. The slender rods of varied metals lying parallel to one another, never touching, on a velvet cloth on the middle shelf. Runes carved from stag bone lying in a jumble on top of a thick wool pouch – their creamy surfaces giving off a gentle glow in the winter sun when the light from the nearby window hit them just right. The tools of his trade, Gwydion would say with a wry note to his voice.

My father, the diviner.

He was in demand by high-level business types of all stripes to help them 'strategise for the future'. His official job title was 'forecasting consultant' because no one would ever admit to hiring a witch. The only real difference between him and the cheap fortune tellers who sat behind satin curtains was that he did it for a lot more money.

I used to be fascinated by each shiny thing on display in those cabinets, handling them as often as Gwydion would let me, willing them to show me all the secret truths of my bewitching little world. But it wasn't the divination tools I had come for. Not today.

It was the notebooks.

The printed books on magical theory filling out the black bookcase underneath the window were well-thumbed – my sister, Thalia, had a pile of them in her room at any given time, creased and broken open at various pages – but in addition to those, on the top shelf of the cabinet next to the door sat a bunched row of plain leather notebooks.

When we were young, Fenrin had told me they were our father's personal diaries, full of secret, embarrassing thoughts and scandalous anecdotes about everyone we knew. Thalia had dismissed them as notes on his clients, guarded simply because of the sensitive information they held. When I had quizzed Gwydion, he had said they were his notes on the craft, gathered over years of personal research – his own Book of Shadows.

He had shown me once, flipping one quickly under my nose, a woefully inadequate attempt to sate what he had always called my 'curiosity monster'. All my eager eyes had caught were pages and pages of handwritten notes in Gwydion's scrabbly, looping style, broken up with the occasional sketch of a symbol or talisman.

I'd yearned to read them properly but I'd never been allowed to, and none of the study cabinets opened without the tiny brass key that Gwydion always kept in his wallet.

The same tiny brass key that had a copy in the hidden drawer of his desk.

Not long ago I had found the drawer, and subsequently the key, completely by accident – and then promptly put it out of my mind. It was not my business to know.

But now?

Gwydion was away on a business trip, and Esther had left Fenrin, Thalia and me home alone for the morning to run an errand in town. We were taking the train back to boarding school in less than three hours. There would never be a better time.

I liberated the cabinet key from its secret drawer and pulled the first set of notebooks from the top shelf. Then I sat on the rug underneath the bookcase, drowsy winter light falling over my shoulders through the window. Hot coffee steamed its way into the air from the mug at my hip. Soft rain pattered at the glass, and the sky was a bright, dense grey at my back.

I opened the first notebook with a churning sense of guilt, dreading that Fenrin had been on the money and I was about to get some far too personal insights into my own father – no, no, and dear *god*, no – but I was relieved to discover that they were as Gwydion had said: scrapbooks filled with fragments of myth and lore that he had picked up from all over the place, bits of scribbled ritual and spells in his sometimes esoteric shorthand, and theories of magic that I'd never even heard of before. It wasn't until I'd skim-read through three notebooks and opened the fourth that I found what I was looking for.

The first page boasted a title in Gwydion's careful looping style:

On the nature of enakelgh

Every page after that was covered in typed words instead of Gwydion's handwriting. I might have assumed that he had, for whatever puzzling reason, decided to print out his typed-up thoughts and stick them onto the pages of his notebook . . . were it not for the fact that at the bottom of each printed page was a URL: thetruthaboutthegraces.com.

Marcus's website.

I had no idea that Gwydion was even aware of it. As with a startling number of subjects in our family, it had simply never been discussed, and I wasn't going to be the one to pile on my sister's acute misery over Marcus by pointing out its existence to anyone. I was aware in theory that our parents might know a lot more about the secrets of our tangled relationships than they let on, but being confronted with the evidence was unsettling.

The first printed page began in what I immediately recognised as Marcus's formal storyteller style:

> Have you ever wondered about the Graces' division of their magic into four elemental powers? Its source can be found within the Four Bells folklore that everyone local to them has likely heard of at some point in their lives.

I remembered this section of the website all too well. It was a detailed dive into the origins of the Grace curse.

> What you might not know is that the Four Bells story has older, pre-Christian roots, and those roots are firmly embedded within the Grace family. So if you haven't heard the older version, here's a quick summary:
>
> Once upon a time a demon comes to town disguised as a young man. As is the nature of such creatures, he gets busy spreading trouble and darkness among all the townsfolk, causing death and destruction with much glee. During this chaotic spree he ends up meeting the daughter of a family of witches and, in a fit of passionate lust, tries to spirit her away with him.

Naturally her family isn't pleased with the idea, but the crafty and highly persuasive demon ends up turning half the town against them. He is only defeated when four of the witches join their power together to drive him out with a banishing curse.

Just before he is pushed out of town, though, the demon inflicts a curse of his own on the witch family – if he can't be happy with a witch, then no one can.

Since that day, so the legend goes, every Grace witch tends to be dramatically unlucky in love. Whether this is a self-perpetuating prophecy or not (if you believe you're cursed in love, do you subconsciously encourage situations that reinforce the belief?) is something no one can answer for sure.

Regardless, that centuries-old tale of myth has perpetuated a tradition in the Grace family. When each member reaches the age of ten, they are asked to choose an inclination: earth, air, fire or water. Each of these inclinations has its own particular talents and personality traits [click here to navigate to the elements section of the website for fuller detail] and each witch works with those talents ever after.

Four witches joined together from each element create a formidable team, one powerful enough to defeat a demon. All such stories begin rooted in some nugget of truth, no matter how distorted they become in the retelling.

But what about the demon? If the Graces are descended from that original witch family, shouldn't there be someone supposedly descended from him – an opposing force of huge power that threatens the order of things?

Here, Marcus's typing stopped and Gwydion's handwriting took over. He had scribbled:

This seems to be where the idea of the 'spirit' element originally comes from. A spirit witch = an outsider who wasn't necessarily brought up as a witch and might be unaware of the power they have. There are documented past instances of such outsiders being brought into an established circle as the fourth.

When four are bound together, and include a spirit witch, this soul circle, or 'enakelgh', supposedly gives every member huge potential power, more than they ever could have dreamed of without the spirit witch — but this element is by its very nature chaotic, and therefore whoever represents it also brings with them huge potential <u>darkness</u>.

Binding a spirit witch to you is a tricky, dangerous business. Yes, it means you can control them and their power, but that influence goes both ways — their power is now inside you, too. This is the upside and the downside of enakelgh. It's a two-way street. You bleed into one another until it's hard to say where you end and their chaos begins. You might even start thinking that it's <u>your</u> chaos and act on it ...

It's far safer for everyone to stay away from outsiders altogether. Enakelgh covens have a tendency to end badly. (Lest we ever forget what happened with E's cousin ...)

My breath seemed to get stuck in my throat.

I read and reread those few sentences over and over until the links began to form. I knew that witch covens – in our family, at least – were always in groups of four, one for each element. I was an air witch, Fenrin was a water witch, and Thalia was earth. *Enakelgh*, though, had *spirit* as one of the four. An outsider who brought both huge power and huge darkness with them.

It was River.

Last year, she had taken the role of earth witch when we had tried a spell to break the curse without Thalia, who was usually the earth witch in our rituals – but I knew at the time that earth wasn't who or what she was. Earth was grounded, characterised by a deep connection of the senses, but that wasn't River. I had always felt that she was something other than that.

Now I knew why.

E's cousin. Gwydion had to be talking about Esther. I tried to picture all the cousins of hers that I knew, but she had a few. I couldn't remember something bad happening to a cousin of hers, but then again my parents were not exactly forthcoming with details on the myriad tragedies in our sprawling family.

When our grandmother was alive, she would relish regaling us with morbid anecdotes of previous generations, but Esther hated her doing that and would usually put a stop to it before she could get too far into the tale. She'd rather we lived in ignorance than know the truth, as if ignorance was an effective defence against pain.

It was all because of the curse, of course.

None of us had ever managed to discover if and

how it had manifested in our parents' generation. Esther seemed to be one of the few Graces who had successfully kept out of its reach, and everyone knew how she had done it.

She had married someone she wasn't in love with.

I slid sharply away from pursuing that thought trail. Thalia was obsessed with our parents' relationship, but I preferred not to dwell on it at all. Careful pairing was a tradition in our family. Though we fell short of arranged marriages, we didn't fall *that* far short.

Thankfully, I had yet to suffer any suggestive nudging, but Thalia hadn't been so lucky. It was hoped, maybe even assumed, that she and Wolf might solidify their friendship into something more, but the idea had always been vastly distasteful to them both. Thalia saw Wolf as a cousin, and Wolf saw Fenrin as ... Well, I wondered if Esther would ever catch which way the wind was blowing there.

As if evoking my mother in my thoughts had acted like a conjuring spell, I heard the unmistakable sound of the car pulling into the driveway.

She was back.

I leapt into action, scooping up the notebooks by their spines, winging them shut and hoisting them up to the top shelf of the open cabinet, trying to stack them in the order I had found them. In my hasty ramming, the edge of a notebook caught on something, and I could only watch as an object slithered past, dropping heavily to the floor with an audible thud.

'Shit!' I hissed in dismay.

The object must have been pushed right to the back of the bookcase. I had vaguely noticed before that half the notebook stack always stuck out a bit too far over the edge of their shelf, but the top of the cabinet was too high for me to see why.

I glanced down at what had fallen. Something weighty, judging by the thump, shaped in a slim rectangular block made of black velvet. I'd have to drag the swivel chair over and stand on it to get this back up on the shelf. I had visions of the chair rotating under my precariously stretched body and me falling to the ground in a very loud, very noticeable heap, possibly killing myself in the process.

There was no time. I'd just have to put it back later.

I reached up and tidied the notebooks, closed the cabinet door, and wrestled the little brass key from my jeans pocket. As I locked the cabinet and winced at the little click, I heard footsteps in the hallway. I turned to the desk and dropped to my knees, wriggling underneath it and feeling around for the catch I knew was there – it had to be there, somehow it had moved ... My probing fingers found it, pressed it, slid the key into the drawer, pressed it shut. I pushed myself back out, rocked back on my heels and breathed out a steady breath. The footsteps grew louder, and then I heard the telltale creak of the middle step on the stairs to the first floor.

I bent down and picked up the velvet block. It was a drawstring bag with something inside it, almost as long as my hand but slender enough to slide underneath my sweater and into the waistband of my jeans. I sucked in my stomach to give it room, pushed it down, and then I sidled out of the study, peering into the corridor.

Esther was crossing the first-floor landing outside my room to go up the stairs to the boys' floor. Doubtless she wanted to take a quick look at Wolf and make sure he was all right, just as she had been doing approximately every half an hour since he had arrived for the weekend.

Right now Wolf's bad luck was my good luck. I waited until I heard a door being opened with an answering male grumble, then stole quietly along the corridor. I reached my room and eased the door open, closing it with a palpable relief.

Pulling the velvet bag out from under my jumper, I balanced its weight on my palm. The drawstrings trailed from its top, tempting me to open it up. If it had been put out of sight behind Gwydion's notebooks, we were not supposed to know about it.

How I loved knowing things that I was not supposed to know about.

I tugged on the twisted little ropes, opening up the bag and sliding out its contents. A block wrapped tightly in black muslin sat on my palm. There were too many layers to tell for sure, but it felt like an oversized pack of cards.

'Summer?' came my mother's voice from the first-floor landing.

I stuffed the muslin bundle back into the bag, dropped it onto my rug and kicked it under my bed, turning round just as my door opened. Privacy in this house was currently at an all-time premium. I'd look at the contents the first chance I got, but in the meantime—

'I've been doing my homework all morning,' I said brightly.

Esther had a deeply sceptical look on her face.

Rude.

CHAPTER 4

At first, I hadn't understood what it was about River that attracted me.

She had been like an itch I couldn't reach to scratch. I was the one who had sent Fenrin looking for River in the library last year on the day we had introduced ourselves to her, intending to charm her into having lunch with us. I was the one who pursued her, invited her over, took over her time and made her spend it with me.

I remembered the words in Gwydion's wiry handwriting, the ones that kept running their thrilling fingers up my spine:

> When four are bound together, and include
> a spirit witch, this soul circle, or 'enakelgh',
> supposedly gives every member huge potential
> power ...

Whatever else I would do with my life, whatever else I would become, inside me there was a bright, burning core that whispered, *witch*. My desire for an existence that breathed *more* was like a kidney or a lung – a vital part of my whole. Without it, I just wouldn't work. I wouldn't be me.

Before I'd ever even known what to call it, I'd been seeking my own *enakelgh*. Had I found it last year, standing right in front of me the whole time in her faded, frayed clothes, with that careful, guarded expression painted across her face?

Gwydion had written in his notebook that *enakelgh* covens tended to end badly. It was too much of a risk. She was too much of a risk.

Wasn't that kind of power worth the risk, though?

Distracted, I didn't even notice Fenrin and Wolf until I was almost on top of them. I walked into the kitchen, catching them leaning their hips into the countertop and leaning into each other even more. Wolf's head was angled in as he whispered into Fenrin's ear. His fingers hovered over Fenrin's belt, brushing at the skin there.

'Oh shit, sorry,' I said, attempting to back-pedal.

I guessed they had resolved the simmering tension between them. I was glad, for Fenrin, for them both. For a while there I'd wondered if they could ever be what they were to each other before.

Honestly, though, what on earth were they doing? We'd all invested a lot of time and energy into keeping their secret for them, and neither could exactly have been accused of being brazen about their feelings towards each other before now. It had always been something to hide. We were a family of closed doors.

Wolf withdrew a little, his eyes lighting on me. He smiled, said something else into the shell of my brother's ear. Then he turned, disappearing through the far door and into the airy conservatory beyond.

I crossed my arms and faced my brother. He looked positively dazed.

'Please put your sex face away,' I said with a gagging sound. 'No one ever needs to see that.'

His gaze focused on me as if he'd only just noticed I was there.

'Listen,' he said. 'We need to get out of that heinous boarding school.'

I raised a brow.

It was no secret that all three of us were having a less than stellar experience at Bishop St James. It boasted one of the most exclusive and expensive educations in the country, but in my experience, just because something was expensive, it didn't mean it was any damn good.

'Wolf,' Fenrin said, with obvious relish, 'is staying here.'

I frowned. 'What do you mean, *staying here*?'

'I don't know how he's done it, but he's managed to persuade everyone that this is the best place for him to overcome his illness. Sea air versus city pollution. Quiet. Restful. No traffic, no noise. A real convalescence. They're going to let him stay until Ostara and then see how he is.'

Ostara, the spring equinox, was still over two months away.

'Isn't that what they do with invalids in Victorian novels?' I grumbled to cover the sudden hope no doubt blooming brightly on my face.

Fenrin galloped past Joke Street and made a hard left into Sincerity Alley.

'We have to be here, Summer,' he said, pinning me with an intense gaze. 'He needs us.'

For a moment I wondered if it was Fenrin's brain or Fenrin's groin doing the thinking for him – but that wasn't fair. Hadn't we all sworn to do whatever was necessary to protect Wolf? Didn't we owe him at least that, and much more, for what he had been through?

'Fen,' I said, 'we already tried, remember, at the end of last term? Gwydion and Esther totally shot us down. We're out of options.'

It was as quick and hasty a reminder as I could make it. That memory belonged to the murky time of Wolf's absence, a time when we'd deliberately checked our consciences at the door to conjure the world's riskiest, coldest plan – kidnap River and threaten her life in order to try and bring Wolf back.

The plan had worked, but that didn't mean I was proud of it.

'Maybe not,' Fenrin mused.

'What does that mean?'

'It means, baby sister, that sometimes you have to take fate into your own hands. It's you of all people who first taught me that.'

'Now I understand what Dr Frankenstein felt like,' I muttered. 'What kind of monster have I created?'

He slung an arm around my shoulders. 'Come on. We have to go and pack.'

I had never given much thought to Wolf's relationship with his parents before.

I'd known Bran and Ivailo Grigorov my whole life – they were thick as thieves with my parents – but they were part of the world of adults and of all that entailed. Wolf's absence and subsequent re-emergence was the first time I'd begun to see them as real. Shadowed eyes, sunken tired faces, vulnerability trembling all over them like a rabbit's nose. It was the first time I'd really understood that, when faced with the stark, unfeeling realities of life, adults very often had no more idea what to do than teenagers.

It was not a comforting thought, but it was a curiously liberating one. If adults weren't as in charge as I'd always been led to believe, that meant I could, as Fenrin had said, make my own fate. The world was changeable, swayed and shaped by the young as much as the old.

Sighing, I tossed the last of my clean socks into the open suitcase at the foot of my bed. There was a mandatory uniform up to the final two years of this school, at which point you could wear your own clothes – within the narrow parameters the good, conservative folk of Bishop St James had set, anyway. The kind of outfits I wore tended not to fit into those parameters so well.

Until Fenrin brought it up, it hadn't occurred to me to fight our fates again, but now the idea began to boil inside me. Considering the trouble and the expense our parents had gone to to get us into Bishop St James, I had thought it selfish to try and wriggle out of it – but as I saw that neat little guilt trap for what it was, my resentment started up a good simmer.

I hated that we had just slid right into that school as if our lives ran on greased rails, hated that the school couldn't care less whether we were dumb as bricks because what it understood was money.

I wondered if my second term there would bring the delights of finding dirt tipped into my bed again because, according to a couple of the girls I shared a dorm house with, I looked like I preferred 'sleeping in a grave'. Or maybe they would carry out last term's idle promise of throwing my black clothes into a tub full of bleach. At least they wouldn't be able to cut my hair off in my sleep like they had threatened to do. As I pictured their faces when they saw the new haircut I had got over the holidays, I couldn't stop a smile of satisfaction surfacing.

Which reminded me. I turned to my dressing table and took up a lacquered pot which had 'Summer's Hair Wax' handwritten on its surface in gold marker pen. An indispensable homemade Christmas present from Thalia, who was becoming more like our mother every day. At least I stood to benefit from her developing beauty-product skills.

I made sure the lid was screwed on tight and then gently lobbed the little pot towards my suitcase, but I overshot. It hit the slant of the suitcase's open top and rolled down the other side, heading deep into the recesses of that nebulous unexplored world – the space under my bed.

Swearing softly, I got on my hands and knees and peered into the darkness beneath. Vague shapes, mingled with dust bunnies that had likely started their own breeding programme, loomed out at me.

I really needed to clean up in here.

I lay down and reached an arm in, feeling for the pot's telltale hard surface, but instead my questing fingers found a soft, blocky object, and I drew it out, puzzled.

The black velvet drawstring bag.

In the circus surrounding Wolf and the impending misery of our boarding school prison, I had almost forgotten about what I had taken from Gwydion's study.

I widened the bag's opening and tipped out the black, muslin-wrapped block. Its length ran from the tip of my middle finger to the base of my palm. The muslin was wound over and over with black ribbon and tightly tied, as if the ribbon were a straitjacket. I picked at the knot without much success until I lost patience and cut it away with scissors. Then I turned the package over and unwrapped the cloth, staring at what lay underneath.

A girl stared back at me.

She wore a heavy green dress that hung in thick, rumpled folds around her feet. A circlet as delicate as a spiderweb rested on her light hair, which hung down over her arm in a thick braid. At her feet scurried two little mice. Three white birds crowned her head. The art was done in a spartan, sweeping style, the lines thin and sure. It reminded me of calligraphy, if calligraphy were more image than word, printed on something like an oversized playing card.

I picked it up, and more lay underneath – a whole deck of images. I spread them out on the ground in front of me. There were more figures, richly dressed, clutching scrolls or swords or candles or a pair of delicate gold scales. Rolling, swirling landscapes in vivid colours. Different symbols made with metal, twig or bone.

They were all strange, all beautiful, and I thought I knew exactly what they were for. My father was a diviner, after all – though I had to admit that they didn't look like any tarot deck I'd ever seen before. None of them had names to identify what they were supposed to represent, presuming that the user would have to come up with their own interpretations, and there was no Major or Minor Arcana that I could see.

If they were supposed to be a divining tool, how come they weren't on display in Gwydion's cabinets like all the others? Why were they hidden away from sight?

Gwydion obviously hadn't noticed the cards were missing. They had been tucked away and forgotten about at the very back of his highest shelf, and the muslin they were wrapped in smelled musty and old. I hazarded a confident guess that he hadn't looked at this deck in a long time. There was something maddeningly familiar about them, as if they told a story I'd heard once before, but I had no time to figure it out now. We were leaving to catch our train in less than half an hour.

That meant I could take them with me.

I looked at my suitcase. I looked at the beautiful, beguiling cards spread out in front of me.

It took me a full microsecond to make the decision, and it was like a warm buzz in my bones. We had been expressly forbidden by our parents from taking anything like this to Bishop St James, in case it 'ruffled any delicate sensibilities'.

Then again, since when had I ever enjoyed doing what I was told?

CHAPTER 5

Bishop St James School was all about appearances.

It had begun life as a huge, grandiose manor house made of elegant, severe stone and rows of tall, gleaming windows, like something from an Edwardian romance. The drive, wide as a boulevard, swept you up to the house as if ushering you in between the twin columns that sentried the front door. The front hallway was dominated by a wood-panelled staircase and lined with plinths showcasing the heads of previous headmasters as marble busts. Not one woman among them, something I had wryly noted on first arriving. A glass table with the world's most impractically enormous china vase towered over everyone's heads in the foyer.

It was rich. Impeccable. Intimidating.

Thalia, Fenrin and I took the train to the local station, where we were greeted by private, dark-grey estate cars lined up like a silent array of sharks. Bishop St James was the kind of school that provided a pick-up service for those who condescended to take public transport, and half its students, it seemed, were coming back today. I had seen quite a few people I recognised on the train ride down. They had ignored me, so I had ignored them. It was an unspoken arrangement that suited me just fine.

The private cars were shared. I stood in the girls' line with Thalia, and Fenrin took the boys' line. The dorms at Bishop St James were segregated, so the boys were driven to the school via a separate entrance. Fen was bundled into a waiting car with three other boys who, judging by their loud discussions of the nubile ladies they had 'fully nailed' and the copious beers they had 'fully drunk' over the holidays, were all great friends.

Thalia was a senior and I was a junior, but today we shared a car with three tiny, chatty Year 8 girls whose nerves at sharing with older girls manifested in great gusts of shrieking giggles that soon gave me a headache. Thalia was silent. There was nothing good to say.

It was another twenty-five minutes before the school loomed in our vision. As we rolled through the school gates accompanied by the muffled crunch of gravel under the tyres, I started to sing softly under my breath.

'*I'm on the highway to hell . . .*'

It wasn't until nearly a week later that we all managed to get together again.

My classes were done for the day and I was lounging in Thalia's room, waiting for Fenrin. Our brother was, as usual, later than he said he'd be. As seniors in their final year, Thalia and Fenrin each got a room all to themselves, but the bedrooms in my dorm house were four girls apiece. Privacy was one luxury Bishop St James did not offer as standard.

Thalia's room was on the ground floor and her window looked out onto the wilderness of the building's small, pretty back garden. In warmer months there would be organised tea parties on the manicured lawns out front, but everyone seemingly ignored the green tangle round the back, tucked away out of sight. It was too small for tea parties but it had other advantages. Providing decent cover when your brother was breaking the rules by sneaking into your girls-only dorm after dark, for example.

I sprawled out on a comfortable mound of cushions on Thalia's bedroom floor while she sat at her desk, forcing her way through a mock exam paper for her advanced physics class, occasionally stopping to huff a frustrated sigh into the air.

People tended to look at my sister and not see someone who should be taking advanced physics, since making assumptions was one of everyone's favourite pastimes. Her teacher, Mr Copley, was a terrifically condescending example of this. The clashes between them mainly stemmed from the fact that Thalia was interested in the kinds of theories that pulled apart the nature of reality, and Copley was only interested in talking about, in Thalia's words, 'things you might teach a six-year-old'.

She hated the way he ran his eyes up and down her pretty skirts, her tousled hair, her big doe eyes ... and consequently wrote her off. When she had once told him to consider the possibility that her looks had nothing to do with her ability to use her brain, he had asked her whether she'd be organising a sit-in. Her classmates had laughed because that was what you did when the people in power made jokes. I said that next time Thalia should suggest Copley insert his head into his own sphincter because this was evidently where it preferred to be.

The window creaked as it was levered open wide from the outside. Then a litany of soft swearing drifted across the room as Fenrin attempted to enter, bulging out the curtains like an insect birthing itself from a pod.

His flustered face poked through the gap in the curtain fabric.

'Hi!' I said brightly.

'You could, I don't know, *help* me,' he wheezed.

I pretended to consider it. 'I would, but I think this is something you need to learn how to do by yourself.'

Fenrin growled and manoeuvred himself through the window gap, balancing on his hands as he pulled his legs through behind him, fetching up in a crumpled heap on the carpet.

'I don't think you're making it obvious enough that a boy is breaking into my room,' Thalia said from the desk, her nose still in the paper before her. 'Could you be a bit louder?'

'Shut up, both of you.' He straightened up, pulling the window closed.

'Also, try to keep your voice down. The walls are thin.'

Fenrin slung himself onto Thalia's bed and settled back against the pillows. 'The girls on either side of you both have boyfriends that regularly sneak over, so I hardly think they're in any position to raise the subject.'

Thalia often complained about the noise her neighbours made when she was trying to sleep.

Grim.

'Spoken to Wolf today?' I asked, as casually as I could.

Fenrin's face darkened. 'Yeah.'

'How's he doing?'

'He's pretty pissed off that we're here and not with him, if I'm honest.' Fenrin's voice dried at the edges. 'Did you know he's been sneaking out of the house?'

Thalia looked around.

I sat up. 'What?'

'Yeah. At night, when everyone's asleep.'

'Where does he go?'

'Walking. Sometimes into town, sometimes into the woods. He gets restless, he says. I don't think he's sleeping very well.' Fenrin shifted to put his hands behind his head, working up to something. 'And he eats like a horse.'

'Oh, let's not be coy, it's more like a whole herd of horses,' I said.

'He's not ... the same, exactly.' Fenrin trailed off. 'I know it's Wolf because everything about him is totally familiar, like I've known him my whole life. In some ways he feels more like he's one of us than he ever used to. You know how damn aloof he always

57

acted, and you could never tell what he was thinking? It's like he doesn't care about that any more. It doesn't even cross his mind to hide what he wants.'

'That's a good thing, isn't it?' I asked cautiously.

A great smile broke out across my brother's face, taking me by surprise. 'It's different. I'm not saying I don't like it, but it's kind of overwhelming, I guess.' He gusted an annoyed sigh. 'I just want him to be okay. You'd think after going to all the trouble of bringing him back, she'd make sure he was, like, version 2.0, you know? Upgraded. Now with adjustable seating and automatic coffeemaker.'

She meant River, but apparently we weren't yet at the point where we casually aired her name between us. Names, as we all knew, had power of their own.

'Why is it that everyone who comes into contact with that girl becomes mysteriously ill, do you think?' Fenrin mused. I had relayed everything Marcus had told me in the car over a week ago to them both.

I frowned. '*We* haven't.'

'Well, that's probably because she hasn't cursed us,' he retorted. 'Yet, anyway.'

'Don't joke about curses,' Thalia muttered. 'And I'm honestly surprised you guys just assume that Marcus is telling the truth.'

'What if there was a way to find out?' I said.

'Such as?' Fenrin slid his hands behind his head.

I reached for my bag. The room's sudden silence settled like a weight as they watched me scrabble in its depths and withdraw the black muslin bundle. I hadn't even been able to snatch a moment of privacy to look at the card deck since coming back to Bishop St James. I'd been waiting for a moment just like this, with all of us together.

My heart beat a little faster as I unwrapped the cloth and spread the cards face up. Seeing them again stirred my blood. Their strange and lovely world beckoned, enticing.

'Where did you get them from?' Thalia said. She had swivelled around in her chair and was frowning down at the spread deck at her feet.

I decided to come clean. 'Gwydion's study. They were hidden on a top shelf in one of the cabinets.'

'And you just . . . took them?'

'Borrowed. Temporarily.'

Thalia blew out a pained breath. 'If he sees they're gone—'

'He won't. He hasn't touched them in years.'

'You're an idiot,' Thalia said. But I could see something in her face, and I thought it was the same kind of eager pull that I had in mine.

'Tarot cards,' Fenrin said, unimpressed.

'They're not just any tarot cards,' I shot back. 'Look at them. Have you ever seen a deck like this before? There are no number cards, no Major or Minor Arcana. Every single one of them is unique, hand painted.'

Fenrin shrugged. 'So they're expensive, one-of-a-kind tarot cards. What a shock that our father should own something like that.'

'Are you going to continue sassing,' I said, 'or do you want to ask them a question you might actually get an answer to?'

I watched with great satisfaction as his mouth opened and closed.

'Do you even know how to use them?' he finally came out with.

'Oh, sure. They teach advanced divination on a Tuesday morning, in between biology and art.' I ran my fingers over the cards, fanning them out a little wider. 'It's like everything to do with magic, dolt. Insert desire, apply will. The rest is instinct.'

'So you're just going to say, "Hello, Mister Tarot Deck, please tell me if our ex-best friend has been cursed by our other ex-best friend,"' Fenrin said. 'And it's just going to tell you?'

Thalia stirred. 'I'm game.'

Fenrin rolled his eyes.

'Two against one,' I taunted him.

He waved a hand, pretending apathy. 'Fine, fine.'

I pointed at the shelf above Thalia's head, which boasted a lone stubby white pillar candle in a hefty clay pot currently serving as a bookend. Thalia handed the candle to me and I lit it with a pack of matches from my bag. White was a good colour. Good for divination, so ritual had always told us. White meant clean, pure, wiping the mind of distraction. White meant opening up and seeing beyond.

As I stared into the candle flame with only the quiet breathing and watchful eyes of my siblings for company, I began to shuffle the cards with careful flicks of the wrists, feeling pleasure unfurl at the way their smooth, lacquered surfaces slid between my hands, a motion that drained my whirling thoughts, leaking them out until all I could see in front of me was Marcus.

I closed my eyes and asked the cards for guidance, letting the need expand in my chest, contract with my breath, expand again, growing bigger with each intake, filling my world.

Then my fingers found the first card and I picked. My eyes opened as I laid it down before me, face up, as bold as could be.

The Trickster. I called this one the Trickster because it was the lone joker card in the deck.

The art depicted a lithe, androgynous figure standing in the midst of a crowd. The figure had a hand cupped around its mouth, leaning into a man's ear as if whispering. The rest of the crowd was a forest of limbs and wide eyes, fighting each other in savage desperation. Fingers were wrapped around throats and bodies were trampled underfoot. Chaos reigned, but the Trickster didn't seem to mind – the ends of the figure's lips were curled upward into pleased little commas.

'Looks like a charmer,' Thalia commented. She had lowered herself to the floor and sat opposite me, leaning over the card to examine it up close while one hand held her hair back from her eyes.

I laid down the next card. It was the girl in the green dress, the first card I had seen after unwrapping the deck. She smiled serenely out from her forested world.

'A devil and a princess,' Thalia said.

I nodded. 'She belongs to the Royal Family set in the deck, for lack of a better name. There's four of them and they all have crowns, so I figured they were supposed to be a king and a queen, and a prince and a princess.'

'Okay, but what does either of them mean?' Fenrin said.

I hesitated. I wasn't sure.

Thalia just shook her head. 'Pick the next one.'

The new card showed a girl straddling a boy, encircling him with her thighs, her face hidden in his neck. His hands crawled up her back, clasping her to him, and her dark hair dripped over his fingers. They were alone in what looked like a forest clearing.

'The Lovers,' I murmured.

'Well, yes,' Thalia said drily, her eyes on the artwork. 'No mistaking what that one is supposed to be about.'

In absence of any better ideas, I peeled a fourth card from the pack and laid it down alongside the other three, hoping that the more cards I laid down, the more sense they would begin to make.

The next card I had dubbed the Coven. It showed a ring of four people with their hands joined as they stood together in a plain, windswept place. They circled a craggy tor, which jutted up into the pale stone sky like a mountain giant's thumb.

Fenrin sighed. 'What is that one even supposed to be?'

I stared down at the cards. The Trickster. The Princess. The Lovers. The Coven.

A feeling of strange familiarity swept over me like a wave, swelling and swelling until I nearly had it, like the tip of a sneeze, the top of a rollercoaster.

Then the sneeze came, the rollercoaster dropped.

I looked up at Fenrin, eagerness straining my words. 'Don't you see it?'

'See what?'

'The meaning,' I urged.

'Summer, you've entirely lost me,' Thalia said. She was as puzzled as her twin, but to me the story was plain as day. I tapped the first card, the Trickster, with my finger.

'Once upon a time,' I said in my best storytelling voice, 'a demon comes to a small town by the sea, disguised as a human boy.' My finger moved to the second card, the Princess smiling softly at us all. 'Then he meets a girl.' My eyes fell on the Lovers. 'The demon and the girl become lovers.' I brushed the final card, the Coven. 'The demon wants to take her away but the girl belongs to a coven of witches . . .'

'Oh my god,' Thalia said, understanding finally glowing on her face. 'It's the origin story of the curse.'

Fenrin snorted. 'That's a fairy tale.'

'So's resurrection,' I shot back.

Fenrin leaned down from his cross-legged vantage point, elbows on his knees, eyes on the cards. He said nothing, and I knew with some triumph that he saw it now, too.

I brushed the Coven card with my fingers. There were four witches painted there.

This was no coincidence. It couldn't be.

'I've got something to tell you guys,' I said slowly.

As I related everything I had learned from Gwydion's notebook, I spread the rest of the cards out as best I could and began to sort them into sets. Some I had already identified, like the Royal Family, and more and more sets presented themselves until I had grouped most of the deck.

It was all so glaringly obvious. Not only did the cards I'd chosen tell the story of the curse, but the deck itself was divided over and over into sets of four. There were the four in the Royal Family, a set for the four seasons – spring, summer, autumn, winter – and four depictions of time: sunrise, midday, dusk and night. There was a set of four shapes, four professions, four virtues and four corresponding vices. The Coven card had four figures in it.

'So what does this all mean?' Thalia said, once I was done.

'*Enakelgh* is the most powerful circle of all,' I replied, 'but it works by binding three witches together with a fourth, an outsider – a spirit witch. You get access to one another's power, and you also influence one another's power. If her power really is out of control and she's cursing people, we need to find a way to temper it. *Enakelgh* could be the way.'

First the notebook, now the cards. Coincidence tended to take a holiday around witches, and there were just too many hints to ignore.

Fenrin stirred. 'Okay. She brought Wolf back for us – thank you so very much – but we agreed to part ways, and I think that's best for everyone. I have no interest in binding myself to someone that dangerous, and neither should you.'

'What about Marcus?' I argued. 'What about anyone else who's been affected?'

'Guys,' Thalia said. She had picked up the Princess card and was peering closely at it.

'Marcus can take care of himself,' Fenrin replied. 'And we are supposed to be staying away from him, too, in case you'd forgotten?'

'Where's your sudden hard-on for the family rules coming from?' I frowned.

'Marcus has issues, Summer.'

'Don't we all?' I snapped back. I was getting annoyed. Marcus might have had problems in the past but he'd never been a liar, and I knew Fenrin still cared about him deeply, whatever front he was putting on. The puzzle pieces were right in front of us. All we had to do was put them together.

'Guys, seriously,' Thalia said. 'There's something painted into this girl's hair. It's like an acronym.

What's I-O-N-A? Does that stand for something, or – wait, maybe it's a name . . .'

'You know, we don't have to go through life being totally selfish all the time,' I said to Fenrin. 'It's okay to use your power to help people—'

'We don't owe anyone anything,' Fenrin interrupted, and then huffed a sigh. 'Altruism doesn't suit your skin tone, baby sister. You've always been pushy about this stuff. You were the one who invited River in. You were the one who made space for her in our lives. You *wanted* this. You've always wanted it.'

'Hey!' I said sharply. 'I didn't want anyone to die.'

'Well, that's what happens when you mess with things you don't understand. People get hurt.'

'IONA,' I heard Thalia say in a thoughtful voice. 'I feel like I've come across it before . . .'

At that moment the card in her hand chose to catch fire.

It happened fast. A thin plume of black smoke shot up past Thalia's nose with a quiet *whumph*. In her hand was a flame, then two, licking straight up her fingers. For one split second I could only watch, mesmerised, as it seemed like she had control of it, as if she had summoned the fire herself and was about to hurl it at an enemy.

This is not a computer game, Summer, screamed the voice in my head.

With a breathless gasp, Thalia dropped the card onto the floor. Smoke roiled up from it to the ceiling, thicker and deadlier. Any minute now the fire alarm would sound, the whole dorm would be evacuated, Fenrin would be found, and we would be in the deepest shit for attempting to burn down the building . . .

. . . with a card that was now lying on the carpet, perfectly fine.

The smoke was gone.

The fire was gone.

There wasn't even a charred edge or a stray wisp of grey.

Confused and panicked, I looked up at Thalia. She was rocked stiff and frozen back on her heels, staring at the clean and unmarked edges of the card in disbelief.

'You saw that, right?' she said eventually, her voice faint.

Fenrin was on all fours at the edge of her bed, staring at the innocent card like a madman.

'What the hell? Do you normally set things on fire to get attention? Because I think that's called clinical pyromania.'

'Oh sure, Fenrin, I did it with my invisible magic Zippo,' Thalia shot back.

'Maybe it caught the edge of the candle?'

'I was nowhere near the candle!'

I sucked in a steadying breath. The air betrayed the faint acrid tang of smoke, now gone. I reached out, cautious, and picked up the card. It was pristine.

'Unless we just joint-manifested the exact same hallucination,' I said slowly, 'that felt real to me. Maybe it's not a question of whether it happened, but when it happened.' I looked round at the twins. 'Come on. These *are* divination cards. Maybe that was a vision of the future.'

'What is that supposed to mean?' Thalia said, her voice still high from aftershock. 'That River's going to cause someone to die in a fire?'

'We'd better hope not,' Fenrin said, a grim look on his face. 'One death was more than enough.'

'Then if *enakelgh* is too risky, our only other option is to try a more traditional binding,' I said, trying to keep calm. 'Or would you rather just sit by and let another potential death play out?'

The twins were silent.

A binding flirted with the border between dark and light magic. It was supposed to keep a person from doing another person harm – not by hurting them back, but by restricting them, or putting them off their behaviour. The added advantage being that the witch casting the binding didn't have to be anywhere near the person they were binding, as long as they had a personal object of theirs.

'I don't suppose anyone brought any supplies with them?' I said hopefully.

Thalia nodded to a little wooden chest sitting innocently under her desk.

'Nice,' I whistled. 'I only brought cards. You brought a whole shop with you.'

'You're not the only rule breaker in the family, baby sis,' Thalia said primly. 'But it's not going to work unless we have something of hers.'

Time to come clean.

'We do,' I said. 'There's this crappy little bracelet made of plastic beads. She bought it in one of the tourist shops when she first got here, and naturally I mocked her for it, but she never took it off.'

'Then how do you have it?'

'Found it in one of the guest bathrooms from when she stayed overnight last year. I guess she must have taken it off after all.' I caught sight of Thalia's face. 'What?'

'Nothing. It's not weird that you kept it.' She paused. 'It's a little bit weird that you have it on you right now, though.'

A million excuses ran through my head. The truth

70

was, I had none. I didn't know why I had kept it. I didn't know what it meant. All I felt was that, however forbidden it was, I still needed a connection to River left open. Just in case.

It seemed now like my instinct had been right.

A bang on Thalia's door made us all jump.

'What's going on in there?' someone said in a tremulous voice.

Thalia hissed under her breath.

'Nothing's going on, Clarabel,' she called out. 'Honestly. Everything's fine.'

Clarabel seemed immune to Thalia's charms.

'You're not alone in there,' she whined. 'I heard other voices. I heard a guy's voice. I smelled *smoke*. What are you *doing*? If you don't tell me, I'm going to call the matron, and you're going to be in so much *trouble*.'

Thalia pressed the heels of her hands to her eyeballs and curled into a fetal position. Fenrin's face bloomed red as his shoulders shook with the effort to keep in his laughter.

'Well, we can't do it here,' I muttered. 'We're going to have to go somewhere else.'

'The woods?' Thalia was bright-eyed.

I nodded. 'Tomorrow night.'

CHAPTER 6

More than once in my life it had occurred to me that buildings could, in a way, be considered alive.

Our own house had a kind of aura. Anyone who had ever visited tended to say that our family had soaked into its bricks over the decades. Sometimes it was as if its mood seemed to change with our own, shifting between dark and charming, silent and brooding, vivacious and bright.

During the day you might hear noises of dinner preparation filtering up through the floor. Strains of music curling their way out of the kitchen. The purr of the oven or fridge. A door click as it was pulled to. But in the deepest velveteen part of the night, there sometimes came the older sounds, sounds that Thalia said had happened in a different time to now and had become impregnated in the walls. The rustling of skirts. Footsteps on wood. The heavy ticking of a grandfather clock. The tinkling rattle of bone china. Soft, rhythmic chanting. Weeping. Laughing. Sounds so soft and vague that in the morning you'd dismiss whatever you had been straining to hear the night before as fantasy or dream, nothing more.

Unless you were anything like my family, of course.

Generations of Graces have lived here, our grandmother used to relish telling us, *and I don't think they ever entirely left.*

Bishop St James was not so different. Its history was proudly summed up in the brochure – it began as the sprawling estate of some lesser royalty member, the memories of hosting kings in its draughty halls. A place took on the character of its occupants, and Bishop St James had always been an old, timeless institution. It was as if those rigid walls had eyes because what happened two days later was nothing short of conspiracy.

The first inkling that something was wrong began as a prickling along my shoulders, a particular feeling I knew all too well from years of experience: people close by were talking about me. Sure enough, when I turned round from packing textbooks into my locker, I found a girl standing not far away, staring at my back.

Her name was Edie, a pretty redhead with a ski tan who claimed to be friends with 'literally everyone'. She was also the same girl who had casually threatened to bleach all my clothes and cut off my hair in my sleep last term.

She was flanked as usual by her two best friends, Tor and Jay, who were whispering to each other and throwing me wide-eyed glances. They were all right on their own – I'd managed a civil conversation or two with Jay, who at least acted as if she had a soul. Together, though, they were heinous enough to have earned the unofficial moniker of the Unholy Trinity. Edie was the Father (the leader), Tor the Son (the follower), and Jay the Holy Ghost (the one who often pretended to be invisible when the other two were at their worst).

I tried not to notice their triple-headed stare, but even guys on the prowl have nothing on the scrutiny of teenage girls. It was like the entire surface of my skin was being pricked with tiny, judgmental forks. So instead I raised my hand and gave them a cheery wave.

They approached me. Edie's eyes had taken on a saucer-round seriousness.

'Summer,' she said, 'are you okay?'

I raised my eyebrows. 'Yes,' I replied, cautiously. 'Why?'

'I heard about what's going on with your brother and sister.'

I gave her my clearest 'gossip is my least-favourite pastime' look. 'I have no idea what you're talking about.'

'They got hauled into the headmaster's office,' said Tor.

'What? Why?'

'You should know. I heard you were there, too.' Tor had a delightedly scandalised look on her face, greedy gaze poised and ready to gobble up my reactions.

'I was where?' I said, floundering in confusion.

Edie's face was plastered with a sympathetic expression.

'Don't listen to the rumours, okay?' she said. 'I keep telling everyone that the whole *Flowers in the Attic* thing is total bullshit. Don't worry, no one really thinks that. People like to say the craziest things just for a reaction, you know?'

'Summer,' called a voice.

I turned to find one of the school's counsellors, Poppy-Jane, approaching me. In an effort to relate, the counsellors insisted students call them by their first names, but for all that, Poppy-Jane was nice and not fake with it.

'Can I talk to you a second?' she said.

I felt the Unholy Trinity's stares on us both as she led me aside.

Poppy-Jane spoke in a low, kind voice. 'The headmaster would like to speak with you. I think you have a free period next?'

She'd checked my schedule. I must have looked unbalanced, but she didn't try to reassure me.

A bad sign.

'Yes,' I managed. 'I was just going to study in the library.'

'Well, hopefully this won't take long. Do you want to come along with me now?'

Ah. A statement phrased as a question, giving the illusion of choice. I followed in Poppy-Jane's wake, my stomach beginning a slow, anticipatory churn. Unfortunately, the path to the headmaster's office took us directly past the Unholy Trinity, who hadn't taken their eyes off us. I tried to walk normally.

'Hey, Summer,' I heard Edie call after me.

I paused and looked back at her.

'Your hair looks really interesting like that.' She smiled at me. 'You could totally pass for a boy from the back.'

One of Edie's most cherished tricks was to sound

like she was giving you a sincere compliment while doing nothing of the sort. She enjoyed watching your smile falter with the realisation that you were being insulted.

'Thank you!' I said with a bright, nasty edge. 'That's one of the things I really love about this place – it's so progressive. Have you ever noticed how people who like to enforce gender norms tend to be intellectually stunted?'

I turned and walked away. Poppy-Jane gave me a measured look but avoided comment.

'Don't be embarrassed,' Edie called. 'If you want to be a boy, you can *totally* be a boy. Wait, I have a name suggestion for you – how about Richard, but your friends call you Dick?'

Their malevolent hoots of laughter followed me all the way down the corridor.

My boots clicked uncomfortably loudly on the lacquered wood floor leading up to the headmaster's office. I had only been inside once, when we had first come here with our parents for an official meet and greet. An ominous hush hung perpetually around this whole area, synonymous with a feeling of numb, guilty dread.

Poppy-Jane knocked on the door and waited a

respectful moment before opening it up and poking her head inside.

A questioning fly-drone noise came from the office.

'Summer Grace, sir,' she said.

At the sound of my name, my heart plunged into the tips of my pointed boots.

Poppy-Jane motioned me to follow her inside. Slowly, reluctantly, I moved forward into the belly of the beast and the door shut heavily behind me.

The headmaster of Bishop St James seemed like a wet tissue of a man. Presumably he'd been a teenager himself once, but he had an unfortunate tendency to relate to anyone under twenty as if he'd read how to do it in an instruction book that somehow sidestepped the most relevant approach, which was to treat teenagers like intelligent human beings.

'Do take a seat,' he said.

I did so warily. He moistened his lips and gazed somewhere in the direction of my left shoulder.

'What we'd like to do, Miss Grace,' he said to the wall behind me, 'is just get your thoughts on what we've been hearing about your nocturnal activities.'

Nocturnal activities?

He hesitated, waiting. Poppy-Jane, standing at his shoulder, picked up her cue.

'The thing is, Summer,' she said, 'the three of you were seen doing something at night in the woods. Perhaps a . . . ritual of some kind?'

The binding on River.

We had left it as late as we could to perform it, sneaking out of our dorms at well past midnight and meeting up just outside of the woods to the south of the school.

The woods were where students went to do anything that might be frowned upon within the school walls. Once upon a time they had been dense, covering the landscape for miles around, but now they were neatly cropped, long ago razed down to bring them under human control. Still, they were big enough for our purposes.

Armed with our talismans and a few scant supplies, we had set up the ritual underneath the bell-like canopy of a huge and beautiful beech tree, well away from the main entrance to the woods. Talismanic magic was reserved for our strongest spells. It was a way to connect back to the family, a way to draw on its collective strength and power, stretching through the ages. I had found my talisman, a carved amber bird, a few years ago on a trip to Sicily, sitting in a basket on a flea market stall, winking in the sun. Talismans drew you to them.

The binding spell was not about hurting River. It was about making it as hard as possible for her to hurt anyone else. That might mean, if she tried, she'd find herself blocked somehow, or that something would always happen to interrupt her, stop her, or take the other person out of her line of sight. How it worked wasn't something we could control.

Magic is unpredictable. Rituals were our way of trying to tame it, to manipulate it to our will.

As rituals went, it was a pretty uncontroversial one. We had kept it as simple as possible, setting up a circle with black candles, burning tied bundles of dried bishop's wort, and using our talismans to focus through. It had been a cold, unremarkable Tuesday night, so we should have been all alone. I thought we were.

Obviously I was wrong.

'The thing is,' Poppy-Jane said, with the reluctant air of someone who wasn't sure how to broach the impending subject, 'your brother's bag was searched, and I'm afraid there were some telling materials discovered.'

I frowned. 'What kind of materials?'

'A bag of dried herbs,' Poppy-Jane said, 'and some wine.'

Shit.

Fenrin's dorm was the closest to the woods, so post-ritual we had given him the remnants of the supplies to store in his room. The idiot must not have taken everything out of his bag.

'It's just ceremonial,' I said hastily. 'The wine.'

All of our rituals involved a mouthful of wine, but a mouthful was all it was. They must have seen how small the bottle was; no one could possibly have gotten drunk off what we had. Well, maybe a mouse.

'Alcohol is not allowed on school premises, Miss Grace,' the headmaster said. 'It's very clear in our charter, so you must be fully aware that we have a zero-tolerance policy for underage drinking, as we do for parties. The woods are not for parties, or gatherings, or rituals of any kind.' He leaned back in his throne. 'Now, I'm afraid we do have to give you an official warning. As this is your first offence, we won't discuss suspension this time.'

Half my dorm had vodka bottles stashed in their cupboards. There was a senior, Maggie Steinberg, who had been caught throwing up on the lawn after an impromptu gathering in her bedroom had turned into a raucous private party. They'd found the empty bottles in her room but she hadn't even been reprimanded. The phrase 'turning a blind eye' was not me reaching – it was the way things were around here.

'But, sir,' I tried again, filled with a desperate need to explain, 'it's not about partying or getting drunk, it's to do with the craft—'

'The *craft*? Is that what they call it these days?' the headmaster murmured to Poppy-Jane, as if I wasn't sitting feet away from him in a terribly quiet room where every creak of his chair carried clear to the door.

I began to wonder if this wasn't about underage drinking at all.

'It's like at church,' I pressed. 'When you take the blood of Christ. It's just a mouthful, right?'

Wrong. I'd gone wrong.

The headmaster's eyes narrowed to slits.

'I'm afraid,' he said stiffly, 'I find it quite offensive that you would compare something as sacred as taking Holy Communion with something that, quite frankly, smacks of Satanism.'

For a moment I was floored. By the look on Poppy-Jane's face, I could see she was equally uncomfortable with the word. The headmaster, by contrast, was entirely impassive.

My mouth opened. Shut. Opened.

'Sir,' I said, 'Satan is a fictional device created by uptight conservatives for the pure purpose of keeping tortured, guilty little sinners in line. He's not part of our "alternative lifestyle" because we don't believe he *exists*.'

Poppy-Jane held up a hand. 'All right, Summer.'

'Though if he did,' I continued, 'you just know he'd have all the best musicians down there with him. I mean, that's almost worth going to hell for. In heaven you'd probably have to listen to Cliff Richard for the rest of eternity, and I'll be damned if that isn't a worse punishment than anything Satan could come up with.'

'Are you sure?' she replied. 'Cliff Richard seems like a straight-to-hell candidate to me.'

I felt myself begin to crush on Poppy-Jane.

'That's quite enough,' the headmaster cut in. He looked damply furious.

I was living in a world in which truth was rewarded with punishment, but I'd never seen the point of that. Power thrives on secrets and mystery. Speak the truth of something and rob it of power. It is one of the oldest and simplest magics there is.

I needed to speak the truth.

'Sir, people can hold whatever beliefs they like,' I said, struggling to keep a leash on my surging sense of injustice. 'I truly think that. But ours don't incorporate any kind of Satanic worship. They just don't.'

'Your thoughts on the matter are hardly relevant right now,' the headmaster snapped. 'We don't allow *rituals* of any kind here, religious or otherwise. You've deliberately broken the rules, and it's about time you learned that your actions have consequences.'

I stared at him, unable to comprehend just how full of shit he was. This school touted itself as a place of openness to people's beliefs. Half the kids had crosses on their necklaces, and more than one girl wore a hijab. There was even a small chapel on school premises where students could go to pray. What was that if not a ritual?

I dug my hands underneath my thighs, trying to hide their shaking.

'What about the Rite of Passage?' I asked.

Poppy-Jane dipped her head to look at the floor. The headmaster didn't move.

I felt a wave of small relief. They both knew exactly what I was talking about.

Everyone knew about the Rite of Passage.

As far as I could tell, it involved a group of the school's best and brightest surprise-kidnapping someone from their bed at midnight, taking them to the small stone chapel in the grounds behind the main manor house, and performing some sort of humiliating ceremony on them while wearing masks and robes so no one could be identified.

It was hard to ignore all the deliciously scandalised

gossip passing in whispers from bed to bed at night in the shared rooms of the lower years. This time-honoured Bishop St James tradition seemed to be based, like so many time-honoured traditions, on ritualised cruelty. It was a stick to beat weird kids with. People were picked for it based on their inability to 'fit in'. In other words, if you were one of the popular crowd, or at least inoffensively bland, you were safe.

If you weren't . . .

'I'm afraid I've never heard of that term,' the headmaster said.

Poppy-Jane gave an almost inaudible sigh.

'You've never heard of how the seniors terrorise other students?' I said.

'If you're suggesting that I wouldn't put a stop to something that harmed students' – the headmaster glared at me meaningfully, as if to communicate that a private ritual out in the woods had somehow caused mass psychological damage to the student body – 'then I take offence at that. The only practice I am aware of is a simple, harmless tradition in which some of the older students welcome newcomers to the school.'

Oh, I thought, *so you* do *know what the Rite of Passage is.*

'Now, that's not exactly in the official brochure.' He punctuated this with a little laugh. 'But we do promote bonding, team-building and communication. These are invaluable life skills. We encourage our students to have a little fun, Miss Grace. Work hard, play hard.'

'Depends on your notion of fun, I guess,' I said, struggling to make my voice even. 'It's not exactly croquet and cakes on the lawn, is it? I apologise for being blunt, sir, but isn't it a little hypocritical to allow one kind of ritual and not another, just because one is familiar to you and the other one isn't?'

'Do you know what the real problem with you is, young lady?' he asked, his face puckering. 'You think it's "cool" to rebel. Well, trust me, one day you'll find the world will run out of patience with that attitude. The world will ask you exactly how you're going to contribute something *useful* and make a *success* of yourself. And what does success look like? I'm sorry, Miss Grace – it doesn't look like you. But!' He stabbed a soft finger into the air. 'It *could* look like you, if you're willing. The most successful people are integrated *into* the system, Summer, not striving *against* it. Now, here at Bishop St James, you have the opportunity to learn how to be the absolute best person you can be. You would do far worse than to examine your peers for behaviours you could adopt.' His hand waved grandly, in his stride. 'Think of it as a personal development project. Study the way they dress, the way they talk and interact with one another. I promise you, it isn't so hard.' His voice took on a jovial, conspiratorial tone. 'It's not as if they're foreigners muttering away in another language, now, is it?'

I was mute. Mute seemed best. Had this man ever even been a real human being, or had he been grown in a vat?

'Do you think that's something you can do?' he asked me.

He looked at me expectantly, as if he was actually waiting for me to reply.

I beamed at him. 'Absolutely.'

'Really?' he said. His eyebrows raised, and his fleshy lips tucked into a smile.

'Totally, sir. Some of the greatest thinkers in history have said exactly the same thing as you. Take Hitler, for instance. I mean, he was really on to something, wasn't he?'

Poppy-Jane's face dropped. 'Summer—'

'No, no, I'm serious.' I rolled my eyes. 'I mean, *yes*, okay, he was a genocidal maniac, and *yes*, okay, he decimated entire populations of people and fucked up the world for generations. I mean, he took it too far, but he had the right *idea*, didn't he? Let's make everyone the same. Because that's how it starts,' I concluded. 'With people like you, being terrified of anything that isn't like you.'

The headmaster leaned forward.

'Since a warning doesn't seem to be enough for you,' he said in a tone filled with something suspiciously like triumph, 'you may now consider yourself officially suspended.'

He thought he'd won. He thought he'd visited on me the absolute worst horror that could be visited upon a human being. Such a tiny little world.

'Was it the "Hitler" thing or the "fucked up" thing?' I asked.

The headmaster closed his eyes gently, as if he couldn't bear to look at me.

I heaved myself out of the chair, picked up my bag and left his office, my feet noiseless on the plush carpet.

Out in the corridor I could no longer stop the shaking.

Oh, your mouth, Summer, I thought. *Your smart, smart mouth.*

A more sensible person would have made sure to hide anything so obviously incompatible with the tenets of Bishop St James when she was a student here, but, well ... I had never been known for my sense. I had talked freely about power, about magic, about passion and desire, and I refused to feel embarrassed or ashamed about doing so.

If there was one thing I abhorred above all else it was people hiding who they really were, myself included. Give me truth and you earned my respect. Give me lies and I'd hate you for it.

So, here I was, suspended. It seemed as though Fenrin's vague wish to find a way out of here was coming true after all. Well, I, for one, was not going to waste the lifeline we'd been thrown.

And as it turned out, once they heard what had happened, the twins weren't going to, either.

It wasn't enough to leave Bishop St James. We'd have to make sure that we would not be coming back.

CHAPTER 7

What I admired most about the plan we came up with to get ourselves a permanent exit from this school was that it pleasingly utilised all three of the headmaster's favourite things: bonding, team-building and communication.

Somehow I doubted he would appreciate that.

That morning, on unlocking his office and stepping inside, the headmaster discovered the overnight addition of some small yet impactful decorative changes. His throne had been elegantly draped with a black cloak, its twin wooden spires making the whole thing resemble some demonic bat about to take flight. The cloak's hood had been stuffed with newspaper in order to fix the empty face with a tacky plastic devil's mask. The mask grinned from between the spires, its rolling eyes fixed on the door.

Stretching out across the floor in front of his

desk was a bedsheet which had been painted with an elemental pentagram in red and black. Fenrin had wanted to paint the pentagram straight onto the carpet, but I wasn't about to punish the cleaner just for having a bigot as a boss. Another bedsheet was hung on the back wall and scrawled with the following message:

> 'Better to be known as a sinner than a hypocrite.'
>   Traditional Proverb

A side effect of painting a bedsheet once it had been hung was that gravity caused the paint to drip and run off the bottom of each letter, giving the whole thing an appearance of bleeding black blood, which in my opinion served as the serendipitous icing on the cake.

My one regret was that I didn't get the opportunity to explain to the headmaster in person just how we had gained entry to his office without a key.

Then again, I doubt he would have believed me.

There was no clever trick to it. It was just that sometimes I had, let's say, a *way* with locks. It wasn't so much an ability to open one on the spot as already finding it unlocked, as if the universe conspired with me to make sure a lock would be open by the time I got to it.

This didn't work with Gwydion's cabinets, but then again, expecting our house to conspire with me against my father, and in his own study, was probably *too* much of a stretch. Like everything else to do with magic, it was an unpredictable skill, but it had served me well last night. If we hadn't been able to get in the headmaster's office we would have decorated his door and the corridor outside, but it would have made less of a statement.

We definitely wanted to make a statement.

The headmaster's office was not the only place we had blessed with a decorative upgrade. Subtle enquiries with some of the quieter, least popular students of this school had revealed a fairly damning consensus about the regular instigators of the Rite of Passage. In mind-numbingly predictable fashion, there weren't even any surprise names on the list. They included everyone we had expected.

When each of those people reached their lockers this morning, they found a crowd gathered, staring and whispering. Each door had been Sharpied with a rune of opening, drawn in carefully fat black lines, the appearance of which was said to help expand people's minds. Each handle had been hung with the same devil's mask that adorned the headmaster's throne, with the addition of a small black muslin bag hanging from a piece of orange ribbon.

Slipped inside each locker through the gap between the door and the frame was a note:

The bag contains both a boon and a bane.
Open it, or don't.
Either way, it's a risk.
With love from the Graces

The muslin bag contained a simple combination of dried mugwort (for opening up the mind), peppermint (for sparking excitation and restlessness), and a tiny tiger's eye (for seeing beyond the mundane).

It was a curiosity charm.

Curiosity is both a boon and a bane, a blessing and a curse. If any of them began to get curious, maybe this world they had been given no choice about inhabiting might start feeling uncomfortably small.

The final piece of our performance was via email. Every student whose locker had not been adorned received a message containing simple instructions on how to weave a protection charm for themselves against anyone who might harm them.

Part of me had wondered whether this would all be enough to get us out, but I needn't have worried.

Later, nestled among our packed clothes and toiletries like a surprise spider, was a letter from the school to take home to our parents. It explained that we had been asked to take some time out from this fine institution for defacing school property and engaging in activity that was 'in direct contrast to the principles and values we uphold here at Bishop St James'.

In other words, for being both different and unashamed about it.

The taxi was waiting just outside the school gates.

Fenrin was already in the back seat. Thalia leaned against its side, ankles and arms casually crossed, watching me as I approached.

'Ready?' she said.

'Hell, yes.' I hefted my suitcase. 'Let's go home.'

A part of me still hoped to one day morph into Captain Tolerance, superwoman of contemporary civilisation. A part of me wondered if I should be more patient and more understanding of the kind of thinking they perpetuated at Bishop St James. Captain Tolerance would accept these idiots for their differences, not loathe them. She'd glide serenely through it all like a damn swan and not lose her temper every time someone said something that made her want to scream.

You should be tolerant of every kind of behaviour, Gwydion once told me, *except ignorance and stupidity. No one should ever tolerate behaviours that ruin the world.*

'We should have put a curse on them all,' Fenrin murmured as we were driven away.

I glanced at him. 'We're better than that.'

'No, we're not,' he sneered.

'They're not all assholes.' I thought of Jay. Poppy-Jane. Countless other students who had never bothered us and just wanted to get by. 'It's only a few. They're loud and obnoxious and draw all the attention, so it seems like they're everyone, but there's always far less of them than you think.'

'Whatever,' Fenrin muttered. 'I'm with Wolf on this one.'

'What's he got to do with this?' I asked, surprised.

He shrugged. 'He said shitty people need to know when they're being shitty. If no one is ever punished, how can the world change? And he's right.'

I supposed he was.

CHAPTER 8

I loved how tiny and provincial our train station at home was, how the ticket office was manned for about an hour a day, how the wooden sign for the cafe on the platform had been corroded over time by the salt in the air. How as soon as the train doors opened and I stepped out, the smell of the sea crawled up my nose and filled my lungs.

Whatever else happened, wherever else I went in my life, this place would cling to my blood. The sea and the sand and the rocks and the cliffs and the dunes, the cobblestones, the sight of the fishing boats beached up on the shore, ready to set out and bring in the next catch, the cute little pastel-striped ice cream parlours and the cries of gulls overhead.

At this exact moment, nothing could dampen my mood.

Which was just as well, since Esther was waiting for us when we got home.

Her car was parked outside. As soon as I saw it, I exchanged a panicked glance with Thalia.

'Better to get it over with now, I guess?' I suggested.

As soon as we were inside, Fenrin dropped his bags with a thump.

'Wolf?' he called. He hadn't warned Wolf about what we'd done – he'd wanted it to be a surprise. It was the middle of the day so no one should have been home, but now that Wolf was staying here full-time, I realised I had no idea what it was that he did all day.

'Wolf?' Fenrin called again and raced up the stairs.

'Fen, wait,' I said, but he ignored me, turning on the landing and continuing up to the second floor.

'She's in the conservatory,' Thalia said quietly.

I sighed. 'I can smell it.'

The air inside the hallway was blanketed in smells, ponderous with soft, cloudy lavender and rich, warm clove. Our mother was making test batches of new products. You never knew what olfactory extravaganza might greet you on testing days, but this one was all soothing, stroking comfort.

'Come on,' I said to Thalia. 'Let's get this over with.'

Thalia gave a grimace and we made our way to

the conservatory, opening up the door and taking the three steps that led downward into the lion's den.

Esther was sitting on the bench at the giant oak table that dominated the conservatory, with a tidy array of vials, dishes and bottles before her. She had her work apron on, hair gathered in a messy pile on her head and stuck with pins. She looked up as we entered.

'Hi,' I ventured, testing the waters.

'Come in,' she said, entirely unreadable.

We inched reluctantly down the steps, letting the door close behind us.

'We thought you'd be at the shop today, or the warehouse,' I said, trying my best not to sound in any way disappointed by reality.

Esther's shop, Nature's Way, was an elegant boutique that sold her various tastefully packaged creams, pastes, tinctures and powders. It sat in a prime spot down near the harbour – not right at the front where the tourist gods reigned, but two streets back, just about where the esoteric began to creep in among the places selling postcards and tinned biscuits with painted coastal views on their lids.

Esther was rarely at the shop herself, preferring to spend most of her time overseeing the mysterious processes by which her small army of alchemists created her products at a huge, airy warehouse just outside town. Either that or she was taking business meetings with some of the biggest chain stores in the country, all vying to buy her various lines to sell at exorbitant prices in the most upmarket department stores.

She carefully laid down the tiny glass dropper she had been wielding and folded her hands in her lap, resting the fine-boned knuckles against her stained apron. I always loved her hands. China doll fingers, pale skin that showed a tracery of green veins at her wrists.

'I was planning to be,' she said. 'But then I received an absolutely fascinating phone call from your headmaster.'

Beside me I felt Thalia give an involuntary twitch.

I could see the jaws of hell rushing to greet us. There was no preparing for this. Much like an oncoming wave, you simply had to ride it out and hope you didn't drown in the process.

'I'm quite angry,' said Esther calmly, and my heart quailed, 'that you didn't see fit to tell us what an awful man he is.'

We were mute.

'I remember him from our meeting back in August, when we decided to transfer you,' she continued. 'He came across as pompous, but largely well-meaning. And I reassured myself that the education you'd get there would be second-to-none, which mattered far more.'

Plus the fact that Bishop St James was a good five-hour journey from home, ensuring that our separation from people like River and Marcus would be far easier to maintain once established.

But now was not the time for such an observation.

'So I went along with it, despite my reservations,' Esther said. 'I thought you could handle yourselves just fine against mediocrity.'

Thalia's hand brushed against mine. Her eyes slid to the vials arranged in their rows on the table in front of my mother. They were vibrating alarmingly in their wooden holders, shivering all by themselves.

Shit.

Now I began to see Esther's absolute, total calm for what it really was – the eye of a storm.

'But you know,' she said, apparently oblivious to the tiny rattling sounds coming from the workbench, 'if the past year has taught me anything, it's that you're still vulnerable, and you're still children, *my* children, and yes, *yes*, I'm disappointed that you didn't have the courage to tell me what you were experiencing at Bishop St James, but I'm really more disappointed in *myself* for pushing you out into the awful banality of that version of the world too soon . . .'

I listened with growing dismay. Did she think so little of us? Would this be another way to keep us here, protected and cosseted from Big Bad Life?

The rattling became unmistakable. I felt my muscles tighten in response, bracing for impact.

'Because if there's one thing that this world has in terrible, abysmal abundance' – Esther's voice was compressed steel, growing colder and tighter, tighter, tighter – 'it's small-minded, narrow-focused, petty, fearful *bigotry*—'

The word seemed to bounce off the walls and fire like a bullet into the row of vibrating vials on the table in front of her. With a high tinkling noise, they cracked and broke.

Every single one of them.

Shards of glass sprayed the workbench, showering the wooden surface with globs of powder and liquid. Esther startled back out of her chair, one hand pressed to her chest. I could almost feel our hearts, thumping collectively, pulsing in time to the fast, fearsome rhythm of the house as we stared at the mess.

It had always been hard to fight in our house, which seemed calibrated to its inhabitants' emotions as keenly as a tuning fork, manifesting them as physical fallout in a variety of hilariously unpredictable ways.

Last year, Thalia, during a distressed confrontation with Marcus, had inadvertently broken every single one of the clay pots filled with herbs that lined the garden path. Just after Wolf's death, Fenrin had made the blue paint on his bedroom walls run like giant tears and completely ruin his floor. The one and only time I had dared push Esther on the subject of the curse – I'd been trying to find out if something had happened to anyone she knew personally, since she would never, ever talk about it – she'd been tight-lipped. Her refusal to engage with me had provoked me to unintentionally set a giant lamb leg – the one she'd been roasting for dinner – on fire. Fearsome flambé, and not in a good way. We'd come close to losing the kitchen.

This house felt us, felt our moods, and responded accordingly. From it I had learned from an early age about the power, and the consequences, of unfettered emotion in a witch. I often thought it was the reason why our parents could never bring themselves to talk through pain, preferring instead to sweep it all under the rug and wrap us in silent, protective blankets.

We did not *discuss* in this household. We bottled ourselves up until we exploded.

'Mama,' I said, a name I hadn't used since childhood. 'All your work—'

Her head gave a tight shake, silencing me. Then her other arm opened up, and we went to her. Our arms crawled up her back, and hers held our shoulders in a hug like a vice.

'The house has spoken,' my mother whispered.

I gave a shaky, relieved laugh. Thalia's fingers curled over mine.

'I'm sorry you had to experience that,' she said eventually, her voice carrying softly above our heads. 'Outsiders never understand. It's a hard lesson to learn, but I hope the events of the past year will make you more resilient. No parent ever wants their child to experience all the disappointment the world has to offer. I'd rather have showed you nothing but magic and opportunity, and those things still exist, in abundance. You just need to work a bit harder to find them out there. All I wanted to do was protect you. You understand that, don't you? I'll do anything to protect you.'

You can't protect us forever, I thought.

Esther pulled away from us, smoothing her hair, and gave us both The Look.

'But if you think you're getting off without punishment, think again,' she said. 'You just got yourselves kicked out from one of the most prestigious schools in the country without a single attempt at discussing your actions with either one of your parents.'

I've got nothing, I silently projected at Thalia. She took the hint.

'We're sorry about what we did,' Thalia said in her very best contrite voice. 'Truly. I know you've told us to just ignore people who hurt us, but sometimes it's too hard. I guess we lost our tempers. But we were really unhappy there. We just wanted to be back home again, near Wolf, and near you. Haven't you missed us?'

It was Esther's turn to sigh. I could practically see the war going on in her head. Her children's happiness versus appearances. I didn't give a rat's ass what anyone there thought of me, but she did.

'It's done,' she said at last, as if the conversation was over. 'When your father gets back from work tonight we'll have a conversation with the headmistress at your old school.'

I froze, hardly daring to breathe. 'Really?'

Esther canted her head. 'Yes, Summer, really. Or would you rather I pull you out of school altogether and have you home tutored?'

'No, no,' I said hastily. 'Farrow's great. We were doing well there, weren't we? Our grades were way better there than at Bishop St James, right?' It was a hard one to dispute – last term's reports had been less than favourable, to say the least. 'And you know, if you think about it positively, we're saving you a ton of money. The fees at that school were *outrageous*.'

'Don't push it,' Esther said. 'Now, go and unpack. And fetch your brother down here, would you?'

Lucky git, I thought viciously as I turned to leave. *He's dodged the worst of it.*

'Summer, stay here a second – I want to ask you something.'

I froze on the steps. Thalia gave me a fleeting worried glance before disappearing out of the conservatory. I turned back to my mother.

'What were you doing in the woods?' she asked. 'The headmaster mentioned a ritual on the phone.'

It was a classic Esther move when she wanted to know something that we weren't telling her. Out of the three of us, I was the worst at lying, and she had always had the most extraordinary ability to make you think that she could read your insides like a book. She reminded me of those ancient soothsayers, hands covered in blood as they turned over animal entrails for glimpses of truths deep and dark.

'We were doing a binding,' I said. 'There was someone at school that we wanted to stop from hurting people.'

Esther assumed that the school I meant was Bishop St James, and I was not about to dissuade her.

'Bindings can be dangerous,' she said. 'They can come back on you in unpredictable ways, especially in regards to the person you're trying to bind.'

'I know,' I said. 'We wouldn't have done it if we didn't think it was important.'

'And did it work?'

'I don't know yet.'

'Does any of this concern Wolf?' Esther asked, watching me.

Intuition. It ran a real streak in our family, and my mother had it in spades. There was no way she could suspect the truth, of course – our family history was not exactly replete with miraculous resurrections – but if she thought something else was going on beyond the accepted explanations for his disappearance, she might send him back home and we'd lose him as soon as we'd risked so much to be with him again.

'Nothing,' I said. 'I promise.'

It wasn't a lie. Binding River had nothing to do with Wolf.

She held me a moment more, then released me with a nod. Relieved, I clattered up the steps. As I headed to my bedroom I couldn't help thinking about how the ingredients that had made up the alchemical magic of last summer seemed to be coming back together. We were home. Wolf was here. We would soon be roaming the same school corridors as River.

Even as I reminded myself of the pact we had made to stay away from one another, I felt an illicit thrill in the pit of me at the thought of seeing her again – for the first time since she had delivered a naked, mute and shivering Wolf to our door on a deep December night.

Would she know that we had tried to bind her? Had she felt it, somehow?

And how would she react when she realised what we had done?

CHAPTER 9

The Graces.

'Back in black.'

I hummed AC/DC lyrics under my breath all the way to Farrow as the promise of thick, miserable rain hung over our heads, and we swung umbrellas from our arms, breath puffing on the air.

It had only been a week since our exit from Bishop St James, and I had to admire how fast my mother got things done. Despite my good mood, I was tired. I'd stayed up too late last night picking out the perfect outfit, trying on four million different combinations of every piece of clothing I owned until I got the ensemble that screamed *SUMMER IS JUST SUCH A DELIGHTFUL BADASS* to everyone who laid eyes on it. I needed the manufactured courage it gave me.

Our house was only fifteen minutes' walk to Farrow. From the lane that sloped downward to our house, a dirt track – which was an ancient fairy path, according to local folklore – led directly to the wall surrounding the school. I'd once been told that no one else dared to use the path because people assumed we had fae blood, and therefore we had a bigger claim to the path than anyone else. I'd just laughed. What were you supposed to say to something like that?

We arrived late. The headmistress of Farrow – who was thankfully a real live human with real live empathy skills – had wanted to interview us as part of the welcome-back routine, so we missed most of our morning lessons. The corridors were silent and deserted, the indoor light gloomy and winter thin. The twins peeled off, making their way to the seniors' wing, separated from the rest of the school by a pair of heavy, windowless doors and a gulf of two years.

As I watched them go, I felt an annoying stab of loneliness in my chest. At least they faced battle with someone always by their side. I had to fight alone. I pushed the feeling away and slunk off to what remained of my English class. This was not Bishop St James, this was Farrow. I fitted here. It wasn't perfect, but it was home.

The slam of the door behind me vibrated through the quiet and rows of faces looked up like a herd of startled deer. My English teacher, Mrs Savoy, blinked.

'Miss Grace,' she said.

Do not look for River, I ordered my eyes.

In absence of a plan, I gave Mrs Savoy a short bow.

Mrs Savoy seemed unimpressed. 'You're late.'

'By about four months, actually,' I said. 'Did you miss me?'

The joke fell into a black hole of silence. Tough crowd.

'Welcome back,' Mrs Savoy said eventually. 'Take a seat.'

Before I could awkwardly pan across the room to see what was available, I noticed a hand go up. It was Lou Chujan waving me to the spare seat next to her, one row from the front. We had long ago cemented our friendship over comparing the attractiveness of various rock stars. I figured she might have gone lukewarm on me – she had every right to. I'd stopped hanging out with her as much when River came into the picture, but not enough to withhold a lifeline, it seemed, and I was grateful.

If there was a spare seat next to wherever River was sitting, I was too late to claim it.

Lou gave me a quick, uneasy smile that darted from cheek to cheek as I slid into the chair. She had bleached the ends of her hair since I had last seen her, and she looked thinner, porous, as if she might wash away on the gentlest tide.

'They told us in form room this morning that you guys were coming back,' she whispered. Her expression was shaded with reproach. 'You could have called, you know. To talk, or whatever. I haven't heard from you for months.'

Maybe she hadn't quite forgiven me after all.

Genuine chagrin softened me. 'I'm sorry.'

'It's okay,' Lou said, mollified. 'I guess you had some heavy stuff going on.'

Mrs Savoy's voice was too frosty to push today. 'If Miss Grace and Miss Chujan could press pause on their no doubt *vital* conversation, perhaps they could pay attention to our exploration of feminist writers of the twentieth century, some of whom are highly likely to feature on their exam paper this year? Thank you *so* much.'

'Lunch,' Lou mouthed and tapped her watch.

I tipped her a wink and leaned back in my chair.

As Mrs Savoy turned her back to write on the board, a folded piece of lined notebook paper was slipped onto my desk. I unfolded it carefully, expecting more questions from Lou, but the handwriting wasn't hers. It was neat and compact, a cramped, introverted style I'd recognise anywhere. My pulse skipped.

The note held only one short sentence:

I didn't know you were coming back.

I was unable to deny the buzz in my fingers, as if the paper itself were impregnated with her power. When the bell rang, I loitered, hoping to catch her, but all I got was a view of her cloud of hair from behind as she left the classroom without so much as a glance tossed my way.

'I'm starving,' said Lou, watching me hopefully.

As we walked into the cafeteria, I thought the noise levels dipped just a little – but Lou soon distracted me as we queued for today's offerings, spinning tales of Christmas with her younger brother ('annoyingly lovable, which means he gets away with everything'), her grandfather ('he doesn't approve of my nose rings'), and her aunts ('every single one of them is batshit insane').

I gave the cafeteria a casual scan as we walked to a half-empty table. If River was among the crowd, she was doing a good job of hiding. All I got were clusters of snatched, hasty stares. I should have been used to it by now, but today something about it made me uneasy. There was an edge to the room, the kind that made the hairs on the back of your neck spindle delicately into the air.

'I can't believe you're back!' exclaimed Gemma, my other musical partner-in-crime and Lou's hetero life mate. 'This place has been dull *AF* without you.'

'Thanks,' Lou retorted.

The third occupant of our table continued poking the limp salad on her plate with a desultory air.

'Hi, Niral,' I said loudly.

She grunted without looking up. I grinned, my mood soaring. I'd even missed her. I carefully balanced my lunch tray on my palms and slid into a spare chair.

'I know Christmas was over a month ago, so this is a *little* belated, but how was it?' Gemma asked.

I shrugged. 'It was okay. Yours?'

I felt the ever-so-tiny pause as they made a game attempt to not reference what they knew about how my Christmas might have gone. Unfortunately, Niral was not so diplomatic.

'Don't you have a junkie living at your house at the moment?' she asked.

The tabletop vibrated. I guessed someone had just tried to kick someone else underneath it.

'Guess so,' I said mechanically and picked up my fork.

'What's that like?'

'Boring.'

She did not appear to notice the warning in my voice. 'I thought he, like, drowned a few months ago.'

'Niral,' Lou said in a warning voice.

'No,' I said shortly. 'He didn't.'

'He took off for a while, got into some bad stuff,' Lou supplied. Her gaze flickered over at me, waiting for confirmation. 'That's what happened, right?'

'Right,' I said.

'Isn't he coming to school?' Gemma asked.

'He finished high school already. He's taking some time out before college. He's planning on working for his dad in the city.'

Lou nudged Gemma. 'Told you he looked older.'

'You've seen him?' I asked, surprised. 'Where?'

'Around town,' Lou said. 'He said he was getting bored stuck at your house all day. Anyway, it was only in passing. He was wandering around the harbour. Looking *fine*.'

'Stop that,' I said, mock appalled.

'*Please*,' said an unrepentant Lou. 'You'd have to be blind not to see it.'

'But you're bringing him to school, right?' Gemma repeated. 'I mean, he could just hang out with us at lunch or something.'

I put down my fork. 'Give me a minute to adjust here. I appear to have wandered into an alternative universe where everyone is now deliriously in love with one of my oldest friends.'

'Sorry if this is offensive or whatever, but I don't find junkies attractive,' Niral said.

I stewed, irritated. It stung to keep having to portray Wolf that way.

Niral was looking at me speculatively.

I speculated right back at her. 'Yes?'

'His meltdown didn't have anything to do with that tricky little new girl, did it?' she asked. 'I mean, it seemed to happen not long after you guys all became friends.'

It took everything I had not to look floored. Had Niral been bitten by a radioactive spider over the holidays and suddenly developed telepathy?

Gemma gave a tortured sigh. 'Niral, come on. A, River isn't exactly new any more. She's been here nearly a year. And B, you seriously have to let your issues with her go. It's gotta be, like, bad for your health.'

I was pretty sure Gemma had no idea just how on the money that last statement was.

Last year, Niral had mysteriously lost her voice. It had gone on so many weeks that her parents had become spooked, arranging an array of doctor visits which had graduated to hospital tests, and finally a monitored overnight stay. All of this had amounted to nothing more than a bemused diagnosis of 'stress-related chronic laryngitis', since they could find absolutely nothing to explain what had happened to her.

If only they had asked me, I'd have told them that Niral had been cursed by a spirit witch for her tendency to get nasty with name-calling and shit-talking when she felt threatened. Of course, if they had, no doctor in their right mind would have believed a word I'd said.

Niral leaned forward and the movement caused the necklace she was wearing to swing, catching the warm electric light swamping the cafeteria. It was an unusually clear crystal hanging heavily from a delicate gold chain – definitely not her normal aesthetic. Niral's taste in jewellery tended towards bright: plastic and as confrontational as the soul it rested against.

'That girl,' she said to me, 'is all kinds of trouble. And one day you're all going to see it for yourselves.'

'Shhh,' Lou hissed. 'She's right behind you.'

My heart spiked.

'She's not going to hear a word I say over this noise,' Niral remarked, supremely unconcerned.

I let my eyes slide over her head.

River was sitting two tables away, and her eyes were on me. She broke the gaze as soon as I found it, flickering away, and I snatched the moment to look her over.

The last time I had seen her in the flesh, she had been soaked to her bones, huddled underneath a blood moon on the freezing sand of the cove, her face an open wound as she had begged us:

Please don't be afraid of me.

That River seemed as far away from this one as it was possible to get. This one was closed, poised. She'd stopped straightening her hair and now it waved around her head in curious wisps. She was wearing faded, loose dungarees that hung off her frame, and a slouchy sweater underneath that looked so old it was likely now cool again.

She looked really good.

Sitting beside her, doing his usual impression of an uneasy crow, was Marcus. We hadn't spoken again since his fainting fit in our garden and I wondered if he still thought River was responsible for it. He seemed to be avoiding catching my eye – his eyes were concentrated on the table in front of him.

I forced my gaze back to my lunch. I had chosen spaghetti bolognese, and my regret was strong. Its sauce was a violent orange – a distinct warning that it had never been near a real tomato – but it was cold today and I'd been jonesing for the comforting blanket of heavy carbohydrates.

'You've never liked her, have you?' I said to Niral. 'How come?'

She snorted. 'Because she thinks she's so special. She's just like the rest of us.'

'Lots of people think they're special.'

'No,' she countered, 'lots of people *hope* they're special. Only a few assholes actually believe it.'

'Such wisdom,' I said with a smile.

'That's me,' Niral agreed. 'Wisdomous.'

'Does it bother you?' I asked.

'What?'

'If I'm honest . . . that you're kind of a bitch.'

I saw Gemma's mouth fall open, but I didn't care. I was still irritated by her junkie comments about Wolf, and it bothered me more than I wanted to admit that she still harboured an intense dislike of River.

To her credit – and to my grudging admiration – Niral sat back in her chair and laughed.

'No,' she said. 'It really doesn't. Bitches don't mind being bitches. We know why we do it – because people need to work their asses off to impress us. Everyone lies, see. Nice people turn out to be dicks, and shitty people turn out to be kind underneath. At least I treat everyone equally, until they do something to change my mind.'

'You pick on people,' I pushed. 'People you think are weaker than you.'

Niral shrugged, her expression suddenly sullen.

In the corner of my eye I was aware of Lou and Gemma watching this avidly, heads switching back and forth like they were at a tennis match.

'Why do you do that?' I asked Niral. I was genuinely curious now, rather than needling, and she seemed to sense it.

'Maybe I can't stand them walking around being so damn vulnerable,' she said. She had attitude on her face, as if to insinuate that this was all a big joke. Delivered as a joke to hide the fact that it was the truth.

'Maybe you see yourself in them,' I mused, 'and you hate what you see, so you go on the attack. A self-loathing gold star for you.'

'Girl,' said Niral, 'I already got a full set.'

'Let's start a club. The Self-Loathing Club.'

'Membership is free. The whole school will probably join.'

I raised a brow. 'You think there are that many screwed up people in one place?'

'*Please*,' said Niral. 'Most people are more screwed up than anyone could possibly imagine. The really normal ones can be the worst – they look normal because they're so much better at hiding pain than the rest of us. But I think that's bad. Hiding is like a poison, you know? It turns you grim on the inside. Much healthier to let it out.'

I thought of my house, of all the secrets deliberately hidden behind its walls. Smashed vials and flambéed lamb.

'You should be a psychologist,' I remarked.

Niral's eyes lit up before she could stop. 'I've always wanted to be.'

'You'd be great. Tough love. You'd see right into people's souls and make them ugly cry, but then you'd fix them.'

Niral's smile faded fast. 'Nah. There's all those exams. I suck at exams, I'm not clever enough.'

'Yes, you are,' I said. She was far cleverer, in fact. She just needed to believe it.

Niral looked up at me, surprised – and was that a shadow of pleasure underneath, just as quickly hidden?

Two tables away, I noticed River shifting in her seat. I caught her eye again, and again she looked away – but not before arching a sassy brow at me.

I swallowed a sudden, glad grin.

Niral's fingers had ascended to touch the pendant dangling around her neck. It seemed an entirely unconscious gesture.

'Nice crystal,' I said, and her hand dropped fast as she realised what she was doing.

'It was a Christmas present,' she said, but she flushed in the lie. She had bought it herself.

I gave her a reassuring smile. 'Good present. They're known for healing and protection.'

Niral looked uncomfortable. 'I didn't know that.'

Another lie. I found myself wondering if it was possible that Niral had known a little more than her doctors about the cause of her chronic laryngitis, and had decided to take matters into her own hands.

'Look,' Niral said, clearly unmollified, 'I'm not really into this magic shit the same way you are, okay?'

'Oh, really?' I asked, amused. 'Didn't I see you in the copse once or twice last year, partaking in a charm or two?'

'Only because those fools dragged me along.' Niral nodded at Lou and Gemma.

'Bullshit,' Lou exclaimed. 'You *wanted* to come.'

'Whatever.' Niral folded her arms and looked out across the cafeteria.

'Whatever schmever,' Lou said. 'You asked me to teach you that last spell that Gem and I did.'

That caught my attention.

'What's this?' I said. 'You guys have been doing spells without me?'

Gemma looked like a dog who had just been discovered rooting in the bin.

'Not really,' she said hastily.

'You weren't here,' Lou supplied. 'Not that that's your fault. Anyway, we were just messing around.'

'Gemma thinks she got her new boyfriend through witchcraft,' Niral said sourly.

'You have a new boyfriend?' I clapped my hands together. 'Now this is the kind of gossip I want to hear about. Spill.'

'His name's Theo,' Gemma said, shyly. 'He's friends with my brother.'

I whistled. 'An older lover. Giiiirl. What spell did you do?'

'A love charm. You said once to use things that represent what you want. So I used fresh chillis, and I made a paste, and I covered a rolled up photograph of him in it . . .'

'She wanted him to get *hot* for her,' Lou said with a crooked grin.

'I didn't mean to,' Gemma cut in quickly. 'I mean, I did, but . . .' She trailed off.

But she hadn't wanted me to know about it.

I put my hand on her arm. 'Gemma. You're acting like you think I'd be angry with you. Why?'

'I'm not like you,' she said, shame leaking out of her. 'I'm not a real witch. I shouldn't be doing it.'

But I wasn't so sure about that.

You've been teaching them magic, the voice in my head whispered. *What did you expect?*

Time and anecdote had established the Graces as 'the witch family'. It was a small town. Perhaps we had always filled it up too much, leaving no room for anyone else. There was a pervasive assumption, especially among Graces, that if you weren't a Grace then you had no business being a witch.

But that didn't mean you *couldn't* be.

It had started as rebellious fun, teaching my friends simple bits of magic – a middle finger to the authority of my parents and the more conservative members of our community. Truth be told, I'd never expected it to take hold quite like this. I thought of the crystal resting on Niral's chest. The chilli oil on Gemma's fingers. They were girls with strong wills – strong enough to have worked a little magic of their own.

'If it worked,' I said, 'then maybe you should be.'

Gemma looked guilty. 'That's the thing. What if he doesn't actually like me and it's just the spell?'

I shook my head. 'Love charms don't work like that. They can't just make desire out of thin air. If he responded to it, it's because the desire was already there. All you did was ... open him up. Make him stop caring about whatever was holding him back from acting on it.'

Gemma was very still.

'Are you sure?' she said finally.

'As sure as eggs, hell, and a devil in London,' I said cheerfully. 'Congratulations, you're a total *witch*.'

'I don't know,' Gemma hedged. 'Maybe it's all just coincidence.'

'Coincidence tends to take a holiday around the craft,' I assured her. 'Trust me. It's all you.'

Maybe I shouldn't have been surprised that they had attempted magic by themselves, and it made me wonder: was it due to the fact that my siblings and I had left town, leaving space for them to breathe? To dare?

Thalia, Fenrin and I didn't believe we had a monopoly on magic, but whether by accident or design, at school we did. We always had. Now that

124

was changing and I couldn't help noticing that it had begun with the arrival of River.

'Summer,' said a voice behind me, interrupting my thoughts.

I turned in my seat.

Standing in front of me was a girl I knew of old and avoided like the plague.

Her name was Ella Drummond and whenever I saw her I flashed back to the last time we had ever spoken, three years ago. Her delicate face had been flushed with a special shade of pink I thought of as 'righteous rose'. In front of the entire lunch queue, she'd accused me of kidnapping neighbourhood cats and sacrificing them to pass my end-of-year exams. I'd laughed so hard I'd got hiccups. Still, the 'cat killer' moniker had stuck all through Year 9, clinging to my back like invisible paint.

People like Ella emphatically did not associate with witches.

'Yes?' I said warily.

'I need to talk to you. Please.'

'About what?'

'In private.'

I'd run out of patience. After Bishop St James, there was no way I'd pit my word against a girl like Ella. She could say or do anything she liked, but this time I'd have sympathetic witnesses.

'No,' I said, calm and still as rock. 'You have something to say, you can say it here because I'm not moving. I don't have any cat-killing tips. You'll just have to google it.'

To my utter and everlasting astonishment, Ella Drummond, five-time winner of the school's Most Likely to Be a Judgmental Ice Queen award, began to cry.

CHAPTER 10

Ella did not pretty cry.

Great big wet blobs tracked messily down her face and her nose turned an alarming shade of red. People around us openly stared.

'Oh my,' I fumbled, unbalanced. 'Okay. Ella, sit. Sit here.'

She sank onto the offered seat. I glanced anxiously around. Lou and Niral were whispering in each other's ears. Kindly, Gemma moved into the chair on the other side of Ella and offered her tissues. Ella took them from underneath her hair, which she had combed forward with her fingers to hide her face. She muttered something that was lost in the cafeteria buzz.

I leaned forward.

'I'm sorry,' she was saying. 'I'm really sorry for what I did. I just need you to take it back. I get it now, okay? I get that it's my punishment, but I didn't mean it.'

'Ella,' I said cautiously. 'What are you talking about? What did you do?'

'I shouldn't have gone there, but she just made me so mad. I don't understand why it's so evil to want to go on a lousy date, I don't even—'

'Slow down,' I tried. 'Slow. Down. Start from the beginning.'

She wiped at her cheeks, peering up at me.

'Didn't you read it?' she asked.

'Read what?'

'My note.'

'Your note? For me?'

'Yeah.'

Confusion reigned. Not one person in this school would have ever assumed that Ella and I had a note-sending relationship.

'I don't think so,' I said. 'But this is my first day back at Farrow. We transferred to another school last term so I haven't been around.'

'I know that,' Ella said, a touch impatiently. 'That's why they told me to do the note.'

Who was they, and why were they telling Ella to write mysterious notes to me?

I'd have to sort that tangle out later. First things first.

'Tell me about the note,' I prompted. 'What did you say in it?'

'It's about Park. The guy in your brother's year.'

'Park the artist, Park?' I asked.

'He asked me out.'

My eyebrows rose.

Three things I knew about our fellow matriculator, Park: he had beautiful hands, an impossibly cheery demeanour that ensured he made friends as easily as breathing, and a precocious talent for art. He'd already won a national under-eighteen show with his sculptures, and he was apparently bound for an apprenticeship at the studio of one of the most acclaimed classical artists in the city.

Also – and just as importantly, since I was a shallow creature – Park was *hot*.

'Are you dating him?' I asked, impressed.

Ella's face darkened. 'No. He just wanted to take me to that little Italian restaurant on the seafront. But my mother said no way, never, because she doesn't think I should date until I'm practically dead, and apparently Park is not, to quote, "a good choice".'

Not a good choice? As far as I could see, the guy was a mother's dream pick.

'I get great grades,' Ella was furiously telling the ground between her feet. 'I work really hard. I never party. The only parties I ever get to go to are chaperoned by adults, and if I have to play charades and drink non-alcoholic punch one more time with the other church kids, I'm going to scream until my throat gives out.'

I listened with growing astonishment. It seemed that prim-and-proper Ella Drummond had her own well of rebellion, just the same as everyone else.

'Park is one of the nicest guys in school. His parents go to the same church as mine. He's the safest date ever. I do everything she wants. Why couldn't she give me this one tiny thing? Why do parents have this need to totally control your life like that?'

'I really have no idea,' I said with sympathetic fervour.

'I prayed, but nothing happened. And I just got so . . .'

Desperate. Angry. Desirous.

Desire, always desire, a relentless clawing inside all our guts.

'And I heard about the clearing,' she continued.

I frowned. 'What clearing?'

'The one in the woods outside of town. You write out what you want on a note, and then you put the note and some money in an envelope, and you go to the clearing and you tie up the envelope to a tree.'

That was our clearing. That was Grace territory. Someone was using our clearing as some kind of *business scam*?

'Money.' I swallowed. 'How much money?'

'Whatever you can spare.'

My jaw clenched.

'I went to the clearing and I tied up my wish,' Ella murmured. 'But all I asked for was one night. Just a stomach bug or something, something that would keep her in bed so I could sneak out and see Park.'

Intuition flared. 'But it's not just a stomach bug, is it?' I said.

A fresh tear sprouted and leaked down her face. 'No. They don't know what it is. They're testing her for cancers. Leukaemia. Everything.'

I felt anger, an acid burn creeping up my throat.

'Can you take it off?' Ella said, drawing me back to her.

'Take what off?'

'The curse on my mother.' Her expression was pure misery.

'Ella ... I'm so sorry, but this wasn't me. I didn't do this to you. I didn't even know about this whole wishes-in-the-clearing thing until now.'

I wasn't sure if she was listening. 'Please. I know it's not you, it's God punishing me. But I don't want my mother to suffer for something I did wrong. Can't you do anything?'

My anger surged.

'You listen to me,' I said fiercely. 'No god worth your love would play such a spiteful trick on you. Because it *is* a trick, and gods don't do tricks. Are you hearing me?'

She just shook her head, her hair shivering around her cheeks. Before I could second-guess the impulse, I reached out and took her hand – but she stiffened and pulled away from me.

'Ella,' I said. 'Who told you to go to the clearing and tie up a wish?'

I knew what she would say before she said it, but I needed to hear it spoken out loud, where the air would claim the name and it could not be taken back.

'Your friend. The new girl.'

Still a new girl, even after a year. Small-town speak.

'You mean River?'

Ella nodded.

I looked up. She was still at her lunch table, watching us both with a guarded expression on her face. Our gazes caught like fish hooks.

'Gemma, stay with Ella a second,' I said and stood abruptly without waiting for an answer.

River watched me approach, eyes widening with mock alarm.

My eyes strayed to Marcus sitting beside her. He watched uneasily. Did he feel light-headed right now, so close to her? Was he about to get some kind of double dose with me there, too?

If he was on the fence about River's power, I was about to provide him with all the evidence he needed.

'Hey,' said River when I was close enough.

'Hi,' I replied while my pulse carved jagged spikes.

Then I just stared at her stupidly as I tried to ignore the little surge I could feel in the pit of my belly. It was the surge I always felt around her, the one that had led me to her last year like a bird to the sky. It was as if she had magnets in her blood, I had iron filings in mine, and we were being pulled to each other.

For one moment I almost forgot what I had come for – then Ella's blobby tears resurfaced in my mind.

River gave a theatrical look-around. 'Isn't the world supposed to implode if we start acknowledging each other's existence again?'

'I think that only happens if we actually touch,' I said.

Last year's River wouldn't have known what to do with that. This year's River just smiled.

I took hold of an empty chair at the next table and dragged it over, while the occupants stared at me owlishly.

'Hey, our friend's coming . . .' one of them said.

'He can sit on your lap,' I told him sweetly.

'So what have you been up to?' asked River as I settled next to her.

'Oh, you know,' I said. 'Overthrowing systemic bigotry, one asshole move at a time. You?'

'Oh, you know. Bringing the dead back, righting general wrongs, one asshole move at a time.'

Pointed, walking-the-line-of-acceptable jokes?

I raised a brow. 'Check out the new sass tail you got going on.'

'It grew in while you were away,' she said.

'Seems like it's not the only thing that did. I've been hearing about your moves towards the post of resident witch.'

For a moment she seemed startled, but she recovered quickly. 'No idea what you mean.'

'I think you do,' I said. 'And I for one think it's *great*.'

She caught the tone. Her jaw tightened. 'Do you.'

'Hell yes. After all, consumers should be offered choices these days, don't you think? A healthy capitalist system thrives on a competitive market.'

For a moment I was winning. She sat there, indecisive.

'I think I'm catching a little jealousy here,' she said eventually. 'Are you scared of the competition?'

'It's not supposed to be a competition, River.'

'More fun when it is, though, right?'

I gave her an easy smile. 'I just think the money-in-the-envelope thing – it's a little *tacky*, that's all.'

That one hurt.

River folded her arms, her expression cold. 'What is that stick up your ass all about, Miss Grace?'

'I'd just rather you didn't use our clearing to tout your little wish-granting business.'

'Ohhhh,' she said, elongating the sound with dawning realisation, 'so this is about your *reputation*. Okay, got it. Well, trust me – I know how hard it is for you to notice this kind of thing, floating around on your little rich cloud, but some people back on earth often struggle to pay the bills.'

'You know I'd help you with that,' I said before I could stop myself.

'If you ever offer me money again,' she said, an angry smile plastered across her mouth, 'I swear to god—'

'Oh, you'll what? Curse me like you did Ella's mother?'

'What?' she said.

'You put her in the hospital, River. Just because she refused to let Ella go on a date. A little *extreme*, don't you think?'

She stared at me, searching.

'That wasn't me,' she said.

'Well, someone took her note – and her money – and it sure as hell wasn't me.'

'Everyone knew about the Park thing,' she protested. 'She was bitching loudly enough for the whole class to hear. It's not like she even needed to put it in a note . . .'

I raised my hands in frustration. 'That is so not the point! River, someone is in *hospital*. You can't keep doing this. Your power is out of control. People get hurt. People die!'

I'd only just become aware of how loud my voice was getting and how quiet other conversations had become, me and her at the centre of an expanding circle of straining ears.

River leaned in close to me. She smelled of cloves. Something else, burnt and smoky. She made me think of winter frost and cold, cold starlight.

'If people die,' she murmured, 'I'll just bring them back, won't I? So what's the problem?'

She was all calm assuredness. I'd never seen her like this before.

'That is so immensely fucked up,' I hissed. 'You can't deliberately do shitty things and then just *fix* them as if nothing's happened, tra la la! There are scars! Wolf is *scarred*.'

'Oh, poor baby's so scarred you're going to throw a welcome-home party to help him get over it,' she said scornfully. 'That's what rich people do to solve their kids' problems, right? Throw parties at them?'

'What?' I said, mystified. 'Party . . . what party?'

River gave a theatrical sigh. 'We both got the invitation.' She nodded to Marcus. 'But don't worry, we're not coming.' Her eyes were full of disdain. 'I've got nothing to prove to you. Not any more.'

With that, she slid off her chair.

'River, wait,' Marcus called. He stood up hastily, shouldering his bag – and then stumbled, catching himself on the table edge with a grasping hand.

'Are you all right?' I asked him, alarmed. Christ, was he going to faint again?

'I'm fine,' he muttered, and turned away from me.

'Wait,' I said. 'What invitation did you get? What's she talking about? Marcus!'

He wasn't listening to me. He caught up with River but she shook him off and marched out of the cafeteria without so much as a backward glance at me.

She had left me behind like it didn't make a difference what I said or did, or what we had done and been through. It was all forgotten, past tense. Over and done. She hadn't even been angry. She hadn't even given me that. It was as if I no longer mattered at all.

As if I never had.

CHAPTER 11

I came home restless under a glowering sky.

The wind pushed me up the porch and to the front door, almost as if it wanted to hurry me inside where it was safe. The house itself was quiet and dark. There was a note from Esther fixed to the kitchen fridge saying she wouldn't be home until after dinner. Gwydion was away until tomorrow morning. Thalia and Fenrin were bogged down with extra tutoring after school and weren't due back until late tonight.

I was alone.

It happened so rarely that, for a moment, I felt lost. I stood in the dimness of the kitchen and listened to the fridge give its quiet purr, trying to suck some of the house's stillness into me and calm my head. I felt like I had a heavy black stone in my stomach, weighing down the core of me with its cold hard mass.

My mind wandered back to the clearing, now full of dangling, desperate wishes.

The whole set-up reminded me very strongly of the night guests who used to come visiting my parents once upon a time. Though there hadn't been any in years, there was a time in my childhood when they had seemed to arrive two or three times a week.

It would begin with a hesitant knock at the front door, usually after we had gone to bed. The visitor would be let in and ushered to Esther's conservatory or sometimes to Gwydion's study. Doors would be firmly shut and secrets would be spilled – the kind that might require a witch's touch to resolve.

Thalia, Fen and I had devised ever quieter footsteps and ghost-like movements to sneak as close as we dared and try to snatch some of those secrets for ourselves. The twins had never lasted much past the first flush of excitement, and they had often fallen asleep next to me as I strained to hear details and requests that could only be talked about in the velvet comfort of deep night behind a closed door.

I was the kind of dragon who hoarded secret truths over gold. I'd always supposed that didn't make me very nice. Though half of what was said went straight over my head at the time, the memories of the stories those visitors had spun, the way they had talked, the longing in their voices – it was through them that I first came to understand desire as the driving force of magic.

They were never allowed to pay in money, but we used to find gifts on the porch. Fresh cakes. Bottles of wine. Rare herbs in clay pots. Huge jars of homemade honey that turned up at the front door so often, child-me had been convinced everyone got honey by getting a honey fairy to bring them some in the middle of the night, like we seemed to do.

It was a very old tradition. They were not so much payments as tokens, left on the porch as the supplicants' side of a bargain. Both the supplicant and the witch had to trade something, to keep a balance between them. Witches do not like to owe anyone and no one should ever owe a witch.

Witches also do not spill their supplicants' secrets. It is why we are so damn good at keeping them. That is the bargain. Break that and break the tenuous threads that link you.

Did River know that? Did she even care?

I was startled out of my thoughts by a noise. A scraping that came low in the pit of my belly, so low that I didn't understand, at first, that it was a sound and not a feeling. I slowed, curious, and then froze when it came again. It felt low because it was coming from beneath me.

The only thing below was the cellar.

The scraping came again.

'Hello?' I called out.

The scraping stopped. I strained, listening, but there was nothing more. Probably the wind, or ... another sound, one I could identify – bottles clinking together. The cellar housed Esther's stores of her infamous homemade wine. Generally speaking, wind couldn't make full, heavy bottles move around.

Either someone was down there or something was broken.

There was absolutely no way I was staying in the house by myself without knowing which one.

'Shit,' I muttered as I approached the cellar door tucked into the corner of the kitchen. The door was normally kept locked, with the key living permanently in the keyhole – but the key was missing, and when I pushed at the door, it swung open.

Beyond was nothing but darkness.

'Shit, shit, shit.'

I reached a hand for the light switch and turned it on, flooding the steps in dull yellow light.

Silence.

'If there's an axe murderer down here, I'm going to be so annoyed,' I called out in a strangled voice.

Silence.

Cursing under my breath, I forced myself down the stairs. The cellar light was a paltry thing, giving the whole place a grimy cast, and it didn't reach the very back wall where most of the wine bottles lived in their dusty stacked holders, which were permanently cast in shadow.

I peered around, every nerve on high alert.

'*Summer*,' hissed a voice from the darkness.

I never screamed when I was shocked. Instead I did this strangled kind of inhale and then forgot how to breathe. The hiss melted into a laugh and from the darkness a shape emerged. A Wolf-shaped shape. He moved from his crouch beside the wine holders, a bottle in his hand.

'You utter *bastard*,' I managed, clutching at my heart. I still wasn't used to the idea of him being here full-time, and it hadn't occurred to me to wonder where he was.

His laugh turned gleeful.

'What the hell are you doing down here, creeping around in the dark?'

'Having fun,' he said, balancing back on his haunches.

I pointed at the bottle in his hand, the hammering of my heart making my voice wobble. 'It's a little bit early in the day, don't you think?'

'It's never too early to have fun,' Wolf said cheerfully.

'This is not fun.'

'Speak for yourself.'

'Wolf, seriously.'

'Seriously?' He broke into another laugh. 'Lighten *up*. Have you had a bad day or something?'

I sighed. 'Something like that.'

'Come here,' he said, parking himself on the ground. It was cold, packed earth, and not exactly cosy.

I eyed him dubiously. 'Why, so you can pretend to axe-murder me?'

He tutted. 'Come here.'

I crossed to him.

'Sit.'

I sank down to the packed earth and copied him, leaning my back against the stacks. His knee pushed against mine, our thighs parallel. He passed me the bottle and fastened my hand around the neck.

'Come on,' I said feebly.

He scoffed. 'It's not poison. You need to relax.' His hand reached over to me and he gave my stomach a brief scrape with his fingertips. 'Feed that illicit little thrill tickling your insides. Just the once.'

There was, indeed, an illicit thrill blooming there,

damn him. I felt a recklessness steal over me and welcomed it like a blanket. It was my old friend, this feeling.

I upended the open bottle into my mouth. Esther's homemade wine tasted like she had somehow bottled a summer storm together with fresh blackberries off the bush. It was earth and plums, just a little salt, and thick, dark syrup. Apple and rain.

'Oh man,' I said, when I could speak again. 'I'd forgotten what this stuff is like.'

The tingle in my throat spread downward, running my veins through with sparks.

'Better, no?' Wolf murmured.

'You're not an alcoholic, are you?' I waved the bottle at him. A third of its contents were already gone and I'd only had a sip.

He laughed. 'Please. There's always an open bottle going down here. Your parents partake of their solitary escapes, on occasion. You know that.'

I was silent. I did know this, having caught sight of them drinking alone once or twice over the years, but the idea of it made me feel uncomfortable somehow.

'So,' Wolf said in an easy tone, 'tell me about your bad day.'

'Well, I've been doing some investigating today. Turns out that River has been going around offering out "wishes" to anyone who wants them, as long as they give her money for it. She gets them to go to our clearing in the woods and then she grants them anonymously—'

'Wait. She's pretending to be you?'

I paused. 'Well, no.' Ella flashed into my head. 'People are just assuming it's us.'

'Wow,' Wolf said, sounding serious. 'It sounds like she wants to be the new Summer Grace.'

I hadn't thought about it like that.

'Do you think?' I said, feeling uneasy.

Wolf shrugged. 'At the very least. It feels a bit sinister to me.'

Sinister. Was that River? I'd never thought of her like that before. I'd always given her the benefit of the doubt, believing her when she said that she never meant to do the harmful things she did. Was I being naive?

'There's more,' I said. 'I think her magic is going wrong, making people sick. But when I confronted her about it, it was like she didn't even care.' I sighed and leaned my head back against the wine stacks behind us. 'I thought she didn't want to hurt people. I thought she had her magic under control but she doesn't, and I don't know what to do.'

'Your binding spell didn't work, then,' Wolf said.

I glanced at him. 'How do you know about that?'

He shrugged. 'Pillow talk.'

'Ew,' I said, scandalised. 'That's my brother.'

'He doesn't mind.'

'Stop.' I subsided. 'I feel weirdly guilty about casting that binding on her.'

'Look,' Wolf said, unperturbed, 'here's a brutal truth that no one seems to have the courage to face: there are people in this world who deserve what they get.'

I tossed him a look. 'Maybe, but that's a bad road to go down. Who's to say who deserves what? What system of justice are you using to determine that one?'

'My own. It's the only one anyone can ever use. Justice as a universal concept is inherently flawed.'

'What about if it's an innocent who gets hurt?'

He gave me a pitying look. 'There is no such thing as an innocent.'

'Ella's mother is only sick because her daughter wanted to go out on a date,' I retorted. 'She hasn't done anything wrong.'

'Oh, but how do you know for sure? You only know what the woman has let slip into the world. What about all the dark and dirty secrets she keeps hidden, the bad things she's capable of? If you knew *them*, would you be so quick to feel sorry for her, or would it make it easier to punish her?'

'How do you know what she's done?'

'Darling,' he said, 'I know everything that's going on in this town. There's a trick to it.'

'What is it?' I asked curiously, caught by the hushed tone in his voice. Some kind of spell?

Wolf raised a hand and wiggled his fingers in a mystical pattern.

'There exists an oracle,' he intoned solemnly. 'If you make a pilgrimage to it, and you sit quietly and open your heart, it will tell you any truth about anyone in this town that you care to know.'

'Where is it?'

'On the bench outside the supermarket near Garner Park. The oracle's names are Mrs Jean Monroe and Ms Agatha Torrence, and they are two of the biggest gossips I've ever met.' He grinned. 'The other week I bought a coffee and sat near them. Within twenty minutes I knew half the current scandals in town. People just seem to find it easy to talk around me.' He affected a modest look.

I rolled my eyes. 'Magical.'

'There's magic in mundanity, if you know where to look.' He gave me a sidelong glance. 'Feeling any better?'

'You know how sometimes your head is so full of a million things that it gets all gloopy, like if you turned it too fast, stuff would start sloshing out of your ears?' I said. 'Sometimes I just want to shut it down. Think about nothing.' I raised the bottle. 'Here's a tried-and-tested method, I guess, though not exactly a healthy one.'

'Needs must when the devil drives,' Wolf replied. He must have picked the expression up from Thalia – it was one of her favourites. 'Though, there is a healthier method.'

His smile was lascivious enough for me to understand exactly what he meant.

'Not a lot of options in that department right now,' I said mournfully. 'I don't even think my old enemy-with-benefits Jase Worthington would consider it. We'd probably have to fight first, maybe call each other some names.'

'That sounds like a lot of work,' Wolf agreed. 'Plus you'd have to leave the house again, and why bother when I'm right here?'

Shock. It made me do that inhaling thing again, which was damn near perilous when in the middle of drinking. I nearly choked and ended up having to spray my mouthful of wine across the floor.

'You're a funny guy,' I wheezed, and then coughed.

Wolf folded his arms and watched me splutter, amused. 'You're right, but the offer is there.'

I searched his face for the joke I knew he was hiding.

'Come on,' I said, bemused.

'Don't tell me you've never thought about it because I know you have.'

I pulled a face, growing embarrassed. 'Shut up, Wolf.'

'Ha,' he said delightedly. 'You *have*.'

'Stop it.' I made to scramble upright but he pulled me down with a laugh.

'Come on, Summer,' he said. 'You've never been a prude before. We're just talking. It's called puberty. Hormones. Everyone experiences it.'

'It was years ago,' I snapped. 'Anyway, you're with Fenrin.'

'Sure.'

'*Sure?*' I mocked, air quoting around the word. 'Nice, Wolf. Nice. I bet he really appreciates that. And here's me thinking he looks so tired because of you, but I guess you're getting your jollies elsewhere.'

'Relax,' Wolf said. 'You're so uptight. Fenrin is the one getting all my jollies, I promise.' He paused, thoughtful. 'Do you really think he looks exhausted? Maybe I'm wearing him out.'

'Boy,' I said, unable to keep the scandalised note

from my voice, 'you have developed a truly *impressive* impulse-control problem.'

'So what? I'm enjoying being alive. Trust me, it's a hell of a lot better than being dead. You want to punish me for that?'

I gazed at his profile. Alcohol had made him expansively eloquent, it seemed, whereas in the past it would have shut him down even more than normal. He sounded so sure of himself. Honest.

'I get it,' I said softly.

He looked away. 'No, you don't.'

'Do you . . . remember any of it?'

He paused so long that I thought I wasn't going to get an answer.

'There was nothing,' he said at last. 'Then there was the beach. And River, next to me, talking to me. I couldn't understand her. I couldn't understand anything at first.' He seemed to shake himself. 'It took a while to get used to . . . being here. But I'm here now and it feels good.' He leaned into me. 'Hey, how about that party you suggested?'

'Huh,' I said sourly. 'If we did that now, she really would think I was mocking her.'

'Hmm?'

'Someone sent River and Marcus fake invitations to a welcome-home party for you.'

'Oh yes,' he said. 'That was me.'

I sat up. 'What?! Why?'

He shrugged. 'You guys mentioned a party. I wanted to get a head start.'

I stared at him.

He blew out a breath. 'Okay. I guess I thought it would be funny.'

'Well, it wasn't,' I retorted. 'Now she hates me.'

'Why do you care, Summer? If anything, I did you a favour. Now it'll be easier for you to stay away from each other. Isn't that what you're supposed to be doing?'

I growled. 'You sound like Fenrin.'

'Because he's right,' Wolf remarked.

'I guess.'

But despite everything, it didn't feel right.

'Hey.' He nudged me with his thigh. 'Don't be sad.'

I tried to smile. 'I'm not.'

'Lies. I know a way to cheer you up.'

I rolled my eyes. 'What?'

Before I quite knew what was happening, he had launched himself at me and tackled me to the ground, pinning me down. I squealed and writhed and wrestled, and it was funny and stupid and fine, and then I felt heat on my neck.

Wolf dipped his head into me and brushed his lips on my skin.

For one moment, I thought it was a mistake. He'd just brushed me awkwardly, that was all. We lay, stilled, one heavy second peeling off after another – and then his lips were on my skin again, making it shiver into his mouth, and that was not a mistake.

I stiffened and pushed him off me, my heart climbing into my mouth.

He sat back on his haunches, watching me.

'What are you doing?' I said, breathless with shock.

'Don't you like it?'

I wanted to lie. I wanted to push him into the dirt and lie.

But I couldn't.

'You're with Fenrin,' I said. 'You're with my *brother*.'

'We're seizing the moment,' he said. '*Carpe diem*, Summer, because tomorrow you might be dead.' The words buzzed like soft bees against my skin, making me feel drunk, suddenly, in a soft and nauseous rush.

As he leaned forward, the hem of his sweater rode up, just enough to show the tail of the lizard tattoo that crawled across his groin next to his hip. I stared

153

at it, hypnotised, and then I felt Wolf's lips meet mine, soft and insistent.

And I didn't stop him.

This was wrong. This was weird. It felt like falling and never hitting ground.

I pulled away.

Fenrin.

'I don't want this,' I said, my voice shaking, scrambling to my feet. 'Okay? You're with Fenrin. I don't want you.'

As I turned and fled up the cellar steps I heard him say softly, 'Liar.'

CHAPTER 12

I was curled up under my bedcovers with my hands clamped around the headphones on my ears, as if I could drown out the awful choices I had recently been making, if I just pushed hard enough.

Over the next three days, my encounter with Wolf in the cellar surfaced in my head at arbitrary moments, causing my entire being to seize up in utter, total and complete numbing shame.

You were drunk.

But I hadn't had enough wine to be drunk.

I'm enjoying being alive, Wolf had said. *Trust me, it's a hell of a lot better than being dead.*

There was such a thing as enjoying life too much.

My first instinct had been to come clean to Fenrin. We had always trusted each other with the truth because we knew what it was like to be kept in the dark. I nearly had, as well, but then I'd found a note underneath my pillow from Wolf.

I'm sorry. It was a drunken mistake and it won't happen again. I won't tell if you don't. Please?

After a long struggle I decided to go along with Wolf's plea. Since then, we had avoided each other like the plague, unable to even catch each other's eye. He seemed as mortified about the whole thing as I was. It was that more than anything else that convinced me he was genuinely sorry.

But I still couldn't get rid of this sickly feeling in my stomach.

Groaning, I pressed the headphones into my ears. Listening to music, for me, was like swimming underwater. Night swimming, cocooned in darkness, the real world high above, muffled and unimportant. Lately, I had spent hours indulging this method of escape, since I badly needed to sever my connection to the reality of my life.

From beyond the beats burring through my skull, I heard knocking on my bedroom door. I was in no mood to entertain a visitor and ignored them, hoping they would go away. The knocking only got more insistent.

I dragged off my headphones.

'Who is it?' I asked. *Please, please, not Fenrin.*

'It's me,' came my sister's voice.

My pounding heart eased.

'I'm busy,' I informed my bedroom door. The door didn't seem to give a rat's ass about my current mood, swinging open without a care in the world.

'Traitor,' I told the door.

'Who's a traitor?' Thalia said as she came in.

'No one.'

'Summer, you've been moping around like this for a couple of days. Are you okay?'

I sighed. It was hard to force a lie out of a guilty throat.

'I don't want to talk about it yet,' I said. 'Okay? Can we just focus on something else?'

Thalia closed the door behind her, navigating my room on swift bare feet to flump onto the bottom of my bed. She crossed her legs, sat up straight, and regarded me with serious eyes.

'You know, when you're ready, you can talk to me, right?'

I nodded mutely, feeling miserable.

'Okay.' Thalia held up a hand. 'I have something that will take your mind off it.'

'What?' I grumped.

'I-O-N-A.'

'I wasn't paying attention in acronyms class, Thalia.'

'It's not an acronym, it's a name. Iona.' Thalia gave me a triumphant look. 'I know who that girl on the Princess card is in the divination deck you found.'

I frowned. 'She's just a painting.'

'No she's not, she's a real person. Or at least she *was*.'

My stomach dropped, as if it had worked out what was coming next before I had.

'Her family name was Webber, but she was a Grace – her father was married to one of our great aunts, or something. She was the last one before Wolf to die from the curse.' There was a feverish catch to Thalia's voice. 'She died in a fire.'

I remembered the vision of the card burning, smoke roiling up from its edges, and Thalia's hand as a curiously beautiful fireball.

'Don't be weird,' I said uneasily.

Thalia's head gave a vehement shake. 'I'm not, I promise you. Ask our parents about it. Or ... well, you can try. You know what it's like talking to them about the curse.'

Yes, we all knew what that was like. Head, meet brick wall.

I eyed her. 'Then how do you know about Iona?'

'Because it happened when I was, like, eight,'

Thalia said. 'I remember the phone call Esther got to tell her that Iona had died. It was pretty bad.'

'I don't remember any of this,' I protested, but that wasn't quite true. I had vague stirrings of a time in my childhood suffused with the feeling of something gone wrong. We had gone on a trip to see cousins without my parents, and their absence had seemed like forever to little six-year-old me.

'Well, I do,' Thalia declared. 'It was her – and her boyfriend, Nathaniel Dowl.'

'Did he die in the fire, too?' I asked.

'No, I think he managed to escape. Imagine having to cope with that for the rest of your life. They die, but you live.'

I gave a soft laugh. 'Yeah. Imagine. So the grand conclusion from this exciting episode of *The Twilight Zone* is . . . what, exactly?'

Thalia brought her hand around from her back. In it was a folded piece of paper, which she tossed into my lap. At first glance it seemed to be some sort of boring administration form with typed answers in each blank box. It wasn't until I glanced up at the top and caught the word *Death* – the simplest title possible for such a form – and then the name *Iona Webber* that I understood what I was looking at.

'Thalia,' I said slowly, 'is this what I think it is?'

'If you think it's Iona Webber's death certificate, then yes,' Thalia said solemnly.

'Holy crap.' I looked at her from over the top of the paper. 'How did you get hold of this?'

'Requested it online.'

'You can do that?' I said, impressed.

Thalia ignored this. 'Check out the *cause of death* box near the bottom.'

I scanned, greedy for more. 'Asphyxiation due to smoke inhalation from a fire.'

Thalia was soft. 'I was right.'

I kept scanning. Iona Webber. Her age was a stab in the chest: just twenty-three when she died. Judging by her parents' address, she had grown up in the city only a couple of hours away.

'You were right,' I confirmed. 'But how does this help us?'

'Summer, this is our chance. We've never had a way of finding out more about the curse without having to ask our own, entirely unchatty family – until now.'

'How?'

Thalia tapped the death certificate in my hands. 'There's her last known address – same as her parents' address. I bet they still live there.'

'So call them up and check.'

'I'm not scaring them off. We need to visit them in person. It's harder to say no to someone in person.'

'Presuming they even let us in the door,' I said. 'What makes you think they're going to be any more forthcoming on the curse than our parents?'

'Have we ever met the Webbers?' Thalia asked. 'In fact, do you remember the name Iona or indeed Webber ever being mentioned? Has a Webber come to a single one of our Yule parties?'

I thought. 'No. I'd never even heard of her until you said her name.'

Thalia was satisfied. 'I think they're estranged from the rest of our family, and I really want to know why.'

I took a long look at my sister.

Thalia had always been obsessed with the curse, its history, its source – even more so since she and Marcus had split. She was the one who had first told him the very oldest version of the Four Bells, the origin story of our family's *malediction d'amour*.

I remembered that moment last year when I had uncovered a fox heart, half buried between the thick roots of the guard dog. I remembered the cool, dry feel of it on my cupped palms, a tiny, earthy, squashed ball. And I'd never forgotten the crawling sensation under my ribs when I realised what it meant – that my sister had tried black magic to break the curse.

By herself.

Thalia had a way, sometimes, of taking matters into her own hands.

'So when exactly are we supposed to get the chance to travel to the city without being missed?' I asked.

'This weekend.' Thalia was triumphant. 'Esther has to go up north for some hideously dull meeting with her shareholders, and Gwydion has a business trip he refuses to get out of. Neither of them will be back until Sunday morning.'

I frowned, surprised. 'They're leaving us alone overnight?'

It would be the first time they had dared to do so since Wolf came back.

'They're leaving you in the care of your incredibly mature and responsible older sister,' Thalia said with studied casualness. 'I've already written out meal plans and chore lists and a studying timetable because that, baby sister, is the sort of thing that I do.'

Delight began its warm trickle into my guts. 'You're so organised. And so deeply manipulative.'

Thalia surveyed me archly. 'Needs must when the devil drives.'

CHAPTER 13

'*Summer*. Wake up.'

'I'm tired,' I muttered into my pillow. 'Leave me alone.'

'No way. You have to get up now.'

'I do not,' I retorted.

'Come on, come on.' Thalia bounced happily on the end of my bed.

I wrenched the bedcover back and heaved myself into a sitting position. 'Fine. FINE. I'm awake.'

'It stirs!' Thalia declared. 'And the villagers flee before it, screaming in horror!'

'Shut up.' I checked the time on the black plastic clock shaped liked a skull that sat on my bedside table. Thalia thought it was the tackiest thing she'd ever seen, which was half the reason I had bought it. With the way my sister's eyes crinkled ever so slightly with distaste whenever her gaze fell on it, the clock had paid for itself several times over already.

'Are the others up yet?' I said.

'Nope, they're still asleep, and Esther and Gwydion left over an hour ago. Which means we get breakfast all to ourselves, if you're quick.' Thalia leapt up with a tinkling of belled anklets and whipped out of the door, leaving me staring after her in bleary surprise.

Two hours later I stood in the hallway, impatiently tapping my foot as my sister sashayed down the stairs clutching her favourite purse.

'I got up *after* you,' I shot at her.

'It takes work to look this good.'

'It takes nothing. You look the same as you did when you woke up, which is one of the most annoying things about you.'

'Just get in the taxi.' She shoved me towards the front door.

We took the train to Iona's parents' house, and gradually, as an ever-changing landscape slid past my window in a comforting roll, some of the cloud I'd been living under recently began to lift. Just for a little while, maybe I could forget all that weighed heavy on me.

I glanced at my sister sitting opposite. The ends of

her bobbed blonde hair skirted gently under the line of her chin as she painted a vibrant shade of red on her lips. The shadows under her eyes, the lips, the hair – it gave her a fragile 1920s air, something of a Daisy Buchanan about her.

'You do *not* wear red,' I said, delighted.

'Felt like a change.'

'I didn't even know you owned that colour.'

'I don't. It's yours.' Thalia grinned.

'Thief.' I looked out of the window, pretending to grump.

'I kind of wish Fenrin and Wolf had wanted to come,' she said, putting the cover back on my lipstick with a satisfying click.

I didn't.

'I think it's good for them to get some alone time,' I hazarded.

'Are you kidding? It's the first time in forever they get the house to themselves. *Someone needs to stay behind and look after Wolf,*' Thalia said, mimicking my brother's pitiful excuse to us. 'Yes, Fenrin, we all know what "looking after" means.'

I tried not to squirm.

Thalia pulled a face. 'They need to stop. Fenrin looks terrible at the moment. He says he's not sleeping well and three guesses what that means, but whenever

165

I tell him off about it, he just laughs at me. They're too reckless. It's like everything else comes second to their appetites.' She leaned into me. 'I think Wolf is a bad influence on him.'

I could not roll my eyes fast enough. Wolf was a bad influence on more than Fenrin.

They had always had this strange, itching tension between them, Fenrin and Wolf. In the beginning, I chalked it up to that peculiar thing boys seemed to do around other boys, that competitiveness they displayed. It wasn't there all the time. Whole days passed in our summers together where it was too warm, too fun, too busy for them to let it in much. The back garden became another world, since we were adept at spinning fantasy. Every tree potentially led to another land and wars between mythical races were fought and won in the grove.

But finally, I noticed a secret suspended between them, a connection that some instinctive part of me recognised the shape of, even as I struggled to understand what it meant.

The worst thing was that they kept it from me – all three of them, Thalia complicit. They fancied themselves practically adults and it was their secret game, one I wasn't allowed to know about or participate in because I was only fourteen, the baby sister. It drove me absolutely crazy. I'd watch them whisper to one another when they knew I couldn't hear, or drop oblique clues into normal conversations, using code words and silences to communicate over my head.

I reacted the only way I knew how. I marched into Fenrin's bedroom one evening and confronted him, threatening to tell our parents unless he confessed. I remembered Fenrin's coyness, the flush in his cheeks as he told me that he liked Wolf and Wolf liked him.

For the rest of that summer holiday I became a co-conspirator, helping find ever-more-elaborate ways for Fenrin and Wolf to spend time with each other away from curious eyes. It wasn't hard, as the adults largely let us be as long as we were all together, but the fun of the game depended on us pretending that it was.

They struggled around each other in those early days, though. Fenrin was afraid of how vulnerable his feelings for Wolf made him, and Wolf was the world's most taciturn boy. Now I was glad that at least one positive thing had come from everything Wolf had been through. He no longer saw any point in hiding their desire, and it was obvious how happy that made Fenrin.

It was that thought that made me come to a decision. No more brooding. I would get over what had happened in the cellar, and fast. I would not, could not, let anything come between them.

Not when they were finally finding some kind of happiness.

Iona Webber had grown up in a fashionable part of the city.

Her house was a beautiful, slender town house at the end of a row in a leafy residential street. In the distance you could hear the general hum of a city turning, but here it was calm and quiet. A graceful set of steps led upward to a black lacquered front door, and a tiny grilled window was just visible above ground, presumably as part of a cellar. The tall bay windows by the front door were swathed in plain white curtains. Weak winter sunlight shone on the glass, betraying nothing of the world inside.

'What if they're not in?' I murmured.

Beside me, Thalia shrugged. 'We go shopping, taking time out to drink some ridiculous mocha-locha-latte-choco coffee with marshmallows, and eat seven-layer cake in an achingly cool cafe. Then we come back and try again later.'

I contemplated this. 'I kind of hope they're not in.'

She flashed me a smile and took the first step, but as her foot touched it, I felt a sudden spike of dark, skittering nerves.

'Thalia,' I said. 'Let's not. Let's just go back home.'

She tossed an annoyed glance at me.

'What? Let's at least see if they're here. We came all this way.'

Before I could stop her, she walked lightly up the rest of the steps, paused at the door, and rang the bell.

For a long moment, nothing happened. Thalia rang it again, but I could see by the set of her shoulders she was already preparing to come back down, resigned. Just as her foot drew back, there was a click and a rattle and the door unlocked, swinging back inside.

A man stood there, blinking in the light, dressed in a loose V-neck and faded, ripped jeans that hung pleasingly from his hips. He was in his twenties, lanky and gently rumpled in a way that, it must be said, was immediately easy on the eye. Disappointingly, he was way too young to be Iona's father – much closer to our age than our parents'.

His gaze fastened on Thalia.

'Can I help you?' he said in a soft voice, puzzled curiosity wrinkling his features.

'I'm sorry,' Thalia said. 'I think we came to the wrong place.'

She skated back from him and I put my foot on the first step in ready support.

The man's eyes flicked down to me.

'Who are you looking for?' he asked.

Thalia seemed unable to speak.

'Mr and Mrs Webber,' I called up, wondering at my sister's sudden nerves. 'But they're totally old. You're not . . .' I left it hanging.

'Ah,' he said in sudden understanding. 'They did live here, but they sold the house to me a few years ago. I'm not sure where they are now.'

Disappointment rolled through me. Despite my earlier misgivings, I'd let Thalia sweep me along on her tide of confidence, but it had only ever been a complete shot in the dark.

'Never mind,' I said. 'Sorry to have bothered you.'

The man leaned against the doorframe, an unconsciously louche gesture that made him even nicer to look at. 'Well, what did you want to talk to them about? Maybe I can help you.'

'It was about their daughter, Iona,' Thalia said, finally finding her voice again. 'We just wanted to ask some questions about her, that's all.'

The man's gaze switched between us both, back and forth, back and forth, like the lashing tail of a cat.

'You're Graces,' he said at last.

A chill ran through me, propelling me up the steps to stand beside Thalia.

'How d'you know that?' I asked.

This close, the man's loveliness was just a little too much. Clear eyes like sparkling liquid. A razor edge of a jawline countered by a soft, full mouth. Thick, ruffled, dark hair that gave him the air of a slouchy rock star. Gorgeous, dishevelled, with a wild, bohemian air.

I could see why Thalia was tongue-tied.

Instead of answering my question, he countered with another. 'You have no idea who I am, do you?' He took our silence for assent and his lips curled into a faint smile. 'I guess I'm not surprised.'

'Uh huh,' I said, getting impatient. 'Are you going to let us in on the joke?'

'It's no joke,' he assured me. 'You want to know about Iona? You can talk to me.'

'We can?'

He pushed off the doorframe. 'Want to come in?'

My eyebrows rose into my hair. 'Don't you want to know who we are, first?'

His forehead crumpled with mild condescension. 'You're Esther's girls. I can see her in your faces.'

Beside me, I felt Thalia stir excitedly, ready to accept his invitation, but I wasn't.

'Then we're at a disadvantage,' I said coolly. 'I'm assuming you knew Iona?'

His smile widened, but his eyes were downcast, giving it a wistfulness.

'You could say that,' he replied. 'We were in love.'

I stared. Standing relaxed before us, as if fate were the most natural thing in the world, was Iona's boyfriend, Nathaniel. The one who had escaped the fire.

The one who had escaped the curse.

CHAPTER 14

Nathaniel padded further into the narrow hallway on bare feet, beckoning us inward.

The walls were covered in sketches and paintings, some framed, some not. The living-room door was ajar and I caught a flash of various-sized canvases stacked against one wall as I passed. It looked like Nathaniel was an artist.

He led us to the kitchen and to a small fold-out table next to the back door that could just about sit four. He pulled out two chairs for us, but I couldn't sit, not yet. I watched his tanned feet brush over the floor's coloured tiles as he moved around the room, opening up the blinds and flooding the space with sunlight.

'Coffee, tea?' he asked.

'Let me help you,' Thalia offered.

'No, no. Please, sit. Now, what can I get you?'

We settled on a pot of coffee between the three of us. I leaned awkwardly against a countertop as Thalia took a seat at the table with her back to the garden, her eyes not quite on our host.

In our kitchen back home everything was in its right place, shut up neatly in cupboards of muted wood, calm and in control. Nathaniel's kitchen, by contrast, was a mess of brazen colour. French tin prints lined the walls, old reproduced adverts for soaps and riotous shows at the Folies-Bergère nestled in between sketches of nudes stretched out on divans or undressing in front of floor-length mirrors.

Nudes. In the kitchen.

Esther would pitch a fit.

'So how did you end up living here?' I asked, watching Nathaniel busy himself with a cafetière.

'You mean, how come I bought the house of my dead girlfriend?' he said baldly. 'Yeah, I appreciate that it looks a little weird. After what happened, her parents were the only ones who didn't turn their backs on me and we stayed friends. They ended up not wanting to live here any more. Too many memories, I guess. I needed a studio space and they were willing to sell the place to someone they knew at a cut price, so it all just kind of worked out.'

Thalia frowned. 'Who turned their backs on you?'

Nathaniel was quiet, but it didn't take a genius to figure it out.

'Our parents,' I said. 'Right?'

He shrugged. 'We haven't spoken for a long time.'

'Why not?'

He switched the kettle on and turned to face me, mirroring my stance by leaning against the countertop behind his hips.

'You're the forthright one,' he said, a smile spreading languidly across his mouth. 'There's always a forthright one.'

'I'll take that as a compliment.'

'You should.'

'I'm sorry,' Thalia interjected, 'we're so rude. We haven't even told you our names.'

Nathaniel held up a long finger. 'Let me see if I can remember. There was the youngest, Summer.'

'That's me,' I said.

He gave me an amused nod. 'Then the elder twins. Was it Thalia and Fenrir?'

'Rin,' I corrected. 'Fenrin.'

His hand went to his chest and he bowed his head. 'Forgive me.'

Fenrin might have to give up his King of Charming crown to this guy.

'So how come you fell out with our family?' I said.

Thalia hissed my name.

Nathaniel shrugged. 'It was because of Iona.' There was a microsecond's hesitation before he said her name. Just enough for me to understand that she might still, after ten years, be causing him pain.

I immediately felt a rush of guilt.

'You don't have to . . .' I began.

He just smiled in response. 'You came here to talk about her. It's fine.'

But I wasn't sure if it was, and now I saw the imposition we were making. Turning up unannounced, expecting a stranger to unburden himself to us.

Nathaniel busied himself with finishing up the coffee, carrying the cafetière over to the kitchen table, along with three mugs. The sugar bowl was a clay fish, I noticed, painted a deep, gorgeous blue. You had to spoon the sugar from out of its mouth.

Nathaniel took the chair opposite Thalia and wrapped his hands around his mug.

'Your family blamed me for Iona's death,' he began. 'But look, I get it. It's just what happens when someone dies from the curse. The survivor bears the brunt of the family's pain, especially if the survivor is the outsider.'

So Iona's boyfriend had been an outsider. Like River.

'They completely ostracised me,' Nathaniel said, staring into his mug. 'First I lost her, and then I lost everyone else. You have to understand what it's like coming into your family. You fall for one Grace, you fall for them all. It's like a package deal. And when all of that is taken away ...' His smile this time was tired and bruised.

'I'm so sorry,' Thalia murmured.

He tutted. 'You should never try to bear the burdens of previous generations. Their mistakes are theirs and not yours. Anyway, I'm not blaming Esther. I think it's difficult for any of you to think straight when it comes to the curse. Living under that kind of weight ... it can make you do crazy things.' His eyes held a warning note.

Too late, Nathaniel, I thought sourly. *We're all insane already.*

'And Iona in particular was ... beloved,' he continued. 'She lit up a room when she walked into it, you know? She was so full of passion and joy. Talented. Extraordinary. It was devastating for everyone to lose her.'

The silence this time was heavy.

He tried to rally. 'God, listen to me being so fucking maudlin. Ask me any question you like about her.'

The swear word jolted me. I might cut oaths like a sailor, but all the adults I knew never swore in front of me. I'd never heard Esther utter so much as a 'shit' in all my life.

I glanced at Thalia. She was the one who had got us here.

'How did you two meet?' she asked.

Nathaniel's face broke into a wild grin, at odds with the lazy, cultivated smiles so far. 'She tried to run me over.'

'Say what?' I cut in.

It was all the invitation he needed. He launched into the story of his time with Iona with joy, talking animatedly and delightedly as his coffee grew cold, untouched.

He hardly needed encouragement but Thalia gave it, and sweetly. I knew she was trying to be kind. I also knew that she wanted more from him than just information. Flirtatious Thalia was normally an immensely subtle thing – she once said she had to pin Marcus down and kiss him before he would believe that she wanted him – but with Nathaniel, I could see it on her plain as day.

The more Nathaniel chatted, the clearer it became, too, that he knew our mother far better than she had ever deigned to let on. I felt a seed of cold anger plant itself in my heart, yearning to grow. I couldn't believe that she had cut him off from us just because of the curse.

I knew she was controlling. I knew she always wanted to keep the curse well away from us, as if she could protect us better if she kept us in the dark, but I had never resented her so much for that as I did now. What was so bad about knowing all there was to know about what we faced? Did she think so little of us that she didn't see fit to arm us with the truth?

We were two coffee pots and three hours in before I realised just how much time had passed. Nathaniel stirred in his chair and my stomach growled in annoyance.

'Christ, I'm starving,' I said without thinking.

'That's because it's lunchtime,' Nathaniel replied with a crooked grin. 'Let me make you something.'

'Oh no,' Thalia demurred. 'We wouldn't want to put you to the trouble.'

'It's zero trouble. In fact it's in minus figures – I made this, dare I say it myself, astonishingly delicious coq au vin last night for a dinner party, but I only had five people over and I seem to have made enough for twenty. Help me finish it?' He gave us a pleading look, liquid eyes huge in his face.

Thalia did her very best casual face. 'If you're sure,' she said.

'Positive. Leftovers are a crime against the planet.' Nathaniel leapt to his feet. 'But I should make some potatoes to go with ... Give me, mm, twenty minutes?' He twirled a hand. 'Go hang out in the living room if you like.'

'Do you mind if we look around your house?' I asked.

'Sure. It's a mess, sorry. And, erm ... I beg of you, don't go into my bedroom upstairs. I don't want you to think so badly of me when we've only just met.' His smile turned embarrassed and his hands clasped together self-consciously.

'Please,' Thalia sniffed. 'If your room is any worse than Summer's, I'll die of shock.'

'That'd be reason enough for me,' I shot back, stung. 'Don't worry, we won't go into your room, we'll stay on the ground floor.' I jerked on Thalia's hand, my voice sweet venom. 'Come, sister.'

I pulled her out of the kitchen and down the corridor, hauling her into the living room.

'Ow,' she whined.

I heard the distant clang of a cooking pot from the kitchen and felt reassured that Nathaniel couldn't hear us.

'What are you playing at?' I hissed at her.

'What are you talking about?'

'Stop flirting with him.'

Thalia's expression dropped.

'I'm not,' she said, annoyed.

'Are you kidding me?'

She rolled her eyes, as if I was too immature for words. 'What's the real problem here, Summer?'

'What's the problem?' I echoed. 'The problem is that we came here to find out about Iona and the curse, not to engage in a three-hour round of who can flirt the most!'

She paused. 'You think he's interested?'

It was my turn to roll my eyes.

'The man would flirt with a wall,' I retorted. 'It's clearly just how he is.'

She was all scorn. 'You've only just met him but now you think you know him?'

I raised my eyebrows meaningfully. 'Back at you.'

My sister tried to stare me down, and lost.

'We'll get to it,' she whispered. 'Let's just have lunch with the guy before we ask him to recount probably the most painful night of his life, okay?'

'Fine,' I hissed back. 'I'm going to check out the house. You coming?'

We set off to explore. Nathaniel's house was a

seductive rat maze of a place, light and airy in stark contrast to ours, with bare wooden floors and plain white walls covered in framed film posters and old-school vinyl discs, not to mention all the art – a lot of it Nathaniel's. I found I could tell, after a while, which art he had made. He had a certain style that I found familiar.

Nathanial's studio was down in the cellar, he had told us, spattered in paint and covered in half-finished sculptures and canvases. I longed to see it but I knew better than to ask such a thing from him when we'd only just met.

By the time we circled back to the hallway, the whole place was suffused with the most mouth-watering smells. In the living room, Nathaniel had set up a long, low coffee table with lunch, and he had clay cups of fresh lemon tea at the ready to, as he said, cleanse the palate.

I sat in Nathaniel's living room, sipping tea, working my way through one of the most delicious meals I'd ever had the luck to be fed, and listening to some impossibly good band I'd never heard of (he told me, with a mischievous grin, that the name of the band was All Them Witches).

Nathaniel talked about music and art and film, and I thought about what an amazing life he must have. He had surrounded himself with everything that he was passionate about, everything that fed his soul and his senses. There was no one to tell him what to do or how to be. That he was wrong. Bad. Weird. He was himself, and nothing held him back.

There was an easy freedom in his conversation, a sense that you could tell him anything and he'd happily give you bits of his soul in return. Talking to anyone in my family was like trying to navigate a minefield, but with Nathaniel, it felt like there were no secrets.

After lunch, Thalia put on some music and started pulling books and films off shelves, examining them while swaying through the room, her mug dangling from her fingers.

'Thalia kind of looks like her, you know,' Nathaniel said to me, offhand.

'Who?' I asked, though I already knew.

'Iona. You haven't noticed?'

'I'm not sure what she looks like,' I admitted.

'There's a photo of her on that top shelf,' he said with a small smile, pointing towards a bookcase in the far corner.

I went to it, running my fingers over the spines of the books on the shelves. I hadn't noticed before, but now I realised every single one of them was on witchcraft and magic.

I snagged a photo in a frame from the top shelf.

It was set beside some others of a grinning Nathaniel with what I presumed were family and friends. This one was a girl by herself, caught in the act of twirling, her face swung off to the side, exposing her neck, long blonde hair sprayed out into the air.

It was strange to see her in the flesh. Real Iona was neither as swooping nor as sure as her painted counterpart, but she was lovely, squinting against the light, eyes crinkled in something that looked like happiness even if it had only been protection against the glare, frozen and haloed in sun gold.

If Thalia hadn't cut her hair, I'd have called them sisters.

'The resemblance is a little creepy, Nathaniel,' I said, returning to him with the photo in hand.

He frowned. 'Wait, what? Shit, I didn't mean it like that.'

I burst out laughing at his stricken face. 'Too late. Ah, don't worry, it's not so bad. She's eighteen, and you're, what – like, thirty-six?'

'I'm twenty-seven,' he said, aggrieved, and then caught my sly smile and shoved my shoulder. 'You're a terrible person.'

We settled, watching Thalia twirl for a moment. A comfortable haze settled behind my eyes, stretching and compressing the time and space around us. The world beyond lay behind a curtain I didn't want to open.

'It was so fast,' said Nathaniel softly. 'The fire.'

I kept staring straight ahead, afraid of doing anything to stop him talking.

'We used to meet in this abandoned shepherd's cabin, up on the moors. We'd go there for an hour or two after school. Late at night, sometimes, if we could sneak out. Her parents didn't approve, so we met up in secret. I didn't understand why I was such a bad choice for a long time, not until Iona explained the curse to me. I thought it was the most ridiculous thing I'd ever heard. Until she died. That fire . . . it came out of nowhere. Bad wiring, they said. But it came out of nowhere.'

The pause squeezed my heart.

'I loved her more than anything.' His voice was calm, steady. 'And I'd do anything to bring her back.'

My gaze travelled to those books of magic on his bookshelves.

'You've tried, haven't you?' I asked quietly. 'You've researched it.'

'I've researched,' he admitted. 'When you have to upend the laws of nature, you need someone so powerful that reality finds itself bending to fit around their desire. Of course, finding someone like that is hardly easy.'

I felt the room revolve slowly around me as more puzzle pieces clicked into place with an inevitable weight.

'You need a spirit witch,' I said.

'You know about those?' he said with surprise. 'They're incredibly rare.'

'I've met one.'

Why had I told him that? I felt loose, like all my secrets were on the tip of my tongue, ready to tumble off.

His glance was probing sharp. 'You have? Who?'

'A girl my age. She's scary powerful. And then I found out about *enakelgh*, and I thought . . . I thought maybe that was what I had with her, you know. I felt it, that night on the beach. *Enakelgh*. We all did. I know it, even if the others won't admit it.'

With a start, I realised truths were coming out that I had barely admitted to myself. What the hell was wrong with me?

'You have an *enakelgh*?' Nathaniel said, soft and curious. I could tell he didn't quite believe me.

'Yes,' I insisted, affronted at his doubt. 'I felt it, I'm telling you. I just wish I knew how to get it back.'

He blew out a breath. 'Well, Summer, if you truly have one, you need to tread carefully.'

'Don't tell me,' I said wearily. 'It's too dangerous.'

'Yes, it's dangerous,' he agreed, 'but that doesn't mean it's not worth the risk.' His face was alive with excitement. 'A true *enakelgh* is one of the most incredible things in the world. Each member becomes more powerful, and collectively you are capable of the most incredible magic you can dream of. The things you could do. The changes you could make. Think how you might shape the world.'

His words were like fingertips trailing on my spine, thrilling me.

'How do you know so much about this?' I asked.

'Oh, good old research,' he replied drily. 'For years I was convinced I could bring Iona back somehow. I came across *enakelgh* fairly early on and it seemed like the only way it might actually be possible, so I gathered up as much knowledge about it as I could. It's a fairly useless specialist subject, let me tell you. It'll never get me on a game show. I paint about it a lot, actually, though you'd be one of the few to recognise the references.'

The realisation hit me like a slap.

'Holy crap,' I said. 'You're the one who painted the tarot cards.'

Nathaniel straightened.

'You have them?' he said feverishly. 'Iona's cards?'

'They were hers?'

'It was my artwork, but all her specifications. She chose each card, all the symbols, the backgrounds. It was like a giant art project that we created between us.'

It all made crazy sense. The Princess. The fire that had engulfed her card in front of our eyes. The story of the curse built into the artwork. No wonder the cards had led us to Iona.

They had been hers to begin with.

'I have them,' I assured him. 'They're safe.'

His face fell. 'Not with you?'

'No.'

'Ah.' He looked out across the room. 'I don't know if you've tried to use them yourself, but I wouldn't bother. They only ever worked for her, and when she died, no one else could get them to make any sense.'

I decided not to mention that they seemed to work fine for me.

'I'll bring them with me next time, I promise.'

He smiled. 'There'll be a next time?'

I snorted. 'With your cooking? Count on it.'

His smile widened and he shook his head.

'I can't believe we found each other after all this time,' he said. 'I don't believe in fate, but ... ah, it's the corniest thing ever.'

'What?' I pressed.

He shrugged, bashful. 'Maybe it's Iona, guiding you. I don't know. Sometimes I feel like she's still around.'

'You're right, it's the corniest thing ever.'

We both laughed.

'Doesn't make it not true, though,' I said. 'I don't think the people we love ever really leave us. Not if we don't want them to.'

Nathaniel leaned back. 'She must be sick of hanging around me then,' he replied. 'I've never stopped wanting her to just . . . walk through that door. I keep thinking it'll happen one day. It's stupid, I know that, but I can't stop thinking it.'

My heart ached for him. I had felt such loss when Wolf died, but only for a few months. How must it be to endure that for ten years?

It was out of my mouth before I could stop it.

'What if there was a way to bring Iona back?' I said. 'Would you take it? Even if it meant risking everything?'

He bit his lip, staring at nothing.

'Of course,' he said at last. 'But I think you knew that already.'

You can't bring everyone back who didn't deserve to die, the voice in my head cautioned.

But what good then was the power that the

enakelgh offered if you didn't use it to right such a grievous wrong?

'Come back to me.'

Nathaniel's gaze flickered between me and my sister as he lingered at the front door.

'We will,' I said.

'Promise?' Nathaniel replied with a light smile.

'Promise,' murmured Thalia.

We walked down the steps of his house and into the waiting taxi that would take us to the train station and back home. He waved to us from the doorway of his house as we pulled away, leaving him behind.

I knew what we had done to him. We had made him hope again, and hope was a powerful thing. There were no certainties in magic, especially not magic as powerful as this – but we had already brought someone back once. We could do it again.

In order to live, really live, you had to risk.

CHAPTER 15

Back at school, things took a turn for the worse.

On Monday, Della De Luca was missing from form room. Della's parents were splitting up, according to Gemma. Della's mum had caught her dad bundling Della's younger brother into the back of the car without explaining where he was going. The consequent screaming match between them had turned violent and the police had been called out.

On Tuesday, the halls were abuzz with the news that Mr Sherman, the ancient art teacher, had walked out of his job and apparently embarked on an impromptu trip around the world. His shocked wife of forty-three years had no explanation – he'd simply left her behind.

On Wednesday, Fenrin got into a fight.

I was hustling between classes, preoccupied with thoughts of Nathaniel. I kept seeing his face when we talked about *enakelgh*, the wonder and excitement in his voice. He was so different to my parents. They were shut down and closed off, but he wore his pain on his sleeve because he didn't see it as a weakness. Where they saw danger, he saw potential. Where they saw the bad, he saw only the good – and wasn't that their choice? Couldn't it be a matter of perspective? If you thought something was going to turn out badly, it very often would. Whether it was the power of suggestion or something deeper, we all had an immense capacity to shape our lives. Given the choice, I'd rather live in hope than in fear.

I'd rather live like Nathaniel.

I was passing through the corridor between the science and history buildings when a strange grouping caught my eye. First I recognised Ben Mills, a strapping football captain, awkward and jovial. I'd never heard of him getting into trouble or even raising his voice, but his face was flushed a livid red as he leaned into another guy – Fenrin, my brother.

Pinned in the middle and stuck against the wall, with a water fountain pressed against his side, was Marcus.

I slowed, puzzled. A more incongruous three I could not imagine. They were talking, and as I watched, Fenrin turned his head towards me, a look of supremely dismissive boredom on his face. My heart skipped – I knew what that meant. He was angry.

Before I could do anything, Ben's hand came up and pushed Fenrin in the chest, forcing him back into a stumble. There was a long, ugly pause, then Fenrin's arms flashed out and he heaved his hands bodily into the barrel chest before him.

'Stop!' The word burst out of me, but no one listened. I ran towards them as they fought in earnest. The water fountain shuddered as Fenrin's hip smashed into it. His hand found Ben's throat and gripped. They were tipping, tipping towards the floor as Marcus slid hastily out of the way, wide-eyed . . .

Reaching them, I gave a shout of utter wrath. Without thinking, I slammed my hand down on the fountain lever, causing water to come out of the tap with such savage force that a great gout bounced right off the bowl and gushed furiously over the sides, soaking Fenrin's back and hitting Ben square in the groin.

I'd once seen a YouTube video of someone turning a hose on two scrapping dogs. This was so similar that I wanted to laugh. Fenrin and Ben sprang apart with barks of alarm and stood panting, staring in disbelief.

I released the water fountain lever. Fenrin's Converse shoes were planted in a rapidly expanding puddle that spread across the linoleum as if staking a claim.

'What the f—' Ben looked down at his trousers.

'Someone needs to call for a caretaker,' I said as calmly as I could.

Ben focused on me, then my brother. For one second I saw him contemplate starting up again. Then he sneered.

'Graces,' he spat, and loped off. I watched him bang his way through the bathroom door halfway down the corridor.

'Nice one, sis,' Fenrin said, his words ragged and his mouth open in an amused grin. 'You totally made it look like he wet himself.'

I rounded on him, riding hard on the adrenaline kick of my actions. I wasn't sure how I'd got such a violent spray out of the fountain. I'd only meant to distract them with a little water. Had the fight pushed a little furious magic out of me?

'What the hell is *wrong* with you?' I demanded.

His grin mutated into a frown. 'What?'

'You can't just start shoving people around, Fen! That's not like you!'

Fenrin's eyes narrowed. 'You're *defending* that meat sack? The guy was about to punch out Marcus. Should I have just walked on by?'

I laser-gazed Marcus, who was hugging the wall.

'It's fine,' Marcus muttered. 'I mean, I could handle it.'

Marcus didn't look like he could handle it. He looked like the wall was the only thing keeping him upright.

'You okay?' I asked him

'Just a bit light-headed.'

His face was drained and his eyes were glassy – he wasn't faking. When he said he'd started getting sick around magic, I hadn't really taken him seriously, but this was getting a little weird.

Was it my fault, or was it just a coincidence?

'You know,' Fenrin said in a dangerously even tone, 'there are times when violence is justified, baby Sum.'

'Don't goddamn "baby Sum" me to piss me off,' I retorted. 'We just got ourselves kicked out of one school. Do you *seriously* want to be homeschooled?'

He hesitated. I could practically see the thought running through his head.

'Don't even,' I warned. 'You think the kind of tutor Esther hires is going to let you sneak off with Wolf all day?'

Fenrin huffed. 'Fine.'

I eyed him. 'It's not over. Ben could make a complaint.'

'He won't,' Marcus said. 'He'll be too embarrassed, trust me.'

'What was that all about, anyway?' I asked.

Marcus rubbed his forehead. 'River.'

A loud, irritated sigh ripped out of my brother. 'So what else is new? Christ, that girl is literally the root of all evil round here, isn't she?'

'It's not her fault,' Marcus said.

'Not her fault – are you serious?'

Marcus snapped. 'Fenrin, just shut up. You don't know what you're talking about.'

Fenrin blinked.

'You steamrolled right in here without even asking me what was going on,' Marcus said, heating up. 'You know what Ben was mad about? River's been collecting all the wishes people have been tying up in the clearing and giving them back – including the money. He got his wish and his money back in his locker, and he got mad and decided to flex his muscles at me so I'd force her to carry out his wish anyway. But I'm not going to do that, no matter how many assholes come and hassle me. She refuses to touch any of those wishes now because *you* totally freaked her out about them.' He turned on me.

'You were the one who came to us to do something about her!' I said, taken aback.

'Yes, but I didn't mean by intimidating her in front of the entire cafeteria. Where's your compassion? Both of you? What do you reckon everyone thinks about her after a Grace treats her like that? People follow your every move. You keep treating someone like a monster, pretty soon everyone will believe it.'

'It doesn't matter what she tries to do afterwards, the damage is already done,' Fenrin began, but there was no stopping the passionate onslaught rolling our way.

'So every time someone makes a mistake, they should be punished for it forever?' Marcus said. 'Instead of helping her, you're doing exactly what you usually do – burying your heads in the sand and pretending none of this has anything to do with you, when it does. All of it does. You're the damn witches. You should have taken her under your wing as soon as you knew what she was. Instead you kidnapped her and terrorised her into getting what you wanted, and then you discarded her.' He gave a sarcastic clap of his hands. 'Well done. Really.'

I'd never seen Marcus so angry.

Well, that wasn't true. I remembered when Thalia told him that they couldn't see each other any more. I thought he might have been miserable, but instead he'd been livid. Marcus angry was a rare and discomforting sight.

'Come on, Fen,' I murmured, trying to diffuse the tension. 'That was a pretty big thing she did, giving them all back. She needs that money.'

Fenrin crossed his arms. If he could feel the clinging wetness of his sweater on his skin, he was doing a fine job of ignoring it.

'Just . . . think about helping her instead of judging her,' Marcus said, deflating. 'That's all.'

Fenrin opened his mouth. Shut it.

The bell rang, drowning out all further conversation. As soon as its drilling noise had died away, Marcus hoisted his bag.

'I have to go,' he mumbled. 'See you around.'

'Sorry,' Fenrin said suddenly. 'About . . . jumping in with Ben. I didn't mean to just assume you couldn't handle it, okay?'

Marcus's mouth quirked. 'I'll just call you Captain Grace, Defender of the Weak.'

'It wasn't like that.'

'Yeah.'

'You're not weak, Marcus. If anything, I'm . . .' Fenrin stopped himself. 'It doesn't matter. Moment of sheer lunacy. Don't worry, it won't happen again.'

It was the most they had spoken between them in more than a year.

Marcus rubbed his nose.

'Thanks, Pinky,' he muttered quickly, and then started to walk away fast.

'No problem, Brain,' Fenrin murmured when he was out of earshot.

It seemed as if neither of them could manage to forget that stupid-ass cartoon.

Fenrin stirred. 'I have to get to class.' He focused on me. 'Have you seen Thalia?'

I shrugged. 'I never see you two any more. Did you lose your twin? That's careless.'

'We had a free study period planned but she never showed.' He pulled a face. 'I'll make her pay for it later. See you at home?'

With that he wandered off.

'I'll just get a mop then, shall I?' I called crossly after his departing back.

CHAPTER 16

I found Thalia on our ancient hallway phone.

To be more accurate, I found the cord of the phone snaking across the floor and underneath the downstairs bathroom door. It was the only trick available when we wanted a private conversation – even though it didn't look like anyone else was home yet. It was odd that she'd come back from school without Fenrin, especially after she stood up their study period. I wondered if she was avoiding him.

I knocked on the door.

She didn't answer.

'Thalia,' I said. 'Who are you talking to?'

A tinkling laugh came from beyond the door.

I knocked again. 'Who are you talking to?'

The door opened a crack.

'What?' Thalia hissed, the phone clutched against her ear.

'What's the big secret?'

'I'm not in the bathroom for fun, Summer. I'm in the bathroom for a private conversation.'

I watched her, suspicion scratching away at me.

Thalia narrowed her eyes.

'That was Summer,' she sighed into the phone. She cupped a hand around it. 'Just give me a minute, will you?'

'Fine,' I huffed.

The door shut in my face.

Scratch, scratch, scratch.

I stood for a moment more, listening to the lilt in Thalia's tone drifting through the wood. Then I made my way up the stairs to my bedroom and waited.

Thalia came in a few minutes later.

'That was Nathaniel,' she said in a studied offhand voice. 'Just catching up.'

'Mm,' I agreed, entirely unsurprised. I'd already worked out who it might be. 'And how is he?'

'He's good.' She flopped onto the end of my bed.

'Mm.'

I watched her fidget.

And I waited.

I knew my sister.

'We were talking about your *enakelgh* idea,' she said. 'I think he's more obsessed with it than you are.

He wants to teach us more about it. He says that we temporarily accessed *enakelgh* on the beach that night to bring Wolf back, but it was unconscious – a moment of high stress that made all our instincts kick at the same time.'

I frowned. 'Whoa, wait. You told him about Wolf?'

She quirked her head. 'Well, yes. Why?'

I threw my hands up. 'What happened to protecting him from anyone finding out?'

'Come on, Summer, we can trust Nathaniel,' Thalia said impatiently. 'He's been ostracised from our entire family for the last ten years. Who's he going to tell?'

I couldn't exactly argue with that. I scrabbled around for more ammunition.

'I thought you didn't want anything more to do with River,' I said.

Thalia raised her eyebrows. 'You said you wanted to help control her magic. People are getting hurt, you said. So, I don't know. Maybe we should take a chance.'

'Mm.'

'Stop saying "mm" like that.'

'Like what?'

'Like all suspiciously.'

'Mmm.'

She picked up a crescent-moon-shaped cushion on my bed and threw it at me. I caught it, which only annoyed her.

'Thalia,' I began carefully, 'I get that you're into him, but . . .'

She just regarded me, no denial on her lips.

'But,' I tried again, 'you understand why he's been researching *enakelgh* all this time, don't you? He wants to find a way to bring Iona back.'

Thalia's shoulders were stiff. 'He doesn't, actually. He told me that he gave up on all that a long time ago. And that since . . .'

I willed myself to keep silent. Thalia didn't enjoy silence so she talked to fill it – and there was obviously something she wanted to say.

'Since we started seeing each other,' she said in a rush. 'Um, he says he just wants to help me. Us. All of us.'

The effect of releasing her secret was immediate. She did not easily blush, but now her cheeks veritably rouged before my eyes.

My head felt heavy with sudden, weighty intuition.

'Thalia,' I said. 'Where were you today?'

She was silent.

'I've only done it once,' she said. 'It's not a big deal.'

My heart skipped. 'You ditched school to go see him.'

'It wasn't his idea,' she said quickly. 'It was all me. When I turned up at the door he tried to make me go back. But then we got to talking, and . . .' A gorgeous, coy smile spread across her face and she ducked her head, making her hair swing forward and graze her throat. 'Well.'

I gazed at her. In the sitcom of our lives, I'd assumed till now that I was in the opening scene of the episode where the plucky heroine selflessly helps her big sister get over her unrequited crush, but it seemed to be very much requited. She had that flush: eye-bright and feverish over a desire that had unfolded quietly in the background of all the past few days' craziness.

Our grandmother had had a maxim on desire. To inflame it, you drank fresh mint tea made with leaves picked straight from the plant because, as everyone knew, mint was just like desire – if left unchecked, it ran wild and fast through a whole garden, muscling every other thing out of its way, until one day mint was all you had left.

Desire was a tricky thing and should never be left unchecked, but magic couldn't manifest without it. Want created will, and will led to action, which was all magic was, reduced to its simplest form: change, in the way the witch wanted it.

Where there is desire, there is usually magic.

'Did you . . . go to bed with him?' I asked.

'Didn't actually make it to a bed,' Thalia mused. 'I haven't even seen the inside of his bedroom yet.'

'Thalia!' I said, scandalised.

She just gave a delighted laugh.

I massaged my forehead. 'Well, this feels like a giant bad idea.'

Her eyebrows rose. 'Why?'

I let out a sigh, willing myself to say the truth that I knew would cut her. 'He's in love with his dead girlfriend.'

She wasn't even angry with me. She shook her head patiently as if I were being particularly slow.

'Don't you realise why he's so into the idea of *enakelgh*?' she asked. 'It's because he wants to help us break the curse.'

I frowned. 'He said that?'

'He really did. Just think about it. Don't you ever want to be with someone, really *be* with them, all unfettered and undone and never having to control yourself just in case you do or say anything that makes it start feeling like love, like something that will get someone killed? Haven't you ever wondered what it would be like to be free?'

Now I understood why Thalia was suddenly so into the idea of *enakelgh*. I reached out and brushed the mustang horse-hair wrap she had in her hair. Her talisman. Touching it was an intimate gesture, one of trust. She only let Fenrin and me do that.

'Of course I have,' I said finally.

She turned to face me, one foot pulled up on the bed, the other dangling over the side.

'This isn't just our chance,' she said. 'This is our *parents'* chance. If we break the curse, they get to be happy. With an outsider. With each other. Whoever they want.'

On hot August nights when we were young, our parents would take us all out of our beds and onto the dunes to stargaze. We would lie on our backs, staring at the bright, vast scatter of lights above us, making up our own stories of how the constellations came to be as we ate the maple pecan muffins Esther had made and drank the ginger tea Gwydion had brewed.

Back then our parents smiled more. Those smiles became increasingly infrequent as we grew, one of many things I felt hurt to lose. We still jumped over a burning stick in late spring under Gwydion's watchful eye, presumably in case our ankles caught fire, and we still had picnics in the woods when the weather was right.

We still had a world filled with gemstones and bread kneaded by hand and days spent in Esther's conservatory, helping to grind flowers to paste in big stone bowls. We still played the apple game at the start of every winter around the bonfire, peeling the skin in one long strip and tossing it to divine the first letter of our future husband or wife.

The older we got though, the closer we were to adolescence, to falling in love. To the age the curse would claim us. The relationship between my parents had once been as solid as iron and stone, but as we grew, it began to show cracks – or maybe I had finally become old enough to see the cracks. All I knew was that Gwydion went away more and more often on business trips, and Esther spent a lot of time on the phone, speaking in strained whispers and hanging up if she saw one of us approaching.

Raised voices behind closed doors. Smiles plastered on when we came into a room.

Gwydion spending the precious little time he was actually in the house locked away in his study. *I'm just so busy*, he always said, regret in his voice. *Next time, Summer, I promise.*

He was an air witch. He felt things, pushed by currents of the unseen like seaweed by water, but it hadn't seemed that way in a long time.

Time had brought a folding inward instead of outward. They had trapped themselves in a relentless limbo of deliberate numbness. Too afraid to feel, too afraid to let go. Two people forever on different orbits, deliberately.

Right after the whole Marcus debacle, Thalia had briefly threatened celibacy. Having your parents discover you fooling around with the boy next door, and then forbidding the relationship and banning the boy from the house when you thoughtlessly protested that you weren't just fooling around, and that you cared about him – well, that might be enough to dampen anyone's libido.

Thalia had spent all her time possessed of an anger vengeful enough to rival any god's, crippled with fear and shame and guilt, her energy driven to finding ways to punish others, but most of all herself, for what she could not control – her feelings for Marcus, and his for her. She had been so frightened of invoking the curse with their relationship that she had resorted to black magic to try to break their hold over each other.

I had to begrudgingly admit that whatever Nathaniel was doing for her, at least he wasn't making her miserable.

'He's older than you,' I tried.

She just gave me a knowing look. 'Trust me, it really makes a difference. I know you're looking out for me and I love you for it, but Nathaniel and I barely know each other. I don't know where it's going but it feels good. That's all I know right now.' She was steady. 'I'm not in love with him, Summer. Don't worry.'

'Fine,' I said, begrudgingly. 'But if he hurts you, I'll set fire to his stuff.'

She grinned. 'If he really hurts me, I'll help you. Hey. Don't tell anyone else for now? I mean, Wolf knows, but maybe not Fenrin, just for the moment.'

'Er, how does *Wolf* know and not your own twin?'

She shrugged. 'He was the one who told me to go for it, actually. I don't know, it was late one night, we were talking . . . He was like, take a chance. What are you so afraid of? And I thought . . . you're right.'

That sounded familiar.

He didn't try to kiss you too, did he? I thought treacherously. Or maybe I was the only one working overtime in the department of sibling betrayal.

Lucky me.

Content now that she had shared her secret with me, Thalia crawled up beside me on the bed to chat away about the European art house films Nathaniel had recommended and the specific South American coffee that Nathaniel liked, and I smiled and nodded while I thought about the absolute best way to approach River without scaring her off.

I needn't have worried. If there was one thing I should have learned about River by now, it was that she had a knack for finding ways to surprise me.

CHAPTER 17

Entering woods was like entering another world. Winding ribbons of mist curled around the bottoms of the slender, silver birch trunks. The sounds of traffic fell away into muffled unimportance, washed out by the land-sea rustling of wind through the treetops.

It was Friday afternoon on a muted February day, and the bird calls were few.

Walking through woods always gave me a sense of quiet, connected power. Everything I passed felt alive and watchful. I enjoyed the feeling. There was no menace to it. The trees could feel me the same way I could feel them, and we liked the experience.

A childhood memory arose as I walked, sparkling clear in my mind.

It was the first time Gwydion had tried to teach me how to access the magic inside myself. A preparation ritual to focus the mind before attempting any kind of spell.

'Please,' I had begged Gwydion, and his clear, clean blue eyes had studied me thoughtfully. 'I'm ready. I can do it.'

'I don't know,' he drawled, the exact same drawl that Fenrin picked up in his early teens. 'Can you listen and concentrate, and do everything I say?'

I knew I'd won, and he knew I knew, and that I'd do anything to comply now that I saw the prize. I nodded seriously.

I was eight and my father meant the world to me.

Gwydion smiled. 'Sit down in front of me then.'

He had chosen the woods as the backdrop for that day's lesson, and I remembered that same land-sea rustling rushing in my ears as I sank cross-legged to the ground underneath an oak tree, soft summer grass scratching gently at my ankles and the outsides of my bare feet. Gwydion did the same, so we faced each other, kneecaps inches apart. He pushed his hair back from his face, that cascade of warm, caramel tones that didn't yet come brushed with so much grey.

'Breathe,' he said, 'and think of stars.'

I watched him, wishing for his stillness, his

surety. Then I closed my eyes and pictured stars, like I had been doing erratically over the previous few weeks, whenever I remembered, whenever it didn't bore me, whenever Thalia reminded me. I wasn't a diligent student. I'd never be like Thalia. It all came so naturally to my sister, but my energy and concentration had always manifested in unpredictable gusts.

Still, I had tried. I had practised turning my mind's eye upward, picturing a black velvet sky speckled with points of light, some clustered, some sparkling at me. I had felt the enormity of the universe, and I drew comfort from it. The woods felt like breathing and thinking of stars. Sometimes you didn't need to focus to feel magic. You just needed to be in a place that breathed it out.

Today, I had come to the woods directly from school on my own – Thalia and Fenrin would meet me later. I didn't tell them why I wanted them to come, just that I wanted to show them something. Once I reached the point where the human world had seemingly been swallowed up far behind me, and I felt like I could wander forever in this cool, twilight place, I found what I was looking for.

The envelopes first appeared as glowing rectangle drops, pale against the inky criss-cross of branches patterned behind them. They were tied to high branches with string, ribbon, wire. Most were low enough to touch. Some, more daring, had been tied to higher branches that required careful shimmying up rough, unreliable bark.

Those are the darkest wishes, I thought.

The envelopes were dotted sparsely around the clearing, which we had spent our life visiting. It wasn't ours the same way the cove was, but it was a place that called to us. We would come here to dance, drink, cast spells, or just be. We had brought River here more than once last year and created magic together while the trees around us had swelled and breathed their land tides.

As if between us we had found a way to stop time, I found River huddled like a strange fairy on the splintering hollow log that served as the clearing's centrepiece. It felt right, as if the universe had been waiting for us to stop posturing, give in, and be what we knew we were supposed to be.

She looked up as I approached. I moved slowly, as if she were a deer that might startle easily. My feet gave out soft crunches on the cold grass, and I sank down onto the log beside her.

'You got my note,' she said. 'I wasn't sure you'd come.'

It had been waiting for me in my locker that morning. A folded sheet of lined notebook paper, adorned with a simple message:

Would it be okay to talk? In the clearing, when school lets out? — River

She hadn't needed to sign it. I knew that handwriting anywhere.

Our breath plumed together on the air.

The silence stretched on.

River stirred. 'I took them down,' she said. 'I returned as many as I could, if I knew who they were from. The rest I left untouched. But when I come back, there are more. I don't know where they're coming from. Some of them aren't even from people at school. There's one in here from some guy who thinks his wife is having an affair with their neighbour.' She had several envelopes clutched tight in her hands. 'There's so much pain in the world.'

'I know,' I said quietly, thinking of those late-night guests.

I watched River's arm lift and point into the trees dead ahead of us.

'That's where Marcus's wish was,' she said. 'I told him to write it out and tie it up here. I told him

I'd make it come true if I could. It was the first one we did.'

'We?'

'Who do you think's been telling people to come here? Marcus came up with the idea of the envelopes and the notes, and he put it on his website. He said that my magic needed a ritual, a way to channel and control it.' Her voice turned bitter. 'Guess he was wrong about that last part.'

'What do you mean?' I asked carefully.

'You know he's sick, right? He told you that.'

'He said something about it,' I admitted.

'Did he tell you that he can't be around me any more, not without feeling weird? I've seen it. He's not faking. He gets all woozy like he's high or something. I haven't seen him for days now. He's avoiding me at school.' She gave a short laugh. 'I'm at the point where I'm physically repulsing the only friend I've got. What's the psychology behind that, do you think?'

He's not the only friend you've got.

Say it out loud, Summer.

'And now Ella Drummond's mum,' River continued. 'You know they think it's some kind of cancer?' She seemed hollow, like her insides had been scooped out and she was nothing but tough, coarse

216

rind. '*Cancer.* Why would I have done that to someone I don't even know? She never did anything to me.'

I was silent, watching her glove-wrapped fingers twist and hook into each other restlessly.

'When Wolf came back,' she said, 'I thought I'd found a way to fix the things I do. Finally, I thought. I can control it. If it goes wrong, I'll just make it okay again. But what if ... what if I can't make it okay? What if I can't do good things at all and I'm just built to hurt people?'

My heart went tumbling into the abyss.

'What does it feel like?' I asked. 'Your magic.'

River stared across the clearing and I let her work up to it.

'Have you ever had an itch,' she said at last. 'One that starts small, just a twitch on your skin, that then grows because you ignore it, and grows until it's more like a burning pain, until your whole body wants to jerk and twitch and you can think of nothing else but the itch, your whole universe is the itch, and there is nothing else for you in that moment, nothing at all, except the overwhelming urge to scratch?'

'You're saying what you do is like an urge?'

'I'm saying people don't get urges to be good. Good takes work. Good takes choice. Bad ... bad is easy. Bad is an instinct.' She stared into nothing.

'Every day there's some new story circulating about some awful thing that's happened to someone. People's parents getting divorced. That guy whose brother was in a car crash on the weekend. The corner store that got robbed. I know that's life and life happens, but everyone keeps saying how crazy it is right now, like the whole town is cursed. And it's ever since I came here, isn't it?'

'Come on, River,' I said. 'That can't all be you.'

'Oh yeah? You want to check all the envelopes, see how many we can match up? What if I've just been drifting around, doing terrible things to people who don't deserve it without even knowing, like some kind of clueless evil fairy? What if all it takes is for me to *exist*?'

'Is that what you want?' I asked quietly.

'What?'

'To be an evil fairy. Is it what you want? God knows we all do it because everyone wants to feel powerful. It's not special to you, it's just human nature.' I contemplated her profile. 'So, do you want it?'

'Sometimes,' she said. 'But no matter what I do, it always seems to go too far.'

I leaned back on my palms, gazing at the darkening sky above the treetops. How much easier it felt to be honest with each other, deep in the woods, away from everything familiar.

'What if there was a way to control what you do?' I said. 'But there's a catch.'

'There always is,' she replied, and her wryness gave me hope. 'What is it?'

'You have to open yourself up to other people. You can't do it alone any more.'

'What other people?'

'Us.'

She seemed spooked, one word from fleeing. 'We can't trust each other.'

'We have to,' I said simply. 'That's the price.'

'Why would you do that? What do you get out of it?'

I shrugged. 'You.'

'But,' she said, so utterly confused that I felt exasperated, 'why would you want that?'

'*Because*,' I said, but I knew that wasn't enough. 'Because wouldn't you rather be that weird girl that half the people around you will do anything to avoid, instead of choosing to spend your life hiding, never trusting or loving anyone because you're too afraid to live your life the way you want, in a way that will make you think *no regrets* when you're on your deathbed? Aren't you curious? I am. Curiosity, it's like a hunger. I won't waste the time I have on this earth just plodding meekly towards death, and I won't play by the rules because they're not *my* rules. I didn't come up with those rules. I don't want to just exist, I want to *live*. And I'm never, ever going to apologise to anyone for that.'

The feeling inside me that I had never dared name out loud to anyone else before spilled out and leaked onto the grass around us, as if my body was a tipped glass.

River was gaping at me.

'Well,' came a new voice in a familiar drawl, 'if you're going to be all *inspirational* about it.'

Fenrin was leaning against a trunk behind us, his arms folded. As I watched, Thalia emerged from the trees at his side. They had crept up on us without me realising, though now it felt like they had always been there, as natural and as right as the trees.

Beside me, River was stiff and ready to run, her face ghostly in the half dark. As the twins came out from the woods and closer to us, I felt that surge inside me again, pulsing like a heartbeat, stronger than ever before. When she was only halfway across the grass, Thalia suddenly halted, her eyes wide.

'What?' I frowned.

'To your left,' she said, in her softest voice.

I turned . . . and stifled a gasp.

The air around River was flashing.

Tiny lights blinked on and off, *flash flash*. They weren't consistent, either. They would come from different points, change again, switch rhythms.

'Summer,' River hissed. 'Something's crawling on my hand.'

'Shut up and don't move,' I said joyfully. 'It's fireflies.'

'What?'

'Fireflies. They're all around you.'

Her mouth dropped open.

Then the clearing exploded with light.

Dancing flashes, flickering and blinking like a living carpet of stars, surrounding each one of us. We were four frozen statues, lost in the strangest, most beautiful moment of our lives. Each face before me looked ethereal in the flashing, dark and strange and somehow more alive than I had ever seen them. I loved them. I wanted them. I'd never felt closer to them.

I could have bathed in that moment forever.

Gradually though, the flashings tapered off and the swarm moved on, spreading out through the trees as fading pinprick ghost lights, leaving us together in the gathering dark.

Beside me, I heard River draw in a steadying breath.

'Have you ever,' I said, 'seen fireflies in these woods before?'

'Never,' said Thalia. 'Never ever.' She laughed and clapped her hands to her mouth. Her eyes were wide at me over the tops of her fingers. Her gaze fell to River.

'If you say something about that being a sign,' Fenrin said in a trembling murmur, 'I will be sarcastic at you.'

'I don't think that was just me,' River said slowly.

'No,' Thalia assured her, 'that was all of us.'

'You felt it?' I looked around at them. 'You all felt it?'

They said nothing, their silence as acknowledgment. They saw it now, too. They saw what we could become if we were only brave enough to take the risk. This was us again, that connection, that surge inside – but this time it was different. It didn't feel the same as that night in the cove, when we had used fear and violence to bring Wolf back. That night had been darkness and pain. This felt like hope.

It didn't have to be all curses. Together, maybe we could bring a little magic back into our lives.

CHAPTER 18

If the previous night in the clearing had been the party, the next morning felt like the hangover.

When I'd eventually got to sleep, I'd had the visceral kind of nightmares that made you burst into tears with relief when you woke from them and realised they weren't real, they weren't your life. In those dreams I had done things, things I never wanted to do in daylight.

Things I hoped I wasn't even capable of.

It was as though something had tried to infect our newfound hope with darkness. A mood hung over the insides of the house, a thick black smoke skirting the ceilings of each room. I thought I could still feel *enakelgh* in the back of my mind like a warm, insistent tickle, but it was insubstantial, light as a feather against the heaviness of my nightmares. Last night's magic felt as fragile as a spider's web, and as easily broken.

I dredged myself reluctantly from the depths of my bed and went downstairs. The breakfast table was a cold affair of irritated silence. I slumped onto a chair, staring aimlessly at the tabletop. I felt exhausted, my head thick and heavy as if my skull was stuffed full of dense rainclouds. At least it was a Saturday. I didn't think I could face school like this.

Wolf was nowhere to be seen. Thalia was pensive and huddled under swathes of scarf, and when Fenrin joined us, he was grumping, shadowed bruises under his eyes, his skin washed out as if he hadn't slept.

He wasn't the only one.

'Bad night?' I asked him.

He grunted. 'Just give me the coffee and leave me alone.'

'The pot is on the table right in front of you.'

Another, former Fenrin would have had an arch retort ready to fling. This one sank onto a chair and gracelessly snatched the pot, spraying drops of coffee across the table from the spout.

'Fucksake!' he snapped.

'Fuck less, sleep more,' I observed.

Fenrin turned to me, his eyes flashing.

'I know how you two love winding each other up for the fun of it,' said Thalia wearily, 'but I was awake half the night and I really can't deal today, so please don't.'

'Why?' I said.

Her answer was short. 'Bad dreams.'

Before I could prod her further, the sound of a sharply raised voice knifed the air.

Gwydion. We exchanged glances. Gwydion never raised his voice.

Another voice answered, high and furious. Esther.

They were in their bedroom arguing, and so loudly we could hear it from the kitchen.

'I heard about this new French-themed cafe that just opened up in Penwallis Street,' Thalia said, her voice betraying a hint of strain. 'Pastries. Caffeine. French waiting staff, apparently.'

Thalia had always harboured a real buzz for French culture, ever since Gwydion had taken us all on a trip to Paris when I was nine. It was one of the last family holidays when we had all been together.

'French waiters? Here, in provincial nowheresville?' I retorted. *'Mon dieu.'*

'I know,' Thalia said. 'What are the chances? Want to get out of the house for a while?'

'Best idea I've heard all morning,' I declared. Millefeuille could shake off any bad mood.

Fenrin shook his head. 'I can't.'

'Come on,' Thalia wheedled. 'We could use the R&R. Besides, shouldn't we talk about what happened last night? And, you know ... What we're going to do next?'

Fenrin shifted. 'I promised Wolf I'd stay with him. He's not well this morning. He's laid up in bed with some kind of virus or something.'

'That sucks,' Thalia said, her forehead furrowed. 'But obviously pastry cures all ills.'

'I don't think it cures the kind of ill that makes you vomit, Thalia.'

'Grim. Is he okay?'

'He had strength enough to growl at me and tell me to go do something anatomically tricky to myself when I tried to check on him,' Fenrin said with an irritated shrug. 'He'll get over it.'

Our parents' argument, which I had successfully tuned out, flooded back into my ears as it crescendoed down the hallway. Outside the kitchen door came a sudden roll of flat smacking sounds, ricocheting through the air and making my ears buzz.

Startled, we looked at one another as one. I scrambled up from the table and crowded impatiently through the door behind the twins. The giant sideboard that dominated our hallway was usually covered with standing picture frames, scattered haphazardly across its surface and punctuated with bowls of dried flower heads and fruit from the grove. Photos of the sprawl of Grace friends, extended family, and our grandparents long gone, but mostly they were of us. Esther and Gwydion and us. Strange and fractured though we may be, we were still a family and we loved one another.

Something seemed to disagree. Though Esther and Gwydion were in their bedroom, every single picture frame in the hallway had fallen over like dominoes savagely swept by an angry, invisible hand. The biggest photo frame at the sideboard's end had slid right off and smashed onto the ground below. Even from my vantage point, I could see a giant crack in its protective glass. It was a photo of Esther and Gwydion from about ten years ago, standing together on the top of a windswept cliff. Regal. Even from a distance, happy.

'Well,' said Fenrin, staring at the fallen frames, 'that's enough of a warning for me. Shall we leave them to it?'

He was doing his usual trick of wry jokes to cover his misery. Gwydion and Esther outright fighting like this was very rare. The air tasted sour.

Suddenly I longed for nothing more than to be away from here and all the weight of being a Grace.

I wanted to be back in the clearing, surrounded by a hundred lights, feeling magic glow in my bones and in the stars above me.

I wanted to be with my *enakelgh*.

'The cafe might be terrible,' Thalia ventured.

'Can't be any worse than here,' Fenrin said, putting his arm around her. 'Come on, let's get away from here and to pastry heaven.'

'What about Wolf?'

'Let's get away from him, too,' Fenrin said shortly, and disappeared upstairs to get dressed.

I followed suit, conflicted.

It seemed like everyone was fighting, which wasn't good – but I couldn't deny the small thrill of relief at knowing that Wolf wouldn't be with us today. I told myself that it was because he'd feel left out if we were going to talk about *enakelgh*, but the truth was that I was happy to avoid him.

Which made me feel guilty.

Everything was so messed up right now.

In contrast to the angry gloom that had settled over our house, the walk into town was bright, breezy, light, sweeping my head clean. The small cobbled streets were aglow in the sun, the air wreathed in the smells from the bakeries and ice-cream parlours. We chatted as we walked and drew the eye of passers-by, the three of us together, but today the gazes couldn't seem to penetrate my armour.

Before we left I called River and she agreed to meet us at the cafe. The prospect of seeing her again so soon after the magic of last night made me feel fluttery and giddy happy. I hoped she felt the same.

In curvaceous script that spoke of older, fancier times, the sign for the new cafe pronounced it to be La Gauloise. The door boasted panels of fleur-de-lis-patterned stained glass. A handful of small round tables, just enough to admit two people sitting close together, hugged its perimeter.

Perched at one of these tables was River, waiting for us. She had on a pair of red plastic Lolita sunglasses, her wispy hair was pinned back into a shapeless bun mass, and her body was drowning in an oversized second-hand military coat. She looked mismatched and odd and, to my eyes, completely awesome.

'That was fast,' I said. She lived much closer to town than we did, but I still hadn't expected her to arrive before us.

She gave me an uneasy smile. 'I was already about to go out when you called, so . . .'

'Oh, sorry. Did we screw up your day?'

'I was only going to the library.'

I pressed a hand to my heart. 'You ditched books for us? I'm flattered.'

'Of course I did,' she said, as if it were the most obvious thing in the world and, frankly, I was an idiot for thinking anything else. I had a sudden, warm urge to wrap my arms around her and fold her into me. I wasn't sure if that was me or *enakelgh* working on us both.

The inside of the cafe was a warm haven of dark wood, rows of wine glasses hanging from the racking overhead, and waiters in white shirts, black trousers and aprons. Cake stands adorned the brass bar top, packed with croissants, pain au chocolat, millefeuille, tarte au citron and tarte tatin.

'Holy shit,' I proclaimed, instantly in love.

Thalia tutted. 'It's far too sophisticated a place for that kind of language.'

'Please, the French swear more than anyone,' Fenrin said. 'Remember Gwydion's friend Jean-Claude and those foul-mouthed kids of his who visited one time for Yuletide?'

A waiter approached us.

'*Bonjour, mademoiselle,*' he said to me in a voice designed to make toes curl.

I smiled winningly at him. 'Lead us to the sugar.'

'Table for four, please,' Thalia put in.

'*Bien sur*. This way.'

He led us across the room and sat us in a corner, furnished with oversized menus. I found my gaze straying longingly to the cake-bedecked bar top.

'One of everything?' I suggested.

Before long our table was littered with plates, our fingers pecking at the scattered remains of cakes and pastries. Everything I ate was so ridiculously delicious that if someone had asked my name just then, I might have been too clapped out on pure sugar lust to remember it.

River was gazing around the room as tendrils of peppermint-infused steam curled upward from the delicate teacup in her hands. Thalia and Fenrin were swatting at each other contentedly, fighting over the last of each other's leftover crumbs.

Now seemed like as good a time as any.

I sucked in my cheeks. 'So now we're fuelled up ... anyone feel like practising?'

'Practising what?' Thalia asked.

'Using the *enakelgh*.'

Ever since last night I had felt restless, charged up and fizzing as if someone had carbonated my blood, and I didn't think I was the only one.

'Practice makes perfect,' I pushed. 'The better we

get at it now, the better chance we have of being able to do the big stuff later – like, oh, I don't know, say, breaking curses?'

Thalia straightened a little, and I swallowed a smile.

River played with the fork resting on her plate. 'Something small,' she mused.

'Any suggestions?' I asked.

'Someone,' Fenrin said, eyeballing Thalia, 'ate my portion of that red velvet cake we ordered.'

'You snooze, you lose,' Thalia said, entirely unrepentant.

'Well, I want some. Let's get them to bring over a free slice.'

Thalia shook her head. 'You know using magic for bad reasons always backfires.'

Fenrin rolled his eyes. 'What's a bad reason? There's no such thing as a universal definition of bad, is there? It's all subjective.'

'I'd say stealing comes under that vague umbrella term,' Thalia shot back.

'It's a slice of cake, Thalia,' Fenrin replied witheringly. 'It's hardly robbery at gunpoint, is it?'

'Fine,' she said with an aloof tone. 'But don't come crying to me when you're doing twenty to life for a bank job gone wrong because that's the way the universe decides to show you that you shouldn't steal.'

Fenrin covered his eyes with a hand. 'Someone help me out here.'

'You have to share the cake with everyone, then,' I informed him. 'We all have to want the same thing for it to work, remember?'

Fenrin pouted. 'What, you don't all have a burning desire for *me* to eat cake?'

'How should we do it?' River asked, eyes alight.

'Just picture a giant slab of red velvet cake on the table,' Fenrin murmured. A nervous smirk hovered on his face. *'As I will it, so will it be.'*

We exchanged glances.

One by one, gazes transferred to a clean spot on the table.

An illicit thrill ran through me.

'Concentrate,' I said.

'This is going to look majorly weird,' River muttered.

I pictured the slice of red velvet cake that we had previously been served. It had been a gloriously stacked wedge with a sponge the deep, dark colour of garnet, and a layer of pale buttercream as thick as a finger running through its middle like cement.

I saw it now in all its virginal, untouched glory,

resting innocently on a clean white plate just waiting for my delicate little fork to stab into its sugared depths and scoop up a disgustingly large mound of it, and the words rose up into my head.

As I will it,

I thought,

so will it be.

All at once I felt the noise of my surroundings come rushing back, a gentle, buzzing mix of undulating voices and the clink of plates being set down on tables.

Much like the plate that had just been set down on ours, in fact.

'The last slice,' the waiter said, winking at me. '*Vous avez de la chance.*' He placed a small leather booklet next to the plate and sashayed off.

As one, we stared at the red velvet cake currently occupying the centre of our world.

Fenrin swallowed. 'No. Way.'

Thalia snatched up the leather booklet and opened it.

'They haven't charged us for it,' she said.

River clapped her hands to her mouth, trying to muffle the snorting laugh she did when she was suffering from shock. Our cheeks were all flushed.

I felt giddy and silly and alive, alive, alive.

I raised my coffee cup. 'A toast,' I announced. 'To the good ship *enakelgh* and all who sail in her.'

'I'll drink to that,' Fenrin grinned.

Thalia's gaze was fixed on the cake. 'This could really work.'

'For someone who was going on about "bad" magic backfiring, you now seem curiously unbothered,' Fenrin remarked to Thalia as she raised a giant forkful of cake to her mouth.

'I'll just have to accept the consequences of my actions later,' she said, clearly overcome with greed. 'We'll probably all be sick tomorrow or something.'

She shovelled the forkful into her mouth.

'I just wish we knew how to use this to help Marcus,' River muttered. 'I don't think free cake is going to fix him.'

'No, but it's a hell of a start,' Fenrin said as he leaned forward to engage in a fork battle over the cake with his twin opponent.

Then he stopped suddenly. He held his fork stiffly, comically in the air, frozen. For one moment I thought he was going to be sick. As I gazed at him, my stomach was enveloped in a sudden, nauseous rush. For one confused moment I didn't know who I was – Summer or Fenrin – because we were both going to be sick, but who was feeling it, which one of us had begun it, and my god, how had we been separating people out all this time? Didn't everyone realise how connected we all were, threads pulled fast and tight between us all until what I felt was what he felt and what we all felt, all of us around the table, shivering under one, pulsing feeling of nausea—

'Something's wrong,' Thalia said. The skin on her face had gone as pale as a bleached skull. 'Something's—'

The bell above the lintel tinkled and the door opened, and a man came staggering into the cafe. He had on a white coat, Jackson Pollock'd in irregular splurges of red. Against that institutional white, those arcing spatters seemed to shine as bright as neon. They looked fake. They looked like paint.

If it was paint, though, why would he have been dipping his hands in it?

Behind him the cafe noise died away, that sense of wrongness billowing across the room with his entrance, ruffling across the backs of the crowd-herd as individuals caught sight of him and began to frown, knowing something was off but not quite there yet, not quite there . . .

I realised I knew the man covered in red paint. His name was Dr Angus Morton and he was the dispenser from the chemist's next door to Nature's

Way. He looked around, dazed and unsure under the stares. Then his eyes slid over us and something seemed to click. He came forward.

His gaze fixed each of us, one by one.

'He was right,' he said calmly. 'It felt good.'

He moved forward, his hand rising from his side, and it wasn't until he was absurdly close that I realised he was holding a pair of scissors, and I wasn't too sure what happened next, only that my chest felt hot and I was on my feet – we all were – standing around our table littered with cake debris, and Dr Morton jerked to a stop as if he'd been lassoed, stumbling and falling to his knees.

The scissors clattered harmlessly to the floor, coming to rest by his knee.

Only then did my brain kick in to calmly inform me that I had been mistaken. His coat and his hands and the scissor blades were not covered in paint.

They were covered in blood.

CHAPTER 19

I had known Dr Morton by sight all my life.

He was a balding hug of a man, affable and smiley, one of those people that no one, no matter how misanthropic, could bring themselves to dislike.

Except that he kind of hated us.

Or rather, Esther in particular seemed to be the object of his wrath. He openly dismissed her products as 'harmful quackery of the highest order', as he had once been quoted in the local paper, and he had more than once tried to get her shop shut down, fortunately without any success. Esther in turn bore his behaviour with her customary blank silence. She'd always said that ignoring people took their power away, and it had certainly seemed to work with Dr Morton.

His life appeared quite regular and relatively peaceful – at least on the outside. His wife was a quiet woman who taught at a local primary school. His neighbour was a booming, hulking man from a family of farmers, who, it transpired, was having an affair with his wife.

As we learned later, Dr Morton found this out by accidentally discovering his wife and his neighbour in a scenario that was rather difficult to explain away.

When the neighbour stopped by the chemist's to try and smooth things over, the affable, smiley Dr Morton took up a pair of bandage scissors from the countertop and stabbed him several times in the chest. Then he had walked out, leaving the neighbour bleeding out on the floor, crossed several streets seemingly without hindrance, entered the cafe, and made a beeline straight for our table.

After that, everything became a hazy swirl of organised chaos – the police arrived, along with an ambulance, its siren swelling. Everyone's emotions felt muffled by the sense of dislocation from real life. There was no sobbing or screaming, just the quiet voices of professionals and my mother's equally soft responses to their questions. I felt utterly calm throughout, only afterwards realising that I had been in shock.

The neighbour survived the stabbing but he was in a serious condition at the local hospital's trauma unit. Dr Morton, unharmed and covered in blood, was arrested for attempted murder.

The town looked on this scene, looked at us, and whispered behind their hands loud enough for us to hear.

'I don't know. He went straight for them like they'd told him to do it.'

'There's something going on there. You know about the feud between him and Esther, right?'

'Do you think . . . some sort of revenge—'

'Did you hear what he said to them?'

All those poison thoughts were drawn to one another like liquid mercury, pooling into one thick, gelatinous mass that hung heavy and threatening over our huddled heads and pointing to one conclusion:

The Graces did this.

School felt unbearable.

We wandered the corridors together when we could, enduring the whispering. Even Gemma and Lou seemed to pull away from me now. All our old friends avoided us.

On Monday, all four of us were sitting together at lunch when Marcus found us. Thalia and Fenrin had been staying in the upper school wing at lunchtimes of late, making use of the basic kitchen facilities they had there – but today they had ventured back into the school's shared cafeteria. We needed each other right now, but those *enakelgh* threads tethering us together, that feeling of oneness, had been shocked out of us – only temporarily, I hoped. We felt separate and alone, which left me with an empty gnawing.

'I read his wish.' River sounded entirely numb. 'Remember the man who found out his wife was having an affair and wanted to do something about it? That was Dr Morton. I read his wish and then I made it happen.'

'You didn't consciously try to though, did you?' Thalia said.

'Doesn't matter. It keeps happening.'

'This shouldn't be possible,' I said, hating the desperation in my voice. '*Enakelgh* should have brought your power under control. That's part of the deal. And we are *enakelgh*. We all felt it, didn't we?'

'Hey,' came a hesitant voice.

I turned in my chair. Behind us stood Marcus, his backpack hanging off one shoulder. He looked serious.

'I wouldn't,' I said.

He frowned. 'Wouldn't what?'

'Hang out with us.' I gave a humourless laugh. 'We're cursed.'

Marcus brushed right over this.

'Can I talk to you? All of you?' he said.

His furtiveness caught me. He was vibrating like a plucked string.

'About what?' asked Thalia, watching him with cautious eyes.

'About the fact that it's not River doing this. It's not her doing any of this.'

I frowned, unable to tell where he was going. 'How do you know?'

'Because it's happened before,' said Marcus. 'Ten years ago. Just like this.'

CHAPTER 20

Midafternoon break had us gathered together in the copse at the back of the school.

When I left class, River was waiting, slouched against the outside wall of the art room, and together we made our way across the crackling grass of the field. River seemed to have no idea what Marcus would tell us – apparently he had kept his cards close to his chest – so as we walked I told her about Iona, Nathaniel, and the fire, their whole tragic story.

I assumed all of this circled back to them, but how? Had there been another spirit witch causing chaos ten years ago? Had Nathaniel found a way to deal with it?

When we reached the copse, Marcus and the twins were already there, huddled and waiting. The five of us sat in a ragged circle, our breath coming out in pale plumes.

'Can we make this quick?' Fenrin burrowed himself into his thick pea coat. 'It's freezing.'

'Five minutes,' Marcus promised. He rifled through his backpack, bringing out a sheaf of assorted papers. I grew curious, seeing they were printed and photocopied newspaper stories.

'Everyone seems to be on edge right now,' he said, thumbing through the papers with nervous hands. 'My dad nearly punched someone out the other day, just for cutting a queue. You know how laid back he is normally. And all the stuff that's been happening recently – the stuff we thought River was responsible for – it's *way* up from normal statistics. The biggest local news before this year was the uproar about the new parking lot across from the green. I mean, nothing happens in this town, right? Nothing like this anyway. Except that it did – once before.'

He spread the sheaf of papers on the hard ground: newspaper clippings, ranging from old fuzzy newspaper photocopies to crisp articles printed off the internet.

A giant, emphatic headline caught my eye:

LOCAL GIRL PERISHES IN FATAL FIRE

'Ten years ago,' Marcus said, 'a girl named Iona

Webber died in a cabin fire. A terrible accident. Bad wiring. Then, a few weeks later, unusual incidents started piling up – vandalism, robberies, fights, car crashes. *Two* stabbings. Stabbings. In *this* town. More drunk and disorderly citations in one week than in the previous five years. This goes on for a few intense days.' He raised his hands. 'Then suddenly . . . *nada*. No more weird stuff. Everything dies down.' He tapped a piece of paper that sported a colour-coded graph. 'The only other time in the last couple of decades that we've had a surge of incidents like this is now. Check out the data.'

'A *graph*?' Fenrin said, amused. 'Jesus Chr—'

'Fenrin,' Thalia cut in. 'Shut up.'

Her face was carved from granite. At times like this, there was no denying the Esther in her.

'Statistics, Fen,' Marcus said simply. 'Data doesn't lie. Look at the graph. It's not just a spike, it's an *astronomical* spike, and there are only two of them like that. Ten years ago, for about a week. Then regular levels for ten years straight. And then again a huge spike, starting two months ago.'

Thalia shook her head. 'What are you saying with this?'

'A Grace, or someone close to a Grace, dies in a horrible accident,' Marcus responded patiently. 'Then bad things suddenly start to happen in a very fast, very

245

unusually concentrated manner. The current data spike starts just before Christmas. When did you bring Wolf back?'

'Just before Christmas.' Thalia sounded pensive.

Fenrin's chin tipped up. 'Look, we know it's River doing all this. It's why we formed this *enakelgh* in the first place, to . . . help her.'

Control her is what he had been going to say.

I glanced uneasily at River. She was staring at the data graph, seemingly lost in thought.

'How can it be River both ten years ago and now?' Marcus asked. 'She's never lived here before. Fenrin, look at the data. It's right there.'

Evidence-based theory was one of Marcus's favourite catchphrases.

'Then there was another spirit witch,' I said. 'They were in town around the time of Iona's death—'

'*After* her death,' Marcus reminded me. 'That's when it starts.'

'So Iona dies and this witch starts spiralling out of control. Maybe Iona's death caused them to spiral? Maybe they were a friend of hers?' I lit up. 'Oh, wow. Maybe it's Nathaniel.'

Thalia was dismissive. 'He's not walking around causing chaos. He researches magic, but he doesn't do any.'

'Maybe he can't,' I said, momentarily caught up in the idea of it. 'Ever since that day he's had to stop himself from doing magic because his grief made him lose control.'

'Stop making it sound romantic,' River said shortly. 'It's not.'

Just jam that foot right into your mouth, Summer, I thought.

'So ten years ago,' Fenrin said, 'there was another spirit witch that, for whatever reason, caused chaos and then was stopped. History repeats itself. You still haven't told us why it's not River this time, when it seems obvious that it is.' Fenrin sounded impatient.

Marcus shuffled his papers, looking anywhere but at us.

'There's something else,' he said. 'It's about my . . . illness.'

Beside me, River went still.

'When I saw Wolf in your back garden, it was a couple of weeks since I'd given River my wish. It got around that you guys were down for the weekend, so I figured I'd risk it. I told you that I'd come to see if I could feel magic around you, but that wasn't the whole truth.' Marcus's fingers twisted a little faster. 'The truth is, ever since River . . . did what she did, I can feel your house. It's not the only place in town, but it's the strongest.'

Fenrin sounded unamused. 'You *feel* our house. Our house makes you sick.'

Marcus swallowed. 'About that. It's not quite *sick*. I mean it is, in a way, but . . .' He was casting around, floundering. I kept my eyes trained on him, willing him to talk.

'Okay,' he said. 'I read this fairy tale once about a woman who ate the heart of a star so she could stay forever young. It reminds me of that. Bright, overwhelming, buzzing. Being anywhere near River is like being constantly a little . . . overloaded.'

He gets all woozy and weird, like he's high or something, River had told me. I thought I knew what he meant. I'd felt an echo of it around her before, the ghost version. Furred skin, quickened heartbeat, as if whatever energy she gave out was dialled up stronger, a hundred-watt bulb to everyone else's twenty-five.

'It's the same with you guys,' Marcus continued. 'I mean, not quite as strong. But your house is more defined to me now, like it's constantly lit up by spotlights. Anyway, I came late at night because I figured you'd all be in bed and I didn't want you to freak out about me being there. But you were all out in the garden.'

He paused. Looked up at us.

'Then I saw Wolf,' he said, and the way he said it gave me a sudden spike of nerves. 'I knew something was wrong. It's ... hard to describe what it's like, being near him. It's as if I'm looking down the side of the Eiffel Tower. Falling and never hitting ground, like my stomach's trying to climb out of my mouth. I started to feel sick. And then I guess I fainted.'

The copse was silent.

Marcus fidgeted. 'You know everyone's talking about him, right? Even people who barely knew who he was before. You guys might have gone into town once or twice whenever he visited, but mostly he stuck to your house, right? Yeah, not now. Pretty much *everyone* has met him. During the day, when you're at school and I guess your parents are at work, he goes wandering and he talks to people. I mean random strangers. I can't describe watching him move through a crowd in town. It's like watching a rock star or the pied piper or something. It all happens when you're at school.'

He's been sneaking out of the house, Fenrin had said. *He goes walking.*

Wolf had told me about grabbing a coffee one day and sitting near two town gossips who confessed everything they knew to him.

People find it easy to talk around me.

'I didn't understand how everyone else was able to act normal around him,' Marcus said. 'To me he's this horrible, churning figure. I can't even look at him straight or I feel like I'm going to throw up. It's not like being around you or River. It's as if he's something that's been forced where it doesn't belong, and it's splintering everything around it. I don't know how else to explain it.'

Marcus's words were dark and awful, eels slipping silently in the ink-black water underneath my feet.

So many twinges of oddness from the past few weeks, which I'd chosen to ignore, now came flooding back, parading through my brain as if to taunt me with my own stupidity. Wolf was so loquacious and erudite nowadays. He had *never* talked like that. He had mumbled and staccatoed his way through sentences, often preferring silence. The Wolf I knew would never have been so constantly self-centred and greedy, so casually callous to his own parents that he'd persuade them to let their only son stay in someone else's house for weeks when they'd only just got him back. The Wolf I knew would never, ever have dreamed of trying to seduce me and betray Fenrin just to satisfy an urge. Now, Wolf acted on impulse without seeming to care if anyone else got hurt. He had come back a different

Wolf – we all knew that – but just how different was he?

Marcus was right. Something was wrong with him.

'Why did you wait until now to tell us all this?' I said.

To my surprise, Marcus gave a soft, dismissive snort.

'Sure, I can imagine how that might have gone. You were all treating me like a crazy stalker. Would you have believed a word I'd said?'

I started to protest, or apologise, I wasn't sure what, but Thalia got there first.

'I'm sorry,' she said.

Marcus brushed this off – not rudely, but as if it were hardly high on his list of priorities.

'It doesn't matter,' he said. 'What matters is that I wasn't going to tell you something so outlandish as, "Oh, hey, so Wolf makes me want to puke – what's up with that?" until I understood more about *why*. And I didn't even know how to describe it to you at first. I've never experienced anything like it before.'

Fenrin stirred. He stood up and brushed himself off.

'Well,' he said. 'This has been a great show and tell, but some of us have class to get back to.'

I gave Fenrin a puzzled look. 'This is a little bit more important than class. It's Wolf.'

'If you want to be a dropout, Summer, that's your shout. I have shit to do.'

'What's up with you?' I said, stung by his dismissive tone.

'What's up with me?' Fenrin gave a disbelieving laugh. 'Oh, come *on*. You all look like you actually believe this. It's ridiculous.' He threw a hand out to Marcus. 'He gets a bad feeling around Wolf, and we're supposed to have a meltdown about that?'

He sounded desperately unsure, a sea swimmer stretching his toes down for the hard graze of rock or soft, shifting sand and finding nothing but endless, watery space. I knew how he felt.

The steady ground of the known was crumbling away underneath us.

'Even if you ignore my feelings,' Marcus said, and from his tone I could tell Fenrin had hurt him, 'look at the pattern. Iona dies and then crazy things start happening. Wolf dies and then crazy things start happening. Isn't it worth understanding what that means?'

'But it was different last time,' Thalia said. 'You're saying that crazy things started happening only after Wolf came back. Well, that didn't happen with Iona. They didn't bring *her* back.'

Marcus was steady. 'How do you know that?'

Thalia and I exchanged a swift, startled glance. We didn't, I realised. Not for sure.

What if they had and we just didn't know about it? In our family that was a distinct and unfortunate possibility. Then again, why would they dread the curse so much, and work so hard to insulate us from outsiders, if there was even a remote possibility that any lost loved one could be resurrected?

There was only one reason.

If the resurrection had gone wrong.

The night Wolf came back, I remembered the shock of seeing him standing at our front door, alive. Naked, trembling, his eyes like scuffed charcoal scribbles. River stood beside him, her hands on his arm, steadying him against her.

We took him inside the house. Thalia ran to get him some clothes. Fenrin tried to talk to him, his voice high with panic. I just stood there, useless until my brother barked at me to call for help, call for an ambulance, call for their parents, call someone. I bolted to the phone only to find flat silence pouring into my ear. The line was dead.

Soon after that, the power in the whole house went out.

And after that ... nothing. Only the persuasive relief that Wolf was back and everything was fine.

It wasn't fine. It was wrong, like the sharp buzzing tang of mould on a tongue expecting fresh bread. Now we were experiencing a just punishment for the sheer arrogance of thinking we could resurrect someone without consequence.

The universe did not like to be tricked.

'You're not getting it,' Fenrin said, startling me from my troubled thoughts. 'So he's not exactly the same as before, but why does that suddenly add up to him being the fount of all evil?'

'There's a lot of evidence here,' River began, but she was cut off.

'Please,' Fenrin sneered. 'You'd just rather pin the blame on anyone but you.'

'Hey,' Marcus said sharply.

Fenrin just shook his head. 'Whatever Wolf is, he's back, and that's better than having no Wolf at all.' Shadow swept his face. 'Would you rather he was gone forever? Is that it? You'd rather he was completely dead?'

'How dare you?' River said, her expression bleak. 'Don't you think I want Marcus to be wrong? Don't you think I'm on your side? Because if I'm not, it's my fault, isn't it? Wolf is still all my fault. Or don't you think I care about that?'

His reply was bitter. 'You don't care about anything. You're a walking curse.'

I sucked in a sharp breath, but my brother did not back down. He turned, pushing blindly through the foliage.

'Fenrin,' I called, incensed, but Thalia shook her head.

'Leave him,' she said. 'He needs space.'

His figure dwindled as it cut across the field away from us, small and alone.

'I'm sorry,' Marcus said. He sounded wretched. 'I didn't know he'd react like that.'

I turned to River. 'You know that he didn't mean it.'

'Yes, he did.' She was frozen over. 'It's okay. He's right, isn't he?'

I scoffed, startling her. 'No, he's not. You know how I know? You wouldn't have given back those wishes if you didn't care so much about people's pain. Look, I'm really sorry to tell you this, but it's going to be pretty hard for you to hide your true feelings from me from now on, and vice versa.' I gave her a pained smile. '*Enakelgh*.'

River stared at me.

'You never said a word about all these terms and conditions,' she replied eventually.

I nodded. 'I know. You should sue.'

I was flooded with relief. She knew I wasn't abandoning her, not this time.

Whatever happened next, we'd deal with it together.

'What are you going to do?' Marcus said tentatively.

'We,' I told him.

'Oh, we're a team now?' he shot back, but I could tell that he was pleased.

I raised a brow. 'Are you kidding? No one can do data compilation like you can.' I glanced at Thalia, who was staring at the newspaper headlines blaring up at us from the ground. 'You know who we need to talk to, right?'

Thalia caught my gaze.

'Let's give him a call,' she said simply.

CHAPTER 21

My bedroom ceiling was covered in plastic glow-in-the-dark stars.

When I was nine, I'd thought they were the coolest. I'd asked for two packs of them for my birthday and spent hours choosing the exact right spot for each one. They were my familiar constant, shining faintly with their accumulated light.

I'd always loved silly, shiny things – bulbous glitter stickers, garish metallic nail polish, rainbow-striped erasers shaped like tiny fat cats. Thalia had always mocked me for my magpie ways, turning her nose up at the junk I collected – but it was in between the floorboards in Thalia's room that I had found one of my purple stick-on face jewels, which I'd presumed lost, and in the bottom drawer of Thalia's pretty, stained-oak bedside table were my pair of clip-on earrings shaped like ice-cream sundaes.

We always desire what we do not have.

Underneath my hand was a notebook:

On the Nature of Enakelgh.

I'd taken it from Gwydion's shelf. Let him notice it was gone. Part of me wanted him to confront me.

He never confronted any of us.

I wanted to go to him and tell him everything we now suspected. He'd have no choice then. He'd have to find a way to deal with us, even if it was to punish us. This one stray thread could unravel an entire blanket, and I wanted to pull it – but I couldn't.

Not after what Nathaniel's phone call had revealed.

I placed the notebook on my lap and read the line again.

It's far safer for everyone to stay away from outsiders altogether. Enakelgh covens have a tendency to end badly. (Lest we ever forget what happened with E's cousin ...)

E's cousin. I'd wondered at the time, and now I knew. He was talking about Iona.

Somehow she had been involved in an *enakelgh* coven – but it wasn't until we'd spoken to Nathaniel that I knew exactly how.

While Marcus, River, Thalia and I had sat in the copse, we had called him from River's phone. It was one of the most surreal conversations of my life – the four of us huddled around the phone's tinny speaker listening to a man we barely knew, but who had been revealed as an intricate part of our lives, calmly explain that, yes, when Iona died there had been an attempt to resurrect her. And it had succeeded.

Sort of.

'Were you involved?' I asked Nathaniel.

'I was there,' he admitted.

'Will you tell us about it? Please?'

He sounded cautious. 'Why do you need to know?'

I remembered how I'd thought he was different to my family because he seemed so free with the truth – but now I understood that everyone has secrets they keep from the world, no matter how open they seem. He obviously had reasons for keeping all this from us.

That meant the reasons had to be bad.

'It's Wolf,' I said. 'The friend we brought back. We think something's wrong with him.'

Silence.

His voice, when it came again, was subdued.

'Tell me everything you know.'

So we did.

When we were finished, there came a long pause.

'Fuck,' Nathaniel said to no one in particular.

I heard rustling as he moved around, settling in, and then give a long sigh.

'*Enakelgh* was your parents' idea,' he said eventually. 'Esther wanted Iona back so badly. She had heard of *enakelgh* and she said it was the only thing strong enough for resurrection. So she roped in Gwydion and then me.'

'Who was the fourth?' River asked. 'The spirit witch.'

A pause. 'Someone you don't know. Who just asked that? How many of you are there right now? Is that your *enakelgh*?'

'Almost,' I said. 'You're on speaker. Do you mind?'

'As long I'm not being broadcast or recorded,' he said wryly.

'You were part of our parents' *enakelgh*?' Thalia cut in. 'You told me you weren't a witch.'

'I wasn't,' he admitted, 'but I wanted her back more than anything. Anyone can perform magic if the desire is strong enough, even if it's only once – and of course, *enakelgh* needs crazy levels of desire to fuel it. The kind of desire that makes you forget everything else, that you'll do anything for.'

Love.

'It wasn't anything like I'd expected. It was ... weird. We did it. We brought her back, and at first we were so grateful that we pretended that we didn't notice how different she was. She knew things about me, secret things I had never told anyone before. She tried to manipulate us. She was ... persuasive. She made me feel like I should just take what I wanted because life was short and it was the natural order of things. It was intoxicating.'

Carpe diem, Summer.

I thought of Dr Morton. What had he said to us in the cafe?

He was right. It felt good.

'What was wrong with her?' Thalia asked with horrified fascination.

Another pause, as if Nathaniel was considering what to tell us.

'Let's just say that she wasn't alone when she came back,' he replied, and at that my skin crawled. 'But listen – if this is really the same thing as Iona, there's a way to banish it. Your parents didn't believe that, but I know there is. With an *enakelgh*, especially one as strong as yours, you could do it.'

'Sorry,' I said, 'but ... are we really talking about possession here?'

His silence told me everything.

'By what?' I demanded.

'Your parents called it a trickster spirit. They had to call it something, I guess. It seemed to fit with its behaviour.'

The Trickster. A lithe, androgynous figure, surrounded by a crowd in chaos, whispering in a man's ear, with a smile on its face.

It had been right in front of me the whole goddamn time. When I'd asked the card deck who was responsible for making Marcus sick, there was the Trickster grinning up at me – but my own judgmental assumptions about River had led me astray.

Nathaniel had *painted the answer right into the cards*, and I still hadn't seen it.

'You really think that's what's wrong with Wolf?' Thalia asked.

'I don't know,' Nathaniel replied, 'not without seeing him myself. Bring him up here to me.'

My sister and I exchanged a resigned glance.

'That might be a bit impossible,' she hedged. 'But what if you came to us?'

His reply was short. 'No.'

Surprised, she tried again. 'I know you fell out with our parents, but you were *enakelgh*. They'd understand, surely, they'd—'

'No!' Nathaniel interrupted, sharp enough to cut.

'Absolutely not.' He sighed. 'Shit. I didn't want you to know this.'

'Know what?' Thalia said.

A horrible suspicion began to form. I looked up and caught River's eye, and it seemed like we were reading each other's mind. I saw what I felt mirrored in her.

'Thalia, honey, please don't think badly of them for this.' Nathaniel sighed again, a pained sound. 'You have to understand how scared they were. The real reason we fell out is because they couldn't deal with what Iona brought back with her. I knew there was another way. I told them, if they just gave me some time to figure it out ... but they didn't want to listen. I forgave them a long time ago for that, but they never forgave me.'

'Forgave them for *what*?' Thalia demanded, but she already knew.

'For ... taking matters into their own hands.'

'They killed her,' I said flatly. 'They killed her to stop that thing inside her.'

Thalia was shaking her head. 'No.'

Nathaniel sounded wretched. 'I'm so sorry.'

'You're saying ...' I bleated a hollow laugh. 'You're saying if we tell them about Wolf, they might *take matters into their own hands*.'

He wouldn't answer.

Was it so very far-fetched to believe that of my parents? Would they not go to any lengths to protect their family? This was what Graces did. We loved each other to death.

'There's more,' Nathaniel said gently. 'If it is a trickster spirit inside Wolf, and they did try banishing it instead of just killing him, it wouldn't work. It's your *enakelgh* it's attached to. No one else's magic will have any kind of effect. It has to be you.'

'Well, this is just getting better and better,' I tried to joke, but I sounded unsteady.

'You're not alone in this, but you have to get him to me,' Nathaniel insisted. 'I have a permanent binding circle set up in my cellar. My whole house is protected from outside influence. If you bring Wolf inside the house, the spirit won't be able to leave. Then you can perform a banishing. You can save Wolf.'

'Why on earth would you have a binding circle set up in your cellar?' I asked curiously.

He hesitated. 'In case . . . it ever came back for me.'

Oh god.

'It hasn't,' he added quickly. 'Once it's banished, it doesn't come back. I'm just paranoid, I guess.'

He sounded sheepish, but I didn't blame him for being paranoid.

'One last thing.' He drew in a steadying breath.

'If there really is a trickster spirit inside your friend, do not act differently around it. If it thinks you know about it, it will start to feel threatened and . . . I don't know what it will do. I know we fell out, but I still love your parents so much. I couldn't forgive myself if something happened to them.'

For a moment I couldn't breathe. I felt Thalia clutch my hand.

She took up the phone then and talked to Nathaniel privately.

Marcus, who had been silent throughout the whole exchange, was watching River, who was watching me. We didn't need to speak to communicate and I knew what she was thinking.

How could our *enakelgh* banish a trickster spirit without Fenrin?

After the gathering in the copse he'd disappeared. For the rest of the afternoon Thalia tried in vain to find him, desperate to relay everything Nathaniel had told us, but Fenrin was nowhere to be seen.

Our brother was avoiding us.

Then again, I had always been pretty good at confrontation, and he couldn't hide forever. He had come home late from school, but he was up in his room right now.

No time like the present.

I put the notebook down and leapt off my bed, determination propelling me. As I reached the landing outside my room, I looked up to the first floor. Where were all the lights? Why was it so dark?

'Fenrin?' I said again. My voice was sucked into the damp hush.

The weight grew as I took the second set of stairs, Fenrin's bedroom door looming dark. I reached the second-floor landing and hesitated, my hand reaching out to the door handle. Stilling.

'Hi, Summer.'

A startled exhale burst its way out of me.

To my right, a shape moved on the landing's small couch.

'What are you doing there in the dark?' I said.

Wolf regarded me, stretched out.

'Relaxing,' he said.

Relaxing outside Fenrin's room?

Relaxing . . . or guarding?

I heard Nathaniel's voice: *do not act differently around it.*

It was Wolf. Wolf, the boy I'd known all my life. Lover of terrible musicals and half moons of watermelon chilled in the fridge, all thick curled hair and sweet eyes.

His eyes were hooded, impossible to read in the low light. I realised I hadn't seen him, really seen him, for days. I hadn't been close to him since the cellar. I hadn't been alone with him until now.

He looked . . . sick. Drained. Pale and wet.

'Are you okay?' I asked.

He took too long to answer.

'Fenrin's asleep,' he replied finally, avoiding my question.

'Tiring him out again?' A little venom seeped through my voice.

'Why?' he said. 'Jealous?'

I stared at him, affronted. 'Don't be gross.'

'Where have you been?'

'School.'

His head tipped. 'No. I meant on Friday.'

Friday? I racked my brain.

'Fenrin said you all met up in the woods.'

The night of the fireflies.

'Sure,' I said cautiously. 'River needed to talk to us.'

Wolf swung his legs off the couch, planting them on the ground.

'So,' he said. 'You're best friends again with the girl who killed me, huh?'

He regarded me, unblinking, while I searched for what to say.

'It's not like that,' I told him finally. 'She needs our help.'

A look of pure, unmistakable revulsion flashed across his face. 'I told you to stay away from her.'

I forced myself to stand still and stare him down.

'That's my decision,' I said.

He tipped his head. 'I guess it is.'

'And she's also the one who brought you back,' I reminded him. He was quiet; he seemed to have no answer to that. Nervous about a conversation that I no longer knew how to play, I took a step towards Fenrin's door. At the same moment Wolf stood up.

'I just want to see Fen,' I explained, trying to seem utterly normal while every instinct whispered that something was very wrong.

'He doesn't want to see you,' Wolf said. 'He's in bed. Leave him alone.'

I scoffed. 'Are you going to stop me seeing my own brother?' I didn't wait for his reply. I barged past him and pushed the door open.

'Just a warning,' I heard him murmur behind me, and my shoulders twitched in an involuntary creep.

Mercifully he made no attempt to follow me in. I shut the door on him and turned to face the room. I could make out the solid lump of a body in Fenrin's bed. The curtains were drawn and the lights were off. A heaviness seemed to gather in the corners of the room, waiting to drip down the walls.

'Fen,' I called. 'Wake the hell up, I need to talk to you.'

Nothing.

Shadows seemed to crawl across the floor. I fought the urge to run.

'Fenrin, seriously,' I said. I was creeped out enough. I needed something normal to happen or I might scream.

'Go away, Summer,' came my brother's tired voice.

'It's not even dinner time,' I pushed. 'Are you ill?'

Silence.

'We need to talk about . . . what we talked about in the copse,' I said. 'Please.'

'I don't want to talk about anything with you.' He sounded tired and thin, but there was no mistaking the tone of flat fury.

'Yeah, well, tough shit.' I was acutely aware of Wolf outside the door and I wondered what he could hear. What did it take to get some privacy with my own brother?

'Okay.' There came a slow rustling as he levered

himself up, propping his head against his pillows. 'You want to talk? Let's talk.'

'What's wrong?' I came forward, intending to flop onto his bed like I always did, like I always had – but something told me that I couldn't, not this time. 'Has something happened?'

He shook his head, mouth twisted in mockery. 'Oh no. Unless you count finding out about your sister betraying you.'

I stopped. 'What?'

'Did you think I wouldn't find out, Summer? Did you think I'm just . . . that . . . dumb?'

My pulse climbed.

'Find out about what?'

Fenrin shook his head. 'Please don't pretend like you don't know what I'm talking about. Please at least say you respect me enough for that.'

I could have, but that felt like almost as much of a betrayal. Instead I was tongue-tied, choked with guilt.

Fenrin watched me with heavy-lidded eyes.

'Wow,' he said bitterly. 'You aren't even going to defend yourself, are you?'

'I should have stopped it as soon as it started,' I said above the unbearable feel of my surging, shameful heart. 'I know that.'

'I just want to know why,' he said in the same dull, flat tone. 'Why you would come on to my boyfriend. Why you kissed him.'

'What?' I said. 'Wait. Is that what he told you, that *I* came onto *him*?'

'Are you calling him a liar?'

That bastard.

'Yes, I'm calling him a liar!' I said, outraged. 'You want to know how it really went down? I came home and I found him in the cellar being creepy. He was down there drinking by himself and we started talking, and then all of a sudden he was talking about seizing the day and—'

'So you weren't drinking too.'

'What? Well, I was, but—'

'Having a private party,' he said. 'Did you plan it?'

'No.' I could feel tears threatening at the sheer injustice of being lied about. 'No, I didn't, I just— I made a bad choice. It was selfish and awful, and I'm so sorry. Fen, I'm sorry. But he's lying to you. I never kissed him, he kissed *me*.'

He had, but I had let him.

It was just for a moment – but a moment was all it took, sometimes, to ruin everything.

'Why didn't you tell me as soon as it happened, if you're so innocent in all this?' Fenrin asked.

Because I was ashamed, I wanted to say – but it wouldn't come out.

My brother shook his head. 'Then who am I supposed to believe, Summer? My boyfriend or my sister? Are you asking me to choose? Are you really asking me to do that?'

'Yes!' I said desperately, but he was shut down, closed off – and oh, it was such a clever hand, Wolf playing us off against each other. Fenrin turned away from me, slumped and wan against his pillows, and I knew suddenly I couldn't bear it.

I marched from his room and I no longer cared who or what Wolf might be. I was going to drag him to my brother and make him tell the truth—

The landing outside Fenrin's room was empty. Of course. Furious, I stalked along the corridor to Wolf's room but he wasn't there either. He had disappeared.

I came down to the first-floor landing and ran into my father who was loping along the corridor, having evidently just come from his study. He gave me a vague smile as he saw me.

'Have you seen Wolf?' I said abruptly.

'And a good evening to you,' he replied in a jovial tone, and then stopped as he caught the edge in me. 'Summer, are you okay?'

'I'm just looking for Wolf.'

Gwydion frowned. 'I heard the front door go. I think he went out.'

For one moment I thought about going after him. Running down the lane, screaming his name – but as much as I was angry, I was also afraid. Afraid of how easily he had driven a wedge between me and my brother, a foundation I had previously thought of as mountain solid.

Afraid of what he might have inside him.

'What's wrong?' Gwydion asked, but his concern didn't reach his eyes. It never reached his eyes.

Wretchedly I remembered Nathaniel's warning. I couldn't talk to him even if I wanted to. I couldn't tell him anything I suspected. A childish part of me ached to run to him, beg him to fix everything, but I couldn't.

I wanted our parents to stop protecting us, didn't I? Well, now I had my wish. They couldn't help me because now I was protecting *them*.

The universe did seem to love a teachable moment.

'Nothing's wrong,' I said, but I couldn't quite stop from sounding bitter.

Gwydion heard it. 'Hey—' he began, but it was too little, too late.

'Why do you care? You're never here anyway.

What does it matter to you?' I said. I knew it wasn't him I was angry at, or maybe it was. This resentment had been building up inside me for years, and it didn't matter that he didn't deserve it *now*; he had deserved it before and he would again, and again.

'Summer,' he said with a frown, but he was still so far away from me, and I was all alone in this.

I turned away from him, making my way into my bedroom and shutting the door.

Come in, I begged him silently. *Shout at me. Be angry. I don't care if it means we accidentally break all the furniture in my room. Just . . . be something.*

After a long moment I heard his tread on the stairs, moving down to the ground floor.

Away from me.

I threw myself on my bed, misery leaking acid into my stomach, and contemplated the mess I had made.

We were divided from our parents and from each other. Separated and alone. That made us weak. To be powerful we had to be together in this. *Enakelgh* wouldn't work if one of its four was separated from the rest.

I wondered if that was what Wolf had wanted all along.

CHAPTER 22

The poppet faced us both, lying sightless and still.

It was made from lengths of raffia and bound with thick garden twine. Plaited carefully into its woven loop of a head were several strands of Wolf's ebony hair, liberated from his hairbrush.

This was a spell our parents didn't even know we'd been taught.

We had learned it from our grandmother, Gwydion's mother, whom we all called Mamm. She died when I was eleven. She had been a singular character, overbearing and fabulous with a famously short temper, and she still cast a long shadow over the household. No one, especially not Gwydion, could tell Mamm how to behave, and in comparison with my tightly closed, ice-calm mother, she had been an attractive kaleidoscope of drama.

Mamm liked to tell us stories about the myriad

275

fates that had befallen the extended Grace family over the years, fates both strange and humdrum, peaceful and pain-filled. Thalia and Fenrin had kept Mamm's stories alive after her death, gently distorted in the retelling through young minds, whispering them to each other in their bedrooms after dark. Those stories left me feeling the first sting of injustice, the kind that cut so deeply it went all the way down into the core – not just blame unearned or a cruel word, but the unfairness of death, the great equaliser. Did good people die so carelessly, so young, so pointlessly too? Was that really the way it all worked?

On cold winter evenings when the dark seemed closer to the skin, Mamm also liked to show us how to work a little of her own devised magic. Simple spells over a candle, charms for good luck or courage, to help you sleep or make sure you grew tall. Sweet, childish things.

Then there were the other kinds of spells.

Spells to tell when a lie had been spoken. I still remembered that one – steep a chunk of obsidian in moonlit water and it would burn cold on your skin when someone lied in your presence. Spells to protect yourself from harm – in particular when the harm was unclear or clouded from a witch's judgment – a ritual that worked as a barrier to rid a person of anything that could be affecting them.

And finally this one. A depossession spell.

Mamm showed it to us in the kitchen one night, not too long before she died, extracting a promise from us that we would not tell our parents. She said it was an all-purpose spell for cleansing someone of bad energy, however they had acquired it. I'd always wondered why she had wanted to teach us such a particular spell.

Now I wondered if it was because of Iona.

Though she hadn't made a career out of it the way Gwydion had, Mamm had been a diviner too. Maybe she had seen this coming. Maybe she was just cautious.

River and I sat opposite each other, cross-legged on the scratchy carpet of her bedroom floor. Between us lay the poppet we had made together. On one side of it sat a bright red candle. On its other side was a bowl half filled with an oily liquid, its slick surface catching the candle flame with a greasy glitter.

The two of us in her bedroom felt like a conspiracy. Thalia should have been here, but she was late back from spending the day with Nathaniel, and she had skipped school to do it – again.

We had made a deal. She would always tell me when she went to see him, as long as I didn't tell anyone else. I was her sister – I was determined not to betray at least one of my siblings – so I kept my promise, but the oppressive atmosphere in the house was too much to bear.

Inaction drove me to distraction. Creating something, whether it was a spell, an argument, or a piece of music, gave a release for all the churning emotion inside me. I couldn't bottle things up the way my parents did. I wouldn't.

So, the next day after school, an innocuous Wednesday like any other, I went over to River's house, armed with supplies and a whole lot of determination. The last time I had visited her there had been just before Christmas when I had lured her into coming out to breakfast with me and Fenrin under the pretence of renewing our friendship, all so we could take her and force her to bring Wolf back from the dead.

There were no innocents here. We had made this mess together and now we had to fix it.

So we set to work.

With a slow, steadying breath, aware of River's eyes on me, I reached out and picked up the poppet.

With a depossession spell, you work backwards, Mamm had said. *Begin with water, to cleanse the body of the invading energy. Then fire, to burn the energy out.*

278

Then air, to blow away the ashes. Then you end with earth, to seal the open body back up so nothing else bad can take root inside it.

Use a bright-coloured candle to draw it out. Energy is attracted to energy. Take some clove oil. Your mother always has some in her cupboards. Pour out a little into a bowl of water. Take the poppet and bathe it in the oil and water, just enough so that it's covered.

I dipped the poppet into the bowl. With its loop of a head pinched between my fingertips, I rolled it gently against the bowl lip to shake off the drips.

Now fire, Mamm had said.

River leaned forward and lit the red candle with the flick of a lighter.

Now, came Mamm's voice. *Stare into the flame and imagine the person you are cleansing. Can you see their hair, their face? What are they wearing? Remember what their hands look like, the changes on their face when they're sad or angry. Once you have them in your mind as fully as you can, close your eyes. Now take the poppet and hold it high over the flame. Be careful now, you don't want to set it on fire. Let the candle smoke bathe it while you stare into the flame once more and say, three times:*

We cast you out.
We cast you out.
We cast you out.

I heard River's chant echoing mine opposite me, her voice low but unyielding.

Now blow the candle out, Mamm had said.

I leaned forward and pictured Wolf's face one last time before snuffing the flame.

Now you take the poppet outside and bury it in the ground. Bury it somewhere where no one's going to disturb it.

Will it stay buried forever? Thalia had asked.

For however long they need the help to keep out those bad energies, Mamm had replied.

Forever, I had said. *Right? I want them to be okay forever.*

Mamm had lifted my hair back from my uplifted face. *There may come a time when they don't need your help any more because they figured out the balance themselves. They know how to shield themselves, and they know when to open themselves up, and bad energy no longer has a home inside them.*

How will I know that they're okay?

You'll be able to tell. That's the trick of a true witch, Summer. Knowing when to stop.

In River's room, I sat back, wired and tired all at once.

'Is it done?' River said. She looked drained, like a depleted battery.

With the wet poppet still clutched in my fingers, I leapt to my feet, unlatched her bedroom window, and pushed it wide open. Cold dusk air came boiling in, prickling my cheeks, and I sucked in a deep breath. Air calmed me – I was an air witch after all – but tonight it was not enough.

'It's done,' I said, eventually. My thumb rubbed absently over the poppet's loop of a head. 'I just need to bury it to make sure it doesn't get ruined and potentially break the spell.'

'What will happen to him?'

'To Wolf? Hopefully nothing. But if there really is something inside him ... this will work. We won't need to do anything else.'

I said it with as much conviction as I could muster. Belief is half the work of magic. If there is no belief, there is no will. No will, no power. Nothing can be created from doubt.

I turned. River was still sat cross-legged, face uptilted to me.

'Do you really think that's what's wrong with him?' she said.

I was starting to.

'I guess we'll soon find out.' I pushed off from the windowsill, the poppet an urgent weight in my hand. 'I should get back.'

Still I hesitated, reluctant. The last thing I wanted to do was go back to that house and face my brother.

'Walk you home?' said River.

I snorted. 'That'll take you hours.'

She shrugged. 'I like walking.'

She could feel my dread, I realised, even if she didn't know what was causing it, and this was her way of trying to help. I hadn't been able to tell her why Fenrin and I had fallen out, only that we had. It was still too raw. I just wanted to forget it, even though I knew I'd have to deal with it sooner or later.

If River walked me back, that might at least mean later.

'I mean, if you like walking so much, who am I to stop you?' I said, trying to make light.

I wrapped up the poppet in a protective strip of muslin and put it in my pocket. We went downstairs and shrugged on our coats to the sound of the television drifting through the crack in the living room door. River lifted her keys from the hook and prepared to leave.

'Wait,' I whispered. 'Shouldn't you clear it with your mum?'

'Did you clear coming here with yours?' she whispered back.

'My parents aren't home until late tonight.'

River just shrugged.

'It feels weird not to at least say hi,' I pressed.

'It's really fine,' she said, but I was already using my free hand to open the living room door.

I heard my name hissed behind me.

'Hi, Mrs Stevenson,' I said, raising my voice above the noise of the television.

River might prefer her self-chosen last name as Page, but I didn't want to presume that her mother felt the same. It felt strange to reference her old name, though I supposed to Mrs Stevenson it was the only one her daughter had ever had.

It took Mrs Stevenson a moment to look up. When she did, her glazed expression, which had been ready to pass over me and get back to her show, stopped and sharpened.

'You're one of those Grace girls,' she said.

By the tone of her voice, it didn't seem like a good thing to be right now. I wasn't quite sure what to say.

'Yes. The crap one,' I added as an afterthought.

Mrs Stevenson did not seem to think this was funny. Her tired, craggy face was screwed up at me.

'Summer, come on,' River said behind me. 'Mum, we're just going for a walk. I won't be too late, I promise.'

'Where are you going? Are you going somewhere with her?' Her mother leaned out of her chair.

I bristled at the 'her', but River was dragging me away.

'Please,' she said. 'It's just better if we go. Summer?'

I let her lead me out of the house.

'What was that about?' I asked, as we walked.

River was tight-lipped.

'Come on, River. We don't do secrets any more, remember?'

'Sorry.' She shook her head. 'I just ... she's been listening to gossip, that's all. She thinks you're a bad influence on me, or something. I guess she wasn't happy when she found out we were friends again.'

'Ah,' I said. I had no idea what to say. I knew River had a difficult relationship with her mother, but I had no right to comment on Mrs Stevenson's feelings towards me.

After all, my parents had felt exactly the same about River.

'Families are tough,' I said gently. 'I know from what I speak, right? Sometimes they're more trouble than they're worth.'

We both knew I was being flippant. Though that might feel true, sometimes, I still couldn't imagine my life without mine. My entire being was shaped around them. Hating them, loving them, protecting them.

They were my every day, my past and my future. My hopes and my fears.

I was filled with me, but the bowl that held me was made of them.

My usual route home was the back way, over the dunes and through the grove at the bottom of the garden. I never normally came the front way, but walking from town and from River's house led us there naturally.

As soon as I arrived at the top of our lane and I saw what was waiting for us there, I knew we had made a mistake.

'Maybe your mother isn't the only one who's been listening to gossip,' I said slowly.

River frowned. 'Why do you say that?'

I pointed wordlessly.

Our normally empty lane was packed full of cars, and even in the half-light of dusk, I knew I didn't recognise a single one of them.

CHAPTER 23

'Are you having a party?' River asked.

I shook my head.

'Dinner? Soirée?' The joke fell flat, swallowed up by the winter dark.

'Whatever this gathering is,' I said slowly, 'it's nothing to do with us.'

We surveyed the parked cars in silence.

'I'll see you to the door,' River said at last.

We started down the lane in the dusk, winter dark at our backs, our feet crunching on loose gravel. It was a fairly steep tip downward to the house, always a little precarious in bad light, and we went slowly.

Halfway down, I heard the unmistakable creak of a car door opening.

'Hey,' said a woman's voice behind us.

Heart spiking, I stopped and looked back.

I recognised the woman. It was Verity

Worthington, mother to my acrimonious ex, Jase. Had she just been sitting in her car in the dark . . . waiting?

Waiting for who?

'Can I help you?' I said.

'Don't pretend like you don't know me,' Verity said, affronted. 'I've known you since you were a baby.'

Verity was a member of what Gwydion, in a rare display of out-and-out hostility, had disparagingly termed the PDGN – the 'Parental Do-Gooders Network.' He called them Pigeons for short, describing them as 'the sort who coo prettily to your face and then openly shit all over your house'.

Pigeons were townsfolk who had apparently decided that many things most well-adjusted people enjoyed doing would inevitably lead to a swift spiral into decadent evil, and as such, they dedicated their spare time to fighting the good fight against moral turpitude.

Apparently the Graces were the poster family for moral turpitude.

I strongly suspected this had been one of the main reasons Jase had been into me in the first place.

'Are you looking for Esther or Gwydion?' I asked as politely as I could.

'They aren't home,' Verity said.

That shouldn't have sent a spike of nerves through me.

'Maybe you should come back when they are, then.'

'Someone's home,' she continued, as if she hadn't heard my reply. 'I saw a light go on.'

There was another heavy creak and the car door of a battered Ford opened up. A thin man with a mop of flyaway hair got out. I'd seen him around but I couldn't remember his name.

'Jesus, how many of them are there?' River muttered.

I resisted a sudden urge to hold her hand.

This was ridiculous. These were adults, my parents' peers, the people in charge. They posed no threat to me, even though every nerve ending in my body kept insisting they did.

'You're friends with the Woodruffs' girl,' said the thin man, coming to stand beside Verity.

Woodruff. He meant Gemma.

I kept silent.

The man turned to Verity. 'D'you hear what Frankie Woodruff found in her daughter's bedroom? Little plastic packets of powder and dried herbs everywhere. She thought it was drugs. She nearly called the police.'

On her own daughter? Why not try talking to her

about it first? Besides, it was Gemma. She might enjoy the occasional vodka shot, but she didn't do any other drugs. No, I knew what the powder and dried herbs meant.

Gemma had been casting charms recently, after all.

'Terrible,' Verity said, shaking her head.

'My kid picked up this ridiculous book all about the parallels between theoretical physics and magic,' the man continued. He was looking at me. 'Can you imagine? It's a load of complete tripe, but he won't stop reading it.'

Congratulations, I thought, *you have a curious kid.*

I wondered who it was and if I could become friends with him.

'I've had such trouble with Jase, recently,' Verity said in an agreeing tone. 'He's been so rebellious, acting out. Terrible moods. Staying out late and lying to me about it.'

Congratulations, you have a teenager.

'It's the company he keeps, no doubt,' the thin man said. 'That's the problem. You can tell them they're making bad choices in their friends till you're blue in the face, but how do you police that?'

The street lamp at the top of the lane, the one that had been broken for months, flickered on with a sudden, angry buzz, throwing the surroundings into sharp relief and startling all of us.

'Did you come here for a reason?' River said, taking advantage of the pause. 'Because we have homework to do.'

The two adults were thrown and considered her for the first time.

'Who's your mother, dear?' Verity asked, finally.

River was steel and frost. 'You wouldn't know her. You don't shop in the same places.'

'They should be ashamed,' said the man, rallying. 'Bringing up their children like this.' He craned his neck, drinking in my house.

I was suddenly struck by a forcible impression of how we must look from the outside.

This house, nestled in a bowl of landscape like it had grown out of it. Herb pots littering the porch, scattered bright stones and symbols painted underneath the doormat, black points poking out from behind its bristled edges. A horseshoe nailed over the door, a bushy thick sprig of protective dried rosemary hanging underneath it, close enough to brush the tops of tall heads as they came inside. Ghostly silent Graces in the dark of the hallway beyond, waiting and judging. One dangerous, teeth-bared thing with many heads, deliberately impenetrable, deliberately unknowable.

Another car door opened, and River swore under her breath.

We'd assumed the cars were empty.

None of them were empty.

We shouldn't have been afraid. This wasn't how it was supposed to go. I was glad for whatever vague sense of precognition had filled me with reluctance to come back on my own. Something hung in the lane, in the gulf between us. Something bad, only held in check by propriety.

'Did you know your mother and Angus Morton were a thing?' Verity said to me as more people gathered behind her. Her head jerked like a spooked hen. 'Oh, she had him dangling on a string all the way through high school, until she tossed him away like he meant nothing. He was the one who came up with the rhyme, did you know that? *Like gets you bed, love gets you dead*. Went through all the boys like wildfire, that rhyme. It's only a pity that some of them chose not to listen to the warning.'

I felt my whole face flush. How dare she try and shame my mother with her past? How dare she stand there and tell her secrets to her own children? Those were Esther's secrets to give, not hers.

'We need to get inside the house,' I muttered. 'Now. Just walk.'

I tugged on River's hand and we moved. The house loomed large in my eyeline, a safe haven.

'And you know your father's been seen coming out of Nicole Popplewell's house,' came Verity's shrill voice behind me. 'I just thought you should know. Get it all out in the open.'

'What the hell is wrong with them?' River asked, spooked. We were half running now, feet rolling over loose shale.

I could only think of the night guests, of the contract of secrets that had existed between my parents and people like Verity. They were breaking that contract now. It was payback for the power we held over them, payback for the wishes in the clearing, for every one of their secrets that had come to light in recent weeks as people fought and stole and lied and, oh god, stabbed the rivals for their wives. The fabric of this town was fraying at the seams, and the town had found who it needed to blame. Us.

The worst thing about it was that they were right.

It was our fault.

'They're following us,' River panted beside me.

'Get to the house,' I repeated. The house would protect us. It always had.

I'd never loved the sound of my feet on the porch so much. We clattered up the steps, fumbling at the front door – oh god, my keys were in my bag, I didn't have time, they were coming – and then stumbling as the door opened by itself.

No, not by itself. Thalia and Fenrin were there, peering out with alarm into the dusk.

'What the fuck?' said Fenrin, but there was no time to explain. We pushed past them both and into the embrace of the hallway's cool air.

Thalia backed away from the door.

'Fenrin, close it,' I urged, but he just stood there like an idiot with it wide open.

Adults crowded onto the porch like seagulls flocking to leftover food. I recognised a maths teacher from school who taught the year above me. And the owner of the Gull, the pub on the stretch of beach next to ours. Verity led them, and now I saw that she had something in her hand. A pale piece of muslin trailed out from her clutched fingers.

The poppet.

It must have fallen out of my pocket.

'Give that back,' I burst out.

Verity raised her hand. 'What is it? Some kind of curse on one of us?'

'Not on *you*,' I retorted before I could think it through.

Her eyes widened.

'How dare you go around cursing innocent people?' she said, and as she spoke she raised the doll, shook it free of its muslin binding and took hold of its loop head with her other hand. 'What has this poor person ever done to deserve it?'

He's only the reason all this is happening, I wanted to scream in her face, but it was too late – I could only watch as her hands pulled in different directions, tearing the woven raffia to shreds.

She dropped the broken pieces on the wooden floorboards of the porch.

I couldn't believe it. I stared at her, my fear mutating to fast, hot fury. She had destroyed my spell. My spell. The spell that was trying to help us all.

I opened my mouth, but I was interrupted by a cry from behind her.

'He's there, I can see him, he's inside!'

I was lost in utter confusion. Were they after *Fenrin*? Then the thin man, galvanised to action, did a stupid thing.

He tried to get in.

I saw it happen and willed myself to move, but something got there first: the house, me – I'd never know which – us? It was us against them. The giant metal horseshoe – the one that my great-great-grandfather, the town's farrier back in the days when such things still existed, had nailed over the lintel of our front door as a good luck charm, the one that had been firmly hammered into the stone wall for more than a hundred years – fell and struck the man on the arm with a flat, sickening *thump*. Its two ends tipped downward to the ground, hanging briefly off his arm like the world's most absurd bracelet.

No, I thought wildly, *all the luck will run out of the ends and we'll be cursed forever.*

The man let out a breathless squeal and snatched his arm back, flinging the horseshoe, which landed with a dull thud on the porch at his feet.

The crowd rippled in dismay. The man's pale skin glowed with a livid red mark where the heavy metal had struck him. He stared down at it in wild incomprehension, then looked up at us with the world's most defeated expression on his face.

'You said you'd help.'

'What?' My brother's voice was high-pitched. 'I don't know what you're talking about.'

'You said it would be okay. You have to make everything better.' The man's voice was trembling. He was gazing, not at Fenrin, but past his shoulder at me.

No, not me.

'Wolf,' called another voice from outside, and my blood ran cold.

The dam broke and they began to talk all at once, clamouring.

Calling his name.

'Wolf, my mother's been holding out on me. Her will—'

'I know he's screwing her on his lunch hour, and I just wish I could—'

'Stole my—'

'I need it—'

'She won't *give* it to me—'

I shoved past a stupefied Fenrin and slammed the front door shut, locking it.

They didn't stop. They knocked on the door. They called his name.

I turned. The object of their desire was standing at the foot of the stairs, lamplit, tousle-haired, and grinning from ear to ear.

'Wow,' he said, wide-eyed under our collective gaze. 'What did you do to make them all so crazy?'

Fenrin found his voice first.

'Wolf,' he said. 'They're asking for you. Why are they asking for you?'

Wolf shrugged. 'No idea.'

No. I was not going to let him get away with another lie.

'They really want to talk to you,' I said. 'Maybe you should oblige them.'

His gaze was decidedly cool. 'I have nothing to say to them.'

'Funny. That's not what we've been hearing. You've been real chatty these last few weeks, right? You told me yourself. Walking around, grabbing a coffee, catching up with the town gossips. You know everything that goes on in this town, you said.'

Wolf laughed. 'So I got bored. You leave me. Every day you leave me by myself.' His eyes fixed on Fenrin. 'You just expect me to sit patiently in the house waiting for you to come home so I get to exist again?'

'Wolf,' Fenrin said, and part of me – a dark, ugly part – rejoiced at the cold suspicion in his voice. 'What did you do to them?'

'Nothing!' Wolf said, edging towards panic. He looked at us all, flitting from one face to the next. He didn't seem to like what he saw.

'Do you talk to people about their problems?' I said, raising my voice above the clamour outside. 'Do you offer them advice? You're so *good* at listening, aren't you?'

I realised that we had begun to move as one, all four of us crowding in, pinning him to the bottom of the stairs. I felt that togetherness at my back, an animal pack. He looked at us like he was prey.

'It's you, isn't it?' Fenrin said. 'It was you all along.'

Wolf stared at us all, cowed. He licked his lips. Started to speak—

When there was a crash from the back door. Shouts.

They had found another way into the house.

I didn't know where the command came from, but it was there, sudden and overwhelming, echoing in my head:

Protect him.

I turned, and as I did, the others turned with me: River and Fenrin and Thalia, our backs to Wolf. Just as the first shapes came groping into the hallway from the back door, I felt a searing fury – how dare they come into our house, *how dare they!* And it wasn't just my fury, it was all of us. We would do anything to protect one of our own, and it was then that the hallway began to glow.

The long, flat lamp sculpted from driftwood and the tall, vase-like lamp on the sideboard among the photo frames grew brighter. The cluster of lights in the ceiling, the kitchen lights, the hallway bathroom – every lamp, every single bulb, rapidly dazzled, highlighting the scene in bright, cold, painful gold until the light seemed to *scream*.

The intruders, caught in the sudden glare, panicked and scattered, fleeing like rabbits the way they came. The back door banged. The light kept pouring out, half-blinding me, obliterating all else.

In the distance I heard the revving of engines.

The noise seemed to break the thread between the four of us. I felt the fury and the overwhelming urge to protect leak out of me. As it did, the lights dimmed, gradually fading to normal levels.

I could think again. I could breathe again. My heart pounded, my nerves jittered.

There came a soft little groan from the direction of the stairs.

Wolf was cowering against the bottom step, scrunched into a ball, his face hidden in his hands. His body shook in minute shivers, as if he were feverish.

'I don't know what's wrong with me,' he whimpered. 'I don't mean to do it, but it keeps happening. I just want to be me again. Please.'

He looked grey and damp, as if he'd sweated so much that his outsides were nothing but water. We stood, looking down at him.

We'd grown up with Wolf – he wasn't our blood, but he was our family.

We would do whatever it took to save him.

CHAPTER 24

I drove.

I only had my provisional driving licence, so if we were stopped we'd have a problem, but I was the only one of us who had ever insisted on learning how. I drove us to the city, towards the wild hope of freedom. I drove to escape the curses at our backs. Wolf was quiet in the back seat. As long as Fenrin was beside him, holding his hand, it seemed as if he could keep his trickster at bay. I could see it in the hungry, needful way he looked at my brother, tracking him with his eyes as if fearful he could be taken away from him at any moment.

I saw it and I wondered if I would ever need someone like that.

Thalia used River's phone to call ahead and warn Nathaniel that we were on our way to him. It would have been hilarious to find that he'd gone away, or was home but hosting one of his many dinner parties. How gloriously awkward it would be to crash it.

Sorry, everyone, ignore us – we just need to get rid of this trickster spirit that seems to have hitched a ride inside our resurrected friend. If you hear screaming coming from the cellar, don't worry. The canapés look good.

Nathaniel was home alone and waiting for us. I had to wonder at the apparent lack of social life for someone so ridiculously attractive and obviously cool, but Thalia said he was over the bright lights, big city thing. He got his kicks from great food and great conversation, which was easier to conjure at his place than overcrowded, overpriced bars and restaurants. I could see why people would come to him: his home had more appeal than any bar. I hadn't wanted to leave it and I'd only been there once.

As I drove, I had time to marvel at the twist of fate that found us someone like Nathaniel in our hour of need. However I might feel about him dating my sister, he had already done more than we had any right to expect of him, and now here he was, offering his home to us without question or compromise. I couldn't imagine my parents doing the same. Every piece of freedom and desire had to be negotiated with them.

Before we left, Fenrin had suggested I leave a note to our parents explaining that we were out at the cinema for the evening and to expect us back late.

That wasn't quite what I had written.

Despite everything, I couldn't face lying to them. I hadn't told them where we were going, but I had told them that Wolf was sick, that it wasn't safe for him to stay in town, and that we were taking him to someone who could help him. Then I'd left River's phone number at the bottom of the note. In case something went wrong, I wanted them to be able to get hold of us. It would be fine. I knew it would be fine.

But just in case.

If they rang and all was well, I'd answer, I'd laugh it off, I'd tell them whatever they needed to hear, and I'd take any punishment they cared to give me. This was our wrong to right, and they could no longer protect us.

Two hours later we pulled up to Nathaniel's town house. Fenrin helped a jittery Wolf out of the car as Thalia ran up the steps and rang the bell. The door opened and we crowded into the hallway. I caught a glimpse of a serious-looking, tousle-haired Nathaniel giving something to my sister as I closed the front door.

He stood with his hands behind his back.

'You're Wolf,' he said, his gaze fixed on him.

Wolf stared back.

It happened fast. Nathaniel moved forward, his arms opening wide, looking for all the world like he was bringing Wolf into him for a hug, but instead he shifted round to Wolf's back and bear-hugged him from behind, pinning his arms to his sides.

'Now,' Nathaniel barked, and my sister sprang forward. In one hand she held handcuffs, in the other a roll of wide, thick duct tape which she tossed to Fenrin. He caught it and turned, ready.

As soon as he realised what was happening, Wolf began to buck in Nathaniel's arms, making it almost impossible to get the handcuffs on him – but between us all, we finally managed it.

He wouldn't stop. He snarled and writhed and screamed.

'Fenrin!' Thalia snapped. 'Gag him.'

But Fenrin was wavering.

'You've already seen the damage it can do,' Nathaniel panted. 'Gag him now.'

'He's still Wolf,' Fenrin said faintly.

'Fen,' Wolf pleaded. 'Don't, don't, don't. I won't fucking forgive you, Fenrin. Don't listen to them! *They want to kill me.*'

I snatched the tape from my brother's unresisting fingers.

'First you kiss me and then you gag me?' Wolf hissed.

'You tried to play that card already,' I informed him, and pressed the tape around his mouth.

'Wolf, please,' Fenrin said. 'We're not going to hurt you, we're trying to help you. *Please*.'

Wolf stared at him, dragging furious breaths in through his nose. Something seemed to pass between them, something I couldn't understand.

Finally, Wolf slumped.

'Let's get him downstairs,' Nathaniel ordered.

Between the two of them, Fenrin and Nathaniel managed to haul Wolf to his feet and take him down into the cellar, an anxious Thalia opening the door and hovering around while I brought up the rear. I followed them down, my boots clattering on the wooden cellar steps.

As she reached the bottom and looked into the room, I heard River give a low whistle, her eyes wide.

I had wondered what we'd find down there. What kind of things were needed to banish a trickster? Maybe the still-fresh hearts and old bones of animals would be scattered around a chalked-up circle. No, chalk was too meek – surely it had to be blood. Blood meant life.

But when it was spilled, it also meant death.

The walls were stacked with metal frames, packed with the detritus of a house. Paint pots, junked bits of furniture. The plain cement floor, however, was entirely clear and dominated by a huge, permanently carved pentacle.

Its outlines had been cut into the cement, a shallow groove running along the outer circle and down each arm of the star shape stretched within it. Running around outside the circle's groove were symbols and markings, carefully lined in stark black paint. The markings sparked recognition in me – the card deck. Something very similar bordered some of the cards – those careful, sweeping lines.

Well, they were by the same artist after all.

Fenrin and Nathaniel deposited Wolf in the heart of the pentagram. He slumped there, glaring up at us.

Nathaniel backed away, wiping his forearm across his forehead.

'I need to prepare the space,' he said, his voice low and his eyes on Wolf. 'It'll only take a few minutes but I need to be alone. You can wait upstairs.'

'I don't think that's a good idea,' Thalia ventured. Her eyes were ghostly wide in the cellar's thin light.

Nathaniel turned back to us, radiating calm.

'Don't worry,' he said. 'His only power lies in talking, persuasion, and we've taken that away from him. Plus, this pentacle? Very strong ward. He can't hurt me.'

Wolf's glare suggested otherwise – but he wasn't moving and he couldn't speak.

'Go,' Nathaniel urged. 'The quicker I can get set up, the quicker we can help him. I'll call you down in a few minutes, I promise.' His eyes found Thalia's. 'You need to trust me.'

We moved ponderously, reluctantly back up the steps. Thalia closed the cellar door behind her, and I led the way to the living room. Its familiarity helped calm me. There were the bookcases, the quirky lamps and the stacked canvases, the languorous sketches on the walls. Scattered on the floorboards next to the fireplace were Nathaniel's books of magic, rife with neon marker tabs. A leather notebook sat beside them, its open page full of spidery scribbly handwriting.

He'd been doing his homework, it seemed.

Fenrin plopped onto the couch, nervously twisting his hands.

'I can't hear any noises,' he said. 'Is that good or bad?'

'He asked us to trust him,' Thalia replied, but

she didn't look reassured herself. She crouched down beside the notebook and brushed her fingers absently over the pages.

'Who is this guy?' River muttered to herself as she examined the art on the walls.

'Old friend of the family,' I said.

Thalia gave a derisive snort.

My hands needed something to do. Thinking of those symbols, I found the card deck was out of my bag and being shuffled by my fingers before my brain had time to intervene. I sorted through them, looking for the ones I knew I had seen adorned with the same symbols as on the pentacle downstairs.

There – the Crescent Moon. It came out of the deck upside down and I had to put it the right way up before I could see it properly.

Together with the Dawn, the Midday Sun and the Dusk, this card was part of the four I had dubbed the Time set. The Crescent Moon depicted a young man with dark hair, narrow eyes, and an arrogant set to his outline, standing in between two shores – one light, one dark – with a ghostly crescent moon hanging above his head. Around the edge of the artwork ran a border of thin, sweeping black symbols.

'He looks kind of familiar,' said River.

I startled. She was standing over me, peering

curiously at the card in my hands. I put it on the floor in front of me in its original upside-down position. She crouched beside me.

I shrugged. 'Maybe he looks like someone famous.'

'Why have you put it upside down?' she asked.

'Sometimes a card is drawn out from the deck that way. It usually means that whatever it represents is actually the opposite of what you assume it to be.'

'So what does it represent?'

'I don't know,' I said. 'I wasn't really thinking of anything when I drew it.'

Well, I had been, I supposed – I'd been thinking of Nathaniel and his pentagram – but it wasn't a question I'd had in mind that needed answering.

'Draw another one,' said River.

I glanced at her. She seemed fascinated. I was willing to bet she hadn't ever seen divination cards before, never mind used them. I wondered what they might be capable of revealing in her hands. Maybe I could teach her. She'd probably outstrip me in less than an hour.

I glanced up. Fenrin and Thalia were arguing about something to do with the notebook they had been examining and were paying no attention to us. I guessed I had a little time to keep going, so I drew the next card. I picked it because it felt a little warmer under my hands than the others, as if it wanted me to notice it.

This one I had named the Sacrifice. It was one of four cards in the entire deck that seemed to belong to no particular set I could make out. It showed a naked figure lying on a stone table, and another figure above it with a knife in their hands, wide sleeves pooled at their shoulders, and their bare arms raised over their head.

'This one is more ominous,' I admitted.

'I'm not feeling too great about our prospects here,' River said.

'Come on, it's not supposed to be literal,' I replied, and then amended, '. . . probably.'

She tossed me a dark, troubled look.

'I was joking,' I protested. Nothing felt very funny right now, but I knew I was right. The Sacrifice didn't mean someone had to actually *be* sacrificed. Maybe something had to be given up. An idea, a desire, a person.

My gaze caught on the Crescent Moon and stayed there. The boy reminded me of someone too. Why was it inverted, though? Whoever or whatever it represented was the opposite of what I assumed.

My train of thought was interrupted by Thalia

leaping up off the floor and hurrying across to the doorway. I saw Nathaniel's face, serious and set as he murmured something to her, and then suddenly it clicked.

I knew exactly who the boy on the Crescent Moon card was, and it wasn't someone famous.

CHAPTER 25

'Nathaniel says we should make a start.'

Thalia came back into the room and stood looking at us expectantly.

'I have to go to the bathroom,' I blurted. 'Can he wait a couple more minutes?'

Fenrin rolled his eyes, nerves making him impatient. 'Come on, Summer.'

'Do you want me to spoil our concentration halfway through because I have a desperate urge to pee?' I turned to Thalia. 'Just tell him I'll be a couple of minutes. I'll meet you guys down there.'

I followed them out of the living room. As they turned right to go to the cellar, I turned left, making my way upstairs to the first floor. I could feel River's eyes tracking me as I went.

Don't follow me, I thought. If I was wrong about this, I didn't want anyone else knowing about my paranoia. The trust between us all was fragile enough right now.

I just needed to know for sure that I was wrong.

River didn't follow me and I reached the first-floor landing alone. Thalia had mentioned to me that Nathaniel's bedroom was the only room in the house she hadn't yet been in, which seemed surprising considering – I tried to push any mental images away – what they had very likely been doing together on her visits up here.

Now I was beginning to wonder if he had something to hide.

I checked every room. There was a bathroom, a separate toilet, two spotless guest bedrooms – either Nathaniel didn't have people stay over very often or he was a neat freak, which surprised me considering the gorgeously artistic chaos of downstairs – and finally a room with a closed door. It was the only door in the house that was fitted with a lock.

It had to be his bedroom.

The key to the door sat innocently in the lock. I took a brief moment to wonder why you'd go to the trouble of fitting a lock to the door only to leave the key inside it, but I suspected that had nothing to do with Nathaniel and everything to do with my talent at finding doors unlocked.

Feeling guilty, suspicious and nervous all at once, I turned the door and went inside.

I stood, waiting for my eyes to adjust to the dimness. I didn't dare turn on a light, but with the door open, the light streaming in from the hallway was just enough to see by, though it gave everything in the room strange shapes and shadows.

In contrast to the guest rooms, this place was organised chaos. The bedframe was elegant, spindly black iron, with belts and scarves and what looked like Venetian masks hanging off all four corner posts. The bedclothes were mussed, with a giant bundle of dark blankets and clothes seemingly dumped in the middle. Another mound of clothes draped the back of a spartan chair. A small desk under the window was covered in artists' detritus – torn sheets of watercolour paper, mugs full of charcoal sticks and fine-line pens.

On the mantelpiece above the fireplace opposite the bed sat a row of photographs in mismatched frames. Most of the photos were of people I'd never seen before, a lifetime's collection of friends and family, connections and intimacies won and maybe now lost. It wasn't until I reached the last photo that a familiar face leapt out at me.

I picked up the battered metal frame and gazed

at Iona Webber. This time she was flanked by two figures. One, after a bit of puzzling, I realised was a teenage Nathaniel. He hadn't yet grown into the quiet assuredness of the version I knew. He was lanky and gawky, in terrible shorts – fashion back then had a lot to answer for – and an unflattering haircut. His eyes promised an intensity that the rest of him wouldn't catch up with, it seemed, until he'd left these awkward years behind.

The other figure made my stomach flip.

This was the sign I'd been looking for.

As far as I could tell from the body it was another boy, but I had nothing more to go on than that because his face had been erased. I thought the scraping might have been done with the edge of a coin, scrubbed over and over and over in the same spot, eating into the photographic paper until any possible feature had been worn away. The faceless boy was holding Iona's hand.

Nathaniel was not.

I carefully freed the photo from the frame and turned it over. On the back was a handwritten date – a warm July from ten years ago. It was only days before she had died.

I turned the photo back over and stared at the faceless boy. It seemed that Nathaniel had tried a witchcraft trick or two in his years of study because I knew exactly what wearing away someone's face like this meant.

It was a curse.

Whoever the faceless boy had been, Nathaniel hated him enough to try wishing him from existence. The only reason to keep a photo defaced in such a way was to keep the curse alive.

I kept going back to the faceless boy holding Iona's hand. I supposed they could have just been really good friends, but something told me they were more than that. Unless Iona had had a radical change of heart just days before her death, it was safe to assume that the faceless boy was her boyfriend.

Not Nathaniel.

I tried hard to sort through my memories. Had he ever outright *told* us that he was Iona's boyfriend, or had we just assumed it? He'd said they were in love. That he was the one who used to meet her in the shepherd's cabin; he was the one who had narrowly escaped the fire that had claimed her life.

Galvanised, I went over to his desk. I needed to find some other evidence, something that would categorically refute the sudden sinking of my heart. I saw nothing in particular, but draped over his chair was a coat. In his coat pocket was a wallet. In his wallet was a bank card, membership cards to various research institutes, and a driving licence with Nathaniel's photo.

Which was fine – except the name on every single card was not Nathaniel. It was some guy called Aurelian Guillory.

My brain made an inevitable sickening slide down a dark, dark slope.

The cards he had painted for Iona, capturing her likeness in the Princess, preserving her forever as a beautiful, untouchable icon. The way he talked about her, full of such longing – all of that was hard to fake. Clearly he had been very much in love with her, but if he wasn't her boyfriend, Nathaniel, then who the hell was he? Some random friend named Aurelian Guillory?

I sat on the edge of the bed, avoiding the lumpy rumple of dark blankets huddled in its middle, and took out the card deck. I had left the Crescent Moon on the top, and now I studied it up close, comparing it with the photo of him as a teenager. Quiet, thin-pressed mouth. Clear, intense eyes. Now that I had a younger reference, it was utterly impossible not to see it. He'd painted himself as the Crescent Moon.

An inverted card usually means that whatever it represents is actually the opposite of what you assume it to be.

He had been lying to us.

Underneath me I felt the mattress shift and creak, but I knew I hadn't moved. Below the room's oppressive quiet I heard a very soft, very faint slithering noise. It was coming from behind me.

With my heart clambering into my mouth, I turned my head.

The blankets on the bed were *moving*.

I leapt up in fright, forgetting that I still had the deck in my hand. It slipped from my grasp, spilling down across the floor in a rain of lacquered card. I looked down and saw that each one of the overturned cards was the Crescent Moon, over and over, as if the whole deck were made of just that one card, as if it were mocking me – or warning me.

The movement on the bed stopped. I peered at the blankets, heart hammering. A pale shape had appeared among the rumpled dark. A face.

A face I knew well.

'Marcus . . . ?' I whispered faintly.

His eyes were closed as if deeply asleep.

'Marcus!' I whispered. 'Wake up!'

I went over to him and pulled the blanket from his face. It was definitely him. I put a hand on his shoulder and shook it, hissing his name, but he didn't stir again.

'What are you doing in here?'

My heart kicked and I inhaled sharply, struggling to breathe.

At the doorway to the bedroom was Nathaniel, blocking out the light.

For a moment we stood, looking at each other, two faceless shapes in the dark. Then he moved forward into the room, between me and the door.

I found my voice. 'What the *fuck* is going on?'

Nathaniel cocked his head. 'Excuse me?'

'Why is Marcus, my friend Marcus, asleep on your bed?'

My voice was high, too high and nervous. *Control it, Summer. Control this.*

He let loose a sigh. 'That's a . . . difficult story.'

'Make it easy!' I demanded. 'Tell me why he won't wake up!'

'He took some sleeping pills. I stopped him before he took more than he should. He'll be okay. He's just out with a bit of a big dose for a kid his size.'

A kid his size. A little patronising. Marcus was almost as tall as Nathaniel.

I shook my head, confused. 'Why . . . why would he do that?'

Nathaniel folded his arms close to his chest, a pitying look on his face. 'He came here, looking for

Thalia. He was … very emotional. I suppose she must have mentioned me. I tried to talk to him but he became very distressed and took out the pills, and then he went and swallowed a handful before I could get them off him. Honestly, I thought it would be best if he just slept it off here, and by then I knew you were all coming, anyway, and that you could look after him.'

I stared at him, trying to think through the nerves kicking inside my chest.

'Why didn't you tell us?' I demanded. 'Why hide him up here?'

'Because I thought you had enough to worry about, with your friend Wolf,' Nathaniel replied with a lilt of exasperation. 'And I knew Thalia would get upset. She's a very caring person. Can you really afford to be distracted right now, when we have a trickster in the cellar?' He sighed, pulling a hand through his hair. 'Look, I want to help you, but this … it was a lot to deal with all at once. I made a call. Maybe a bad call, I don't know.'

Despite everything, I felt guilty at that. How thoroughly we kept upending his life. It was a lot to deal with. *We* were a lot to deal with. He hadn't asked for any of this. My eyes dropped, found the cards scattered at my feet. All those Crescent Moons.

Mocking me – or warning me.

'You brought the card deck back,' he said, following my gaze. 'Thank you. They mean so much to me.'

'What do you see?' I asked.

'Excuse me?'

'What do you see on the cards, right now?'

He hesitated just a little too long.

'Nothing,' he said. 'I told you, they're unreliable. They lie.'

'They brought me to you.'

Again, a pause.

'Then I'm glad they worked out this time,' he said at last. 'Summer, we really need to get downstairs—'

I moved to the mantelpiece and picked up the photograph of Iona standing in between two boys – one of them faceless.

'That's you, isn't it?' I asked. 'With Iona?'

'You can see that it's me,' he said, his voice tightening.

'So who's the guy holding her hand?'

'A friend.'

'Must have been a close friend.'

He let loose a staccato laugh. 'Wow, Summer . . . this feels like an interrogation.'

Because it is. Stop avoiding my questions.

'What happened to this guy?' I pressed, holding out the photo. 'You erased his face. Did you have a falling out?'

I expected him to deny it.

Instead he said, 'Something like that.'

My internal switchboard was now lit up with alarms.

'What was his name?' I asked.

'Aurelian.'

There it is.

'Really?' I said in a bright, brittle tone. 'That's interesting, because I'm pretty sure that's *your* name.'

His long silence jacked up my heart rate to terrifying levels.

He didn't deny it. He just stood there looking at me, as if waiting to see what I would do next.

That was what made me break.

I ran for the door, knowing he would reach out and grab me, knowing he would haul me down, knowing what he would do next, but if he tried to hurt me, I'd fight, I'd scream, I'd kick and tear chunks out of him with my teeth – but none of that happened. He just let me push past him and run down the stairs.

'Summer,' he called behind me, 'you need to just *calm down* . . .'

I wanted to laugh but my heart was hammering

too hard and my brain was shouting too loud – *get out, get out, get the others and get out* – and I heard him start down the stairs behind me as my foot touched the ground floor and, oh god, they were all in the cellar, weren't they? I wasn't going to be one of those idiots in a horror movie who runs further into the house. I was getting out and getting help, but then – what if he had done something to them? No, we were too many, surely, there were five of us, we could overpower him, we could, we—

I got no further than a few steps down the front hallway when my foot caught on the edge of a rug that I swore hadn't been there before, and sent me flying. My contact with the ground sent a jarring buzz of pain shooting up both my forearms, and a moment later I felt him on me, and I *screamed* and I bucked and I tried to twist in his grip to bite, but no one explained that being grabbed from behind made it impossible to fight, *impossible*. My arms were pinned and I couldn't reach him, and he was so *strong*; were all men this strong? This wasn't real, surely? How could I be so helpless? Where was everyone else? I screamed but no one came, and in my head I apologised to all the movie heroines I'd ever mocked for not fleeing sooner and fighting harder, for not breaking free. Aurelian hauled me to the cellar door, which seemed to yawn open by itself, inviting me in. Then he released me with a push and I almost fell down the steps, stumbling on the wooden slats, grazing my hands on the brick wall to keep myself upright, careening into the metal shelves at the bottom and making them judder, pain flaring at my hip and my arm.

The rest of them were there: River and Thalia standing at the far side of the pentacle, Fenrin crouched in its midst next to the handcuffed Wolf, my brother's eyes on me and shocked wide in the cellar light.

CHAPTER 26

The cellar air was suffused with a bitter, acrid smell.

It was oil, I realised. It had been poured into the pentacle's grooves, rendering them dark and glistening wet. As I pushed myself to my feet, my body began to shiver, making standing up a trial I could have done without. I needed to feel strong, but I was scared and furious and weak.

A hand on my arm steadied me. It was River.

'What's going on?' she whispered, but there was no time to answer. Aurelian had reached the bottom of the stairs and stood beside us, and my body reacted on instinct, propelling me across the floor away from him – and from the only escape route, but I couldn't help it.

I was afraid of him, and however much I wanted to rage, my fear controlled me.

'Why didn't you come?' I said to the others, hating the plea in my voice. 'You must have heard me.'

'We tried the door,' Fenrin said. He was crouched protectively near the bound and gagged Wolf. 'When we heard you scream, we all tried to get out. It won't open.'

'Yeah,' Aurelian said in a tone of false regret, 'that's my fault. Sorry.'

'What are you talking about?' Thalia said. She knew something was wrong, but she didn't know what it was yet, and oh god, I didn't want her to know. I didn't want her world to come crashing down, too, but there was no longer a choice.

Aurelian held up a hand. 'It's just a precaution. We can't risk anyone being able to leave until this is done. You have to be all in, no matter what happens, or it won't work.'

But the cellar door had opened for me without being touched, as if someone had been waiting on the other side. Yet somehow it wouldn't open from the inside?

I raised my eyes. He was watching me, and my fury kicked in.

'Are you going to tell them, or shall I?' I asked, despising the tremble in my voice.

'Tell us what?' Thalia turned to me.

'This isn't Nathaniel,' I said. 'His name is Aurelian Guillory. He wasn't Iona's boyfriend. He's been lying to us.'

Again I thought he might deny it, but he just stood there watching us. Now I understood why – he was waiting to see how to play it.

'Nathaniel?' Thalia asked.

He let out a soft, heavy sigh.

'I'm so sorry,' he said. 'She's right. Look, I didn't mean for it to happen. When you turned up at my door, you seemed to think that was who I was, and it just seemed easier to play along. It was so stupid. It's one of those situations like ... you know when someone you've just met gets your name wrong and you don't correct them right away, and five months later they're still calling you by it, and it's just way too late to have to explain, so you start answering to it, and then the whole thing becomes this excruciating comedy routine ...' He trailed off, squirming with contrite embarrassment.

'Where's the real Nathaniel?' I demanded, even though I was frightened of the answer.

'Oh, up-country somewhere,' Aurelian said dismissively. 'He and his family moved away just after Iona died. He was very much of the "I never want to see another witch again in my life" camp, so we

327

obliged by leaving him alone. I expect he's a dentist with five kids now, or something.'

I had no reason to believe this stranger but I couldn't exactly do much else. Wherever Nathaniel was, I hoped he was safe.

'So you weren't in love with Iona?' Thalia said, suffused in confusion. I knew how she felt.

'Oh, I was in love with her.' He gave a sad smile. 'But she was in love with Nathaniel. As it goes. They were happy together, so I made my peace with it.'

From the midst of the pentacle there came a long, low chuckle.

'Oh my,' came Wolf's familiar rasp. 'What a total crock of shit.'

Fenrin lobbed the ball of duct tape into the corner of the cellar. He had ungagged Wolf while we weren't watching.

Wolf shook his head. 'It's a good performance, I'll give you that. But it's just more lies. You want to know the truth?'

'Tape him back up,' Aurelian said. 'Now. Quickly.'

His voice was sharp with fear. I'd only noticed it once before, when we had first come into the house and he had grabbed Wolf, shouting at Thalia to gag him. I'd assumed it to be a natural level of nerves, considering he'd encountered one of these things before.

What if it was more than that?

'Tape him back up,' River echoed, surprising me. She was staring intensely at Fenrin, who stared back, coldly defiant.

'Don't,' I said, my hand on River's arm.

I wanted to know the truth.

Wolf didn't wait. 'He set the fire that killed his girl. He's a murderer. He followed them up to that cabin and tried to kill them both. Jealousy. Unrequited love. All that kind of thing. Oh, he *reeks* of it. He smells delicious.'

His words creeped through me, plucking strange strings. It was the trickster inside him talking. He felt people's darkest, most awful emotions and he pulled them out into the light so he could feed off them.

Shut him up, my brain warned, but not yet – not yet.

Not when it was Aurelian who was scared.

'That fire wasn't for Iona,' he protested. 'She wasn't even supposed to *be* at the cabin, but she lied to me. To me, her best fucking friend. She said she was stuck at some family thing but really she was sneaking out to meet *him*. If she hadn't lied to me, she'd still be alive.'

Out of everything, the awful expression on Thalia's face stung me the most. I could feel her misery rising, threatening to overwhelm her. I could feel it in my gut as if it was mine.

No, I thought. *Don't be sad.*

Be angry.

Aurelian sighed a deep, awful sigh.

'It was a mistake,' he said. 'Haven't you ever made a mistake? All it takes to ruin lives is one split-second decision. Set that crappy little cabin where they always met on fire. Just to scare him. Just so they wouldn't be able to go there any more. That was all it was. Just a stupid, angry mistake. Don't you see that?'

I thought of River catching Wolf and Fenrin together down at the beach that fateful morning and creating a lethal tidal wave out of one moment of pure, unfettered, miserable jealousy.

And I did see that. I saw exactly how it had happened for Aurelian, too.

Keep him talking. That was what you were supposed to do with your captor, wasn't it? That was what movies taught us. Calm voice, steady eyes, sympathetic ear. What movies don't teach is how hard it is to be calm and steady when your heart rate is jacked up to a million, making your eyeballs pulse, screaming at your body to get up and run, get away from this impossible, laughable, ridiculous situation you're in.

'Did you even have anything to do with her resurrection, or did you lie about all that, too?' I asked.

'Did I have anything to do with . . . ?' He gave a disbelieving laugh. 'It was *my idea*. Who do you think created the *enakelgh* with your parents? Who do you think had the actual fucking balls to at least *try* and bring Iona back? They certainly didn't. It was all me.'

'But you *murdered* her,' I said. 'Why would you want to resurrect her?'

'Don't you think I regretted her death?' he asked, his voice high with amazement. 'I just wanted her back. I told you, I'd have done anything to bring her back.' His gaze flickered to Wolf. 'It was a mistake. She came back like *him*. Don't listen to them. They feed off our poison. The one I brought back ruined my life.'

'She told the rest of them what you did, didn't she?' I said. 'She told them that you murdered her.'

Aurelian's face was a gathering storm.

I thought of Esther's protectiveness, her fury when anything threatened her family. Iona had been family.

'What did our family do?' I asked.

It was Thalia who answered. Her voice was soft with wonder, as if she couldn't believe she had never seen it before.

'You get all your food delivered here,' she said. 'You never go out. People always visit you instead. Whenever I suggest going outside and exploring, you always have an excuse. I've never seen you leave this house. You didn't even come outside the front door when we pulled up, even though you knew we might need help bringing Wolf in. Why can't you leave?'

He was staring at her.

'They bound me to the house,' he said at last. 'Your fucking family. I've lived here, within these four walls, for ten years.' He shook his head, expelled a razor-blade laugh. 'Do you have any idea what it's like to be in prison for ten *years*? I live a half life. It's like being blind.' His hands came up, clutched at the air, fell again.

'He offered me a little deal while you were all upstairs,' Wolf said. 'He'd let the trickster in me live if I helped him trick you into releasing his binding.'

'He's lying!' Aurelian said. 'I never did that, I – I just ...' He was getting wild, desperate. 'I just want to be able to use magic again. I just want to *feel* again. To be kept from magic when it crawls in your blood? When it *is* your blood? That restlessness eating you up inside, feeling your precious time on this earth leaking away from you, unspent, nothing mattering any more, no meaning, no freedom?' His eyes slid to

River's and locked there. 'You of all people should understand that.'

For the first time in a long while, I focused on River. Had she been trying to hide it from us, hold it all in? Oh god, now I could *feel* it. She was struggling, a lethal mix of emotions threatening to swamp her. Fear and fury, the two most instinctive emotions, flooded the cellar, were felt by us all – but swimming underneath them was a dark, morbid fascination.

Curiosity. 'You're like me,' River ventured. '*You* were the spirit witch in the *enakelgh* that brought Iona back.'

'Yes,' Aurelian confirmed, his voice urgent.

'Who was the fourth?' she asked.

'Esther's sister, Miranda.' He was getting impatient. 'River, I can feel it leaking from you in waves. Just be careful that they don't chain you. I didn't see it coming until it was too late. Never trust anyone weaker than you—'

'Stop it!' I said sharply. 'Stop trying to divide us because it won't work.'

'Just unbind me, and I'll never bother you again. I won't come near you or your family.' Aurelian's face took on a desperate ache. 'I just want to be free.'

For one moment, River seemed to consider it. Then I felt her hand in mine, and my heart sang.

'No,' she said simply.

Aurelian stared at her. His gaze shifted to Thalia.

'Baby,' he tried. 'Sweetheart, listen—'

'Stay the fuck away from me,' Thalia said, her voice flat and hard.

'You don't need him,' came Wolf's murmur.

'Yes, you do!' Aurelian shouted. 'You don't know how to get rid of that thing without killing your friend! You need me – I can show you!'

'Fenrin,' Wolf said, looking up at my brother. His face held nothing but perfect trust. 'He'll try to trick you. Don't trust him. You don't need him. Listen to me. It's me, it's Wolf, and I love you.'

Fenrin was locked still. I couldn't feel him. I couldn't read him.

I wondered if this was the first time he had ever heard those three words from Wolf.

'I love you,' Wolf said again, and *then* I felt it – a sudden, joyous surge, making my head rush and my blood sing. Wolf continued, 'But you have to hurry. Fen, I don't know . . . I don't know how much longer I can fight this thing. Please.'

His eyes closed, as if speaking the thought hurt him more than anything ever had.

'I need you to save me.'

CHAPTER 27

At Wolf's words, Fenrin's pain lanced through me. His pain was my pain now, too, and I knew I would do anything for him, for any of them.

I'd kill for them.

As one, the four of us turned towards Aurelian. He had tried to take one of our own away from us. He had to be dealt with.

He seemed to shrink before our *enakelgh*, cowed. I wondered at how afraid I'd been of him before, but that was when we were separated, divided. He'd caught me alone – but now with my family at my back, he seemed so small, so inconsequential. A shivering, murderous coward.

No amount of intimidation got the cellar door open, however. It didn't even have a lock, but brute force did nothing, and it remained stubbornly closed. It seemed that being bound to the house had chained

Aurelian's magic to it – if he didn't want us to leave, the house would make sure that we couldn't.

But that didn't mean we had to listen to him.

We took the handcuffs we had used against Wolf and chained Aurelian to the radiator on the back wall, gagging him thoroughly. A little too thoroughly, maybe, but we couldn't risk him breaking our concentration, and it was easy to ignore any muffled noises he was making. I felt nothing but freezing contempt for him. We had come too far and risked too much to let him stop us now.

Wolf sat in the middle of the pentacle. He had his eyes closed and he sucked in deep, regular breaths, swaying very gently on the spot. He looked soft and greased, like a stick of melting butter, and his hair stuck to his forehead in damp, lank tails of sweat. It must have been taking everything he had to keep the trickster inside him subdued – I could imagine how it was fighting him, fighting for control, feeling the noose pulling tighter and tighter around it. It didn't seem like he had a whole lot of time left, but he was doing what he could to eke it out as much as possible.

Now it was up to us.

As *enakelgh*, we surrounded Wolf at four of the pentacle's points, occupying the spaces for earth, air, fire and water. The fifth, the top point, was left empty. For the first time I understood that, in using a pentacle in ritual, there had always been a space left for spirit. It made me wonder if a true coven might not encompass all five elements rather than just the traditional four we had always been aware of.

There was no time to dwell on that now, though. We had our *enakelgh*, a soul circle made of the four of us, and we had to believe in it to have a hope of saving Wolf.

We sat with the oil-soaked groove of the outer circle running just behind our backs. Thalia was at earth and north, furthest from the cellar stairs. River had taken the place of fire in the circle and sat south opposite Thalia. Fenrin was at water and west, furthest from the tiny letterbox window that let in a ghost of moonlight through its grimy pane. I sat opposite him at air and east, the window at my back.

With a flicker of hope sparking, I let my gaze drift around the circle. I felt each pair of eyes click to mine like nails to magnets, and we all were both nails and magnets, one another's attraction, one another's pull. Suddenly, Wolf seemed very much alone, caught like a fly in the midst of the invisible threads that pulled us together.

'Light the candles,' Thalia said.

She was earth, the grounded point, the beginning and the end, the birth and the death.

She struck the long match against its box and touched it to the wick of the green candle on the ground in front of her. On my left, River did the same with her black candle. Fenrin lit his blue, and I my white. As soon as my flame appeared, climbing greedily up into the air, I felt myself calming, settling in. Candle warmth lit the circle from underneath, making buttery-coloured masks of our faces.

Staring at the flame before me, I began to sink.

It didn't take long, or it took forever, it was hard to say in the twilight world of inside. At some point, my eyes closed and my mind unanchored itself, and night could have turned to day again in the sky and still I'd be sitting here, breathing and thinking of stars just like my father had taught me.

The ritual had its own pull, like gravity, like a tidal wave, as sure as the sunset and the moonrise. *Enakelgh* was pure, unfettered desire. Stifling it only ensured that it overwhelmed you.

I felt the others with me, somewhere in the dark, *in* me, until I didn't feel like *I* any more but *we*, one eight-legged, eight-armed creature that breathed *want* into the universe, pure and pulsing, over and over. We pressed on the fabric of everything, firm, pressure down, steady and increasing, until it was forced to bow to us . . .

. . . and then it was as if we changed direction. Something forced us to swerve and go down a new path. One of us was feeling a different want, fracturing us at first – but the pull was too strong, and soon enough *their* want was my want, *our* want, swelling and swelling like the tip of a sneeze, the top of a rollercoaster.

Then the sneeze came and the rollercoaster dropped, and the release was a dizzying, consuming rush.

A ride I couldn't bear to end, but almost as soon as I thought that, it began to slip away from me like water down a drain, and I ached for the loss, even as I felt a peaceful aftermath spread through me, calming as it went.

At its lowest ebb, there came a noise.

Something in the outside world was making a sound. It was so odd that I felt myself getting distracted, pulled away from the black and back to the room. I fought it – I would not be the one to ruin the ritual – but it was a sound I recognised. I knew what it was, but I couldn't quite—

Something was happening in the middle of the pentacle.

A shuffling noise. A pant, a groan.

I opened my eyes.

Wolf had moved. At some point during the ritual, he had crawled towards Fenrin on the opposite side of the pentacle from me, and he had one arm thrown forward into my brother's lap. His hand gripped my brother's wrist like a lifeline, as if he had pulled himself to safety across the floor.

I stared at them both, trying to work out what was happening. As I did, Fenrin's hand began to tug backwards, slipping his wrist from Wolf's grasp. He pulled himself backwards, leaving Wolf's arm to flop heavily onto the ground in front of him and knocking his candle over, where it rolled back and forth on its side, still lit.

Fenrin was outside the pentacle, outside the outer circle's protective embrace and close to the wall behind him when he started to retch. His body bucked violently but nothing came up. The shadows on the walls changed shape as the light from each of our candles suddenly streamed sideways in still air, wrenched by a wind that wasn't there.

And then I felt it.

It came over me in a nauseous wave, like falling and never hitting ground. A lurching sense of wrongness, like a loose flapping thread, forcing me onto my hands and knees, mirroring my brother. Through its haze I was dimly aware that Thalia and River were doing the same, gasping and flopping like dying fish on the floor, but I couldn't help them. I couldn't move.

Not when I was dying too.

The wrongness crawled its way through me, blooming fast, too fast to stop, like a poison had been injected intravenously into our circle, sticky and cloying. It slithered into the deepest parts of me, spreading throughout each nerve ending. It rolled in my belly, making a nest. It fired up the ugliest parts of my soul.

It made me want to hurt.

It made me want to take.

It made me remember every single dark, selfish, violent impulse I had ever had and feel them again. I was powerless to stop it because all those impulses were already inside me, lying in wait. Biding their time until they could be useful.

Gradually the poison receded, a tide pulling away from shore, until I knew again where I was. In front of me, Fenrin had stilled. His head hung down as he braced himself on his palms, the reeds of his hair obscuring his face. The candle flames, flickering uneasily, straightened.

'Fenrin?' I gasped, while the wrongness twisted inside me.

My brother straightened, his skin glistening pale in the candlelight.

'Sorry,' he said, and a faint, greasy smile hovered on his mouth. 'He's not here any more.'

CHAPTER 28

Fenrin pulled himself upright, using the far wall as a lever, and stood on shaky feet, leaning back against the brick.

A deep, scratchy sigh crawled out of him.

'I feel like total shit,' he said to no one in particular. 'Who knew getting a real body would be so exhausting?'

'You're the thing that's been possessing Wolf,' Thalia hissed as she crouched on the ground, looking up at him through the lank waves of her hair. I heard the savagery in her voice, and I knew that it wasn't just me who had been poisoned.

It was all of us.

'Where's my brother?'

'Oh, he's gone. It's just me now.' The skin of Fenrin's face was pale and waxed. His eyes were blank and glazed. He looked like a puppet played by inexpert fingers. 'He put up a good fight, credit where credit's due. I've been trying to get him for weeks, but it just wasn't working. But I knew if I could get you all together, it would happen. You know when you use your *enakelgh*, you open yourselves up wide? You let me slip right on in.' He tilted his head. 'Fenrin helped, of course. I wouldn't have been able to take him if he hadn't wanted me to.'

All those mornings Fenrin had come down looking exhausted. All those times we had noticed his paleness, his tiredness, over and over. His complaints of bad dreams. I'd dismissed it as an overly healthy sex life. I'd dismissed *him*. This thing had been trying to find a way inside my brother, and my brother had been fighting it all alone.

Now it had succeeded because of us.

'I don't understand,' I said. 'Why did you want to be in him instead of staying in Wolf?'

'There was never any Wolf.'

'But we brought you back with him.'

'No, you didn't,' he rasped. 'It was like . . . having to wear a *really* uncomfortable Wolf-shaped suit. Trust me, I was all alone in that suit. It got tiring, you know, having to pretend to be this Wolf guy all the time. I mean, judging by what you've all been telling me about him over the last few weeks, he seemed pretty fucking dull. I don't really understand what Fenrin saw in him.'

'No,' I said, and I could feel my head shaking violently back and forth. 'No. There was Wolf. He was walking around, talking—'

'I don't know what's wrong with me,' Fenrin interrupted, his voice ringing with a piteous whine. 'I don't *mean* to do it, but it keeps happening. I just want to be Wolf again. Please.'

I stared at him.

He dipped his torso in a short, sardonic bow. 'You mean, *I* was walking around and talking. There's never been any Wolf, darling. There's only ever been me.' He paused. 'I think I have a decent shot at an acting career, honestly.'

I stared into my brother's face. I watched his mouth stretch into a grin.

'Surprise!' he said cheerfully.

'Liar.'

It was River. Before I could stop her, she was scrabbling towards Wolf's silent form, discarded and motionless on the concrete. She stretched out a hand to touch him, and let out a soft cry as his outline gave under the pressure of her fingers like gel.

Then it began to melt.

Like butter in the sun, like the blue paint on

Fenrin's walls, like tears, Wolf's body globbed and ran, dripping and pooling until there was only water, seawater, the briny stink of it crawling sharply up my nose. The water ran over the concrete and sank into it, leaving only a black damp patch behind.

We had made him. We had made him from the sea that took his life.

I wanted to throw up. I wanted to scream, cry, rage, anything that would release this awful tightening vice around my heart.

Fenrin leaned his head back and gave a soft, disgustingly pleasurable sound.

'Oh, you taste so good,' he whispered.

He was connected to us, one of our *enakelgh*.

It's a two-way street.

I fell down next to River as she stared, fixated at the damp patch on the concrete. All that was left of the boy she had tried to bring back. The mistake she had tried to fix. From the outside she looked calm, but I could feel her pain. It was overwhelming.

'River, stop,' I said. 'River, you have to stop. Oh god, please stop.'

It flew around the circle, tearing through each of us. The more she felt, the more we all felt, and the more we all felt, the stronger the thing inside Fenrin grew.

'River,' I begged, and I took hold of her. She

flinched, she fought me, but I held on and whispered into her ear while she took hitched, staccato breaths.

Slowly, gradually, she stilled.

Slowly, gradually, I felt myself filling with cold anger, insidiously sweet. It grew, swelled, pushed my fear and my misery aside where I could no longer feel them. It was a numbing, welcoming sensation.

We needed a victim. We needed someone to pour all this pain into.

Aurelian.

I stood up, moving towards him, and as I did I felt the others, River and Thalia, and yes, the trickster inside my brother, drawing together behind my shoulder blades, crowding close.

Getting hungry.

Thalia came forward, crouching before his folded frame with her skirt pooling around her legs. She reached out and launched a hand at his throat, gripping it hard to keep it still while the fingers of her other hand grabbed and peeled and ripped and tore, pulling the black tape off his mouth and half his skin with it. As soon as it had come away from his lips, he gasped against her palm.

'Talk,' Thalia said, her voice dangerously soft. 'Can we bring the real Wolf back, or did you lie about that as well?'

I wanted to believe she was fighting this, but I could feel her desire – *hurt him* – and it was mine. It seemed as if Aurelian could feel it too because I recognised the expression on his face.

He was afraid.

The only sound, for a moment, was the sound of Aurelian's pained breaths.

'I'm sorry,' he said finally. 'It's always the same. No one has ever been able to bring someone back. All we ever do is create something made from us. All the worst parts of us. And then we let it loose on the world. Don't you get it? That's why it feeds off people's pain and jealousy and anger. Those are what it's made from.'

'All you do is lie,' Thalia whispered.

Aurelian shook his head, his eyes pleading with her. 'You think others haven't tried before you? You think we wouldn't have been knee-deep in resurrected loved ones by now? If there was a way, I would have found it. It's not possible. It never has been.'

It was over then. It was done. With that knowledge came a kind of release.

Aurelian stared at us, wild-eyed.

Aurelian Guillory. Liar. Murderer. An out-of-control spirit witch who needed to be put down before he could hurt anyone else ever again. Our parents should have had the spine to end him when they'd had the chance. How dare they leave him alive to ruin more lives?

We should kill him, whispered the *enakelgh* in my ear. I didn't know who it came from, where it began, only that all of us felt it, and I knew that it meant the thing inside Fenrin was winning, but I no longer cared.

Let it win.

Some people deserve what's coming to them, it had told me in our own cellar that night, and it was right.

We drew closer. I let the gorgeous, full anticipation of vengeance squeeze me in its grip. It felt delicious, the sweet release of giving in when I had held out so very, very long. I was tired of holding out. Tired of being good. It was too hard.

Better this way. So much easier.

Aurelian coughed once, the air bursting from his throat unbidden. Then another, and more, and more, until he was spluttering, struggling to breathe, his face darkening with the effort. His hands pulled desperately at the handcuffs, wrestling, frantic, desperate, legs kicking.

He was choking to death, choking on his own lies, and it felt good.

It felt *right*.

Then – a faltering. Aurelian's eyes were bulging out of his head, fixed on something behind us. Behind our backs. There was a noise. A voice. Someone singing.

Badly.

I turned my head. The singing echoed off the cellar walls, cutting through my fog, fracturing me with its horrible, off-key warble. Despite the terrible rendition, I recognised the song: the theme tune to *Pinky and the Brain*.

Fenrin and Marcus's favourite cartoon.

Marcus was standing at the bottom of the stairs on drug-softened colt legs. He was awake. For a moment I wondered how on earth he had got the cellar door open when we couldn't – but then I realised. Aurelian had let him in to save his own life.

Beside me, the trickster inside Fenrin swivelled on the spot, a look of pure disgust on his face. He latched onto the drooping form of Marcus and that shivering choirboy voice faltered.

'What are you doing?' The trickster sounded revolted.

Marcus stared at him.

'Hey, Pinky,' he said.

'Hey, Brain,' my brother's mouth offered.

'Fenrin,' Marcus breathed.

The trickster sneered. 'Fenrin's gone.'

Marcus just shook his head. 'It's no good pretending, I can see you. You're all over him like ... like sunlight. I *see* you, Fenrin.'

Fenrin was frozen.

I felt that sluicing, seductive poison in us slow, hesitate – and then I felt *him*. My brother. I felt him near me, warm and sun-dappled, salt-surf skin, and that high, hysterical laugh only Marcus had ever been able to provoke. He filled my head like a smell, his warm vanilla smell, and he filled the dark spaces in between us.

The trickster had not killed him. My brother was still here.

Our *enakelgh*, the true one, the one made of hope instead of curses, was still intact.

I understood now why the trickster had needed to take Fenrin. It needed to break our *enakelgh*, to make sure one of us was in its control.

Just as in the origin story of the curse, only four witches joined as one, as *enakelgh*, could defeat this thing.

The morning after the clearing, Wolf – the trickster – had taken ill. That very night, when the mob came to our door, the four of us had turned on it and that had made it weak and cowed.

Our *enakelgh* might have made it, but it was also the only thing that could break it.

As soon as I realised it, so did we all.

And so did the trickster, who regarded us through Fenrin's eyes.

And then it broke.

It ran towards the stairs, its foot catching one of the still-burning candles and toppling it over into the pentacle's oil-slicked groove. The oil caught fire. A thin, dense plume of black smoke spiralled up into the air and the ring began to burn, flames licking along the outer circle.

The trickster pushed past a sagging, weakened Marcus and reached the steps.

STOP!

The word and the desire rippled around the circle, and it jerked back, stumbling, tripping on the first stair slat, reeling backwards and falling to the ground.

Those fleeting *enakelgh* ticklings I had felt in the past few days were nothing compared to this. We were one. We didn't know how long it would last. Nothing lasted forever. *Ride it while it's good. Ride it to survive.*

We turned, moving fast, stepping over the smoking pentacle and closing in.

The trickster was on its hands and knees, trembling and sickened. It looked up at me with red-rimmed eyes, its mouth hanging open and grinning in the corners. It was everything I had ever hated. It was every selfish feeling that had ever caused pain to another. It was every time I had taken what I wanted, thoughtlessly, every time I had made the world just that little bit worse, and I yearned to end it. I knew it was the trickster's poison worming its way through me, turning me black and rotten inside, but I couldn't stop it, I couldn't stop it, and I didn't want to because it was my poison too. Because it was me and I was it and we were all each other.

We were still riding the wave but now the tide was turning. The tide was turning as we rounded on it, Thalia and River and me and Fenrin, yes Fenrin, because I could feel him now, closing off the endless loop of our *enakelgh*, a soul circle that I knew I would kill to protect.

On our hands and knees we crowded it, backing it into the wall with no escape. Its spine pressed up against the wall as it surveyed us with wild eyes, a rabbit surrounded by jackals.

'You can't hurt me,' it croaked. 'If you hurt me, you hurt your brother.'

The wildest, most vicious part of me – the part it had deliberately unleashed – was fully awake and straining at its leash, craving death. I had always been afraid of acknowledging this part of me, but now, when I needed it, I embraced it with arms open wide.

'Wait,' hissed the trickster. 'Nothing else makes you feel as good as me. You can punish everyone who deserves it . . .'

There was only one thing I wanted to punish.

Magic pulsed stronger and stronger inside me until I felt like I was made of nothing else. For one clear, heart-bursting moment, drowning in *enakelgh*, I saw the threads that existed between all of us, between everyone and everything in the universe, all life connected like one infinite, endlessly complex and endlessly simple spider web.

'Wait,' came an awful whine, 'wait, I *love* you . . .'

There was only one way to save Fenrin, and we would kill to protect our own.

All the four of us had to do was reach out to the thread between Aurelian and the trickster and . . .

PUSH.

Fenrin's body slumped.

Behind us at the far wall, a voice screamed in utter fury.

Aurelian.

The entire pentacle burst into flame, pushed into impossible fire by the pure fury driving Aurelian's magic. We could barely see him. Smoke plumes crowded the cellar space, blooming into clouds as the oil caught. I looked around wildly for water, anything. Nothing.

Flames licked up a chair in the corner. Cans, terracotta pots, tools flew off metal shelves, hurtling across the room as the trickster's panic infected Aurelian, and through Aurelian, the house. It threw everything at us. I felt something hit me in the side, making me gasp, and dimly I saw the others clambering up the steps, dragging Fenrin's inert form, trying to get away before Aurelian and the trickster killed us all.

A roaring *whumph* sounded behind us; something big caught fire. We ran from death, clattering up the steps. The cellar door had been left open, but it was closing on us. Marcus got there first, wedging his body in the gap, and he gasped words I couldn't hear over the noise of the fire, but I knew he was begging us to get out.

Inside me I felt the burnt pine cones, the cloves, and ice-cold winter frost of River. I felt Thalia as cool grass, bark strips, caramel and cream. I felt Fenrin, salt-surf skin and vanilla and strands of golden hair.

I no longer felt the trickster. Its poison was gone, banished from us and pushed into Aurelian, where it was going to die.

The vicious part of me, the part I had always strived to hide from the world, was glad.

Smoke was so thick we could no longer breathe. We could no longer see. We staggered into the hallway on jelly legs. Marcus went to the front door, wrestling with it, but it wouldn't open. We were going to die in here – but then the door did open, suddenly, flying wide with a violent crash.

We fell through it into oxygen, into the night air, dragging our brother down the steps, falling onto our hands and knees, lungs aglow with choking poison, collapsing into the arms of our parents.

Our parents. My letter.

'Aurelian,' I choked out.

'No,' Esther murmured above my head. She had me in a fierce grip. 'Honey, it's too late.'

CHAPTER 29

When I woke, I woke alone.

I was lying on a bed, its stiff sheets starched a businesslike white. The first time I had woken, my hand, outstretched in my line of vision, had something taped to it, a thin cord running out from beneath the tape and disappearing off into the cool, blurred distance. That was gone now, but I could still feel a ghostly version of the strange and insistent little tug of a needle in my skin.

I didn't remember fading into sleep so much as running smack into a wall of it. Presumably, the doctors had fed me some heavy-duty drugs intravenously and knocked me out cold. I lay there, trying to piece myself back together. It took a moment, a moment strange and profound as I floated blankly, waiting for something to tell me how to feel.

My memories before sleep were a blur of

ambulances, hospital beds covered with paper sheets that crackled stiffly under my shifting body, tests and doctors and blood and coughing up soot-caked phlegm into a bowl until my stomach muscles screamed in protest.

Maybe a day had passed, maybe more. I vaguely remembered being wheeled into this room, a big room with lots of other beds like mine. Beyond the pull-around curtains, the flimsy walls of my current universe, I heard coughs and shifts, mutterings and voices both brisk and kindly, tired and firm. I lay listening, taking comfort from the fact that the world had kept turning with impressive matter-of-factness. It reassured me.

Life was bigger than all I was responsible for.

I shifted, scratchy sheets rustling underneath my weight, and with that tiny movement my body let it be known just what I had put it through. My throat was tight and sore. I had barked my shins and scraped the edges of myself against more than one sharp surface during our blind escape from Aurelian's town house, and each of those minor wounds clamoured for my attention, pulsing little hot points across my body. My head pounded and my eyes were like two roasted raisins rattling around in the dried cups of their sockets. I was vaguely aware that there would be additional complaints lining up to make their presence felt once the drugs fully wore off.

I levered myself up to a sitting position. In the corner of my curtained-off area was an uncomfortable-looking plastic chair, and folded on top of it was the compact frame of my father, his eyes closed.

He was here. With me. He had stayed with me the whole time I had slept.

And it had only taken us making a trickster, killing it, and then almost dying ourselves to get him to stick around.

I watched him for a moment, drinking in his unguarded face, his form. He looked younger when he was asleep. I could see the ghost lines of the boy he had been, the whole life he had led before I had even existed.

They had been there. They had saved us from the fire. Apparently the vague mention of 'someone who could help Wolf' had been enough to set alarm bells ringing. Once Esther had called and confirmed that we weren't at Aunt Miranda's, it hadn't taken the three of them long to figure out where we had gone. Maybe it had been the ghost of their old, broken *enakelgh* giving them a final warning about exactly what their ex-fourth, the spirit witch Aurelian Guillory, was up to.

Esther had laid the binding on the house all those years ago, and though Aurelian might have been in control inside the house, Esther had attacked from the outside, wrenching the front door open to get us out.

She had almost been too late.

Whether due to magic or good old-fashioned flammability, or a combination of both, the fire had consumed everything in the cellar and then climbed, eating up the rest of the house and leaving only ash and bone in its wake.

Everything gone.

After arriving at the hospital, Esther and Gwydion had stood together at the threshold of the examination room, surveying the damage we had done to ourselves. I had been too battered and weary to do anything other than stare at them and wait for the onslaught that would inevitably follow.

'You lied to us about where you were going,' Esther said. 'You lied about Wolf, and Aurelian, and you nearly died.' She was a glacier buckling in the heat. Great slabs of her cracking and falling off with awful crashes. 'You scared me *shitless*.'

Then my mother began to cry.

I'd never seen her cry. Not once. Somehow it was so much worse than the argument I had been dreading because now I knew just how vulnerable we had made her. I could see how much power I had over her, instead of the other way around.

Family seemed like a raw, instinctive kind of *enakelgh*, formed without conscious knowledge. It was innate, lying all the way down in the bones, as hard to forgo as a soul connection with another. As hard to give up as it had been to give up River.

Now that I was awake again, I knew the interrogations were coming, and whatever punishment was waiting for us, the truth would come out. If there was one thing I had learned really quite well over the last few months, it was that the power that existed in secrets could only ever be a sickly, rotting kind that ate you up from the inside out.

Many things could no longer go unsaid.

I sat in my hospital bed, the room buzzing unpleasantly around me, everything too hard and too bright. It might have been the meds, but it felt like there was something tugging at the corners of me, demanding my attention. Something shouting behind glass, in another room. *Goddamn it.* The meds were making me dopey, my senses all foggy and dazed, but something was wrong, I could feel it, a gathering darkness, a spill of ink dropped into water, blooming as it went . . .

Poison ink . . .

'Fenrin,' I said, or tried to say. My throat swelled in protest, raw and throbbing. His name was a razor blade slicing messily over my flesh.

Something was wrong with my brother.

I pulled the covers off and swung my legs out of bed. Annoyingly, my legs seemed to have been replaced with marshmallow, but I persevered, stood and tottered into the curtain, fumbling with it blindly and pulling it aside.

I took a few faltering steps into the ward. It wasn't as busy as I'd thought – there were only a few more closed curtains. Then I heard a loud, trickling laugh, and my blood froze.

The laughter came from another corner of the ward. I staggered over and ripped the curtain open. There was my brother, Fenrin, propped up in bed, very much alive.

'Sister,' he proclaimed in a crackling voice. 'It's good to see you up and about. I thought you were going to sleep into the afternoon.'

An easy smile played on his mouth, the same Fenrin smile I knew so well. He was being tended by a lovely looking nurse who was chatting with him while filling small vials with blood from a needle in his vein.

'Are you all right, miss?' the nurse asked me. 'Is there something you need?'

'Don't worry,' Fenrin replied jauntily. 'She just came to check who I woke up as.'

I stared at him. Darkness, swirling like poison ink.

His eyebrows rose in mocking peaks. 'Verdict?'

There was no trickster inside him. The trickster had died with Aurelian.

'You're Fenrin,' I said, and I should have been relieved, but somehow the certainty made it worse. If the trickster wasn't inside him, then the darkness was Fenrin's alone.

A sickly, horrified feeling swept over me as I realised that it wasn't over. Our selfishness. Our jealousy, our greed, our fury and violence – it was all still there, lying in wait inside us.

We had banished one trickster, but we could always make more.

The pretty nurse swabbed the tiny wound on Fenrin's arm and taped a piece of gauze over it. Then, eyeing us both, he collected the blood vials, carefully packaging them up, and stood.

'Try to get some rest,' he said to Fenrin. 'Someone will be back to check on you later.'

'Will it be you?' Fenrin gave him a flirtatious smile.

The nurse paused. 'I don't . . . um . . .'

Sensing his discomfort, I hissed at my brother. 'Stop it.'

Fenrin pouted as the nurse took his leave, drawing the curtain quietly across behind him.

'What do you think?' he asked me. 'Reckon he and I have a shot?'

'Fenrin—'

'Oh, I'm bored of that name now. I want a cooler one that's more *me*, you know, really captures my essential spirit. Like our friend River. If she can change her name, I can, too, right?'

'Stop this,' I said.

'Stop what?' He was all mock innocence.

'Pretending like you don't care. We have to face it.'

'Face what? It's all over. Wolf's dead. He died six months ago. Boo hoo.'

'We have to face all the things we've done,' I said. 'All the pain we've caused.'

'Why?' Fenrin asked, entirely calm. 'It's pointless. Everything and everyone dies anyway, so why bother?'

He was right. He was right.

No. I fought the feeling. I could not let us become that. I couldn't give up.

'You have to take responsibility for your mistakes,' I croaked. 'We have to. We can't be allowed to just walk away.'

He leaned towards me. 'Why not?'

Did I imagine that dip and flicker in the strip lighting overhead?

'Because . . .' I stumbled over the words, trying to feel them. 'Because, otherwise it's not fair.'

'The world is not a fair place, Summer. Babies die all the time. What have they done to have their lives snatched away from them? Whole swathes of people are obliterated in wars for no reason at all. Diseases rot everyone.'

My heartbeat stuttered. The skin on the back of my neck tingled as if a spider skittered across it. I raised my hand to brush it off and found nothing. It wasn't a spider. It was the tiny hairs embedded in my skin lifting, responding to the charge in the air.

'It doesn't matter how powerful you are,' he continued, 'or how good you are, because the selfless and the selfish alike, we all die. And for what? What good have human beings ever done the world? What do we offer that is just so special and wonderful?'

'Love,' I whispered.

Fenrin snapped like a winter twig.

The pain I felt was shocking – a sudden, heaving mass. I gasped under its weight, crumpling downward. I knew, in a vague, automatic way, that my hand had shot out to grip the bedrail in front of me, and that it was the only thing keeping me from sinking, weak-kneed, to the floor.

Fenrin's pain. Overwhelming – a valve I didn't know how to shut off.

I felt someone beside me, cool, trembling fingers on my arm. Thalia. Her face was pinched and drawn. We didn't need to talk. She had felt it, too. Fenrin was sucking us in and drawing us down with him. I couldn't not feel it. I couldn't not react. His pain and fury were mine.

Enakelgh.

Just because he wasn't a trickster didn't mean he wasn't dangerous.

And so were we.

I was vaguely aware of a sharp sizzle and a pop from somewhere above me, and then every strip light across the ceiling in the entire ward stuttered and died, leaving us in the kind of dim half-light where everything impossible seemed utterly real.

I sank to my knees under the crushing pressure. I tried . . . I tried to breathe and think of stars, but all I could do was stare at the tiled floor underneath my braced hand as I heard an almighty, word-drowning crash over the surging sound of my pounding heart.

There was movement beyond our curtained world, raised voices. Any minute now someone would come – and what would happen, who would we hurt? The power, the power in the hospital – had we brought it all down, life-support machines ...? Were people dying as we sat here, too wrapped up in our own pain to care about anyone else's?

At that awful, dismaying thought, the weight in my chest eased a little, enough to stop filling my world from side to side.

'Fenrin,' came a small voice.

At the curtain, I could just about make out a girl. A shy, plain thing with clouds of leaf-mould-coloured hair, who nevertheless had always glowed to me like heated metal.

Thalia had sunk to her knees beside me, hands braced on the tiling. Fenrin was hunched over in the bed, looking as if he might explode or puke or possibly both.

River stepped forward willingly into our darkness.

'Stay away,' Fenrin whispered. 'Stay away or I'll hurt you.'

River was shivering. Her delicate bird shoulders shook. 'That's okay. That's okay. I want you to.'

He stared at her strangely. 'What?'

No, I tried to scream, but I couldn't make a sound.

'The Sacrifice,' said River, standing tight and pale at the foot of his bed. Her eyes were on me.

'Remember the card you drew, Summer, just before we went into the cellar? It was about me, after all. Sacrifice magic. You began the ritual that night in the cove, when you said you'd sacrifice me to bring Wolf back. Now's your chance. Do it.'

'No.'

'Come on,' River urged. 'Maybe this is the only way you get him back – haven't you thought of that? Of course you have. I killed him, so I should die. You were right. Don't you remember?'

She was scared. Lines of lightning-blue fear streaked my mind like terror rainbows, but underneath it all coiled a feeling of inky black determination. She meant to see this through. She meant to push him until he broke.

'Shut up,' Fenrin rasped. Anger gathered, pounding through my blood. His, mine, ours.

'Oh come on, you fucking coward!' River snapped, losing patience. 'What are you waiting for?'

'You're just going to stand there and order me to kill you?' Fenrin shouted.

'Yes!'

'Why?!'

'Because I *deserve* it, you idiot!'

For one eternal moment, Fenrin gaped at her in silence. And then he let loose a bitter laugh.

'My god, I hate you,' he said. 'You know why? It's because I don't want you to die. Not you, too. If you go, it'll all be so . . . pointless, I won't be able to stand it. What good will it do? Even if it brings Wolf back, you'll still be dead. Why is that okay?'

'It's nothing to do with okay!' River was all billowing, expanding wrath. 'It's not what's okay, it's what's *right!* It's about punishment! I made a mistake and I haven't paid for it! Don't you see? *This is the only way you get him back.*'

Fenrin lowered his eyes. Weariness was seeping slowly through the cracks in his armour and creeping along his veins.

'You don't know that,' he said. 'None of us do. I don't think we're supposed to be able to resurrect anyone. I don't think the universe will let it happen. It's too much of a violation. He's gone. There's only us left.'

River came around to the side of the bed and leaned aggressively into Fenrin's face.

'Don't you go weak on me now,' she said, gripping the bed rail with white knuckles, her voice rising and rising. 'I killed him!'

Fenrin laughed, the sound more like a sob. 'I know. But I don't want anyone else to get hurt because of us, and neither do you.'

He raised a hand to her and she flinched back, expecting violence and somehow steeled for it – so when he touched her cheek briefly with his fingertips, the surprise dissolved her.

'Don't you do that,' she tried to shout, her voice a knotted, fraying string. 'Don't you forgive me. *Don't you dare forgive me.*'

'No choice,' he said simply. He reached forward again and touched her chin, an awkward brush of his fingers.

The touch seemed to undo her entirely. Her anger crested and broke, falling into shameful stutters, and then she burst into furious, chest-racking sobs. Fenrin leaned out of the bed, slid his arms around her, and pulled her close.

She sank against him and wept into his collarbone.

I was coming to realise that truth was a complicated creature.

River was responsible for Wolf's death, but she was also not, depending on what truth you chose to see about her. Where, then, to lay the blame? On a girl whose fear caused her to lash out uncontrollably for just one moment? How were we any different? Look at all we had done.

Darkness would never go away, but we could learn

not to let it control us. We could learn to be better. Power was supposed to be used to make the world – not just our lives – a better place.

Wolf was gone.

We cried for the boy we had lost. The boy with the lizard tattoo and the wiry frame, who was all awkward angular joints until he hit fifteen. The moody kid who used to mutter in Bulgarian when he wanted to insult someone without them knowing. The boy who, when one hot and sticky summer night we had wound our way to the grove to perform a love charm together, stalked off in a huff before we could complete it because he was too scared of us finding out whom he really wanted. The boy who couldn't bear to see anyone mocked or ridiculed, once pushing a visiting cousin into the river because he wouldn't stop calling Thalia 'goat girl' due to her 'bleating voice and knobby stick legs'. Who had once provoked a laughing fit out of me so severe that I'd sprayed a large mouthful of mashed potato across the entire dinner table and got us both into trouble.

Who had loved, *loved*, tacky Christmas baubles, terrible eighties hair metal and old Hollywood musicals, and who had always grinned from ear to ear whenever he'd made us watch *Hello, Dolly!*, singing along to the songs in the grating voice of someone with all the musical talent of a strangled crow.

That was the way I wanted to remember him: with that wild, unexpected grin that lit him up from the inside, the one rare enough that it felt like a gift every time it surfaced.

The furious, grief-stricken weight was gone. In its place was a flood of sadness, washing out any last traces of poison, leaving in its wake a clean kind of emptiness.

CHAPTER 30

It was late on a Saturday morning, a full month after we had been released from hospital, and the Grace kitchen was in mild chaos.

'Where is the caffeine, please?' said Marcus.

He had turned up at the front door a few minutes ago, looking haggard. I took his arm and guided him gently to the pot.

'Here you go, old man.'

He stared at it dubiously. 'If you made it with two spoons of coffee, our friendship is over again.'

'What blasphemy ... ? Four spoons, Marcus. Always four spoons.'

'Thank you,' he said gratefully. 'My dad's idea of coffee is mildly flavoured water.'

I watched him take a mug and begin, carefully, to pour himself a cup of the hallowed liquid.

'On a scale of one to ten,' I muttered into his ear,

'how high do you feel right now, standing in our house with all of us?'

I watched the corner of his mouth curl. 'About a six.'

I gave a soft whistle. 'Nice.'

'It's getting easier to handle,' he murmured. 'Managed three hours straight with Thalia last night, and I only started feeling weird towards the end.'

'You're getting off light,' I informed him. 'She makes everyone else feel weird within about ten minutes of continued contact.'

Fenrin, overhearing our conversation, paused from his breakfast.

'How late did you guys stay up?' he asked Marcus. Honey dripped from the piece of walnut-stuffed bread he held aloft, landing noiselessly on the table to form a tiny amber puddle.

'We were going over everything to make sure we're as prepped as we can be for tonight,' Thalia said.

'"Going over" everything.' Fenrin air quoted with his free hand.

Marcus flushed. Thalia gave Fenrin a look that should have stabbed him to his chair.

'For your information,' she said, 'planning this kind of thing is incredibly complicated, especially in such a short space of time. We have a lot to do

today, so I would ap[pre]...
minimal sarcasm.'

Fenrin gave her [...]
captain.'

'When's River arrivi[ng...] [...a thread]
of anxiety tracing her voi[ce...] [...we need to]
start soon.'

'In an hour,' I replied. [...]

'Do we even know how m[any people are coming?']
Thalia asked the ceiling desp[airingly.]

'We didn't ask for RSVPs,' I pointed out. 'It's an open house. That was sort of the idea, if you recall. Anyone who wants to come just turns up, no expectations and no pressure.'

'Yes, but that was a stupid idea.'

'It was my idea,' I said, affronted.

'Don't worry,' Fenrin cut in airily. 'No one's going to come so we'll have the food and drink all to ourselves. It'll be grand.'

Thalia glowered at him. 'Stop it.'

They continued to bicker over the whistle of the kettle. Ignoring them both, Marcus sat down and helped himself to the teetering pile of toasted bread products currently adorning the centre of the kitchen table. I sighed and turned away, and as I did I caught sight of our mother outlined in the doorway to the

...s were folded as she silently surveyed

...ings were different now.

The events at the hospital had served as a wake-up call. Where there had been a wall, there was now a curtain, and curtains could be opened. Once the storm of police interviews was over and we had been discharged from the hospital, we made our way home together, silent and bruised.

When we got home, I prepared a spell of my own devising, based on a traditional ritual that had its roots in the most ancient practices.

It required only a few ingredients:

- pale yellow candles for simple truth and new beginnings,
- a large bottle of tequila for loosening tongues, warming hearts, and relaxing minds,
- a plate of lemon slices, for making the tequila taste better,
- a bowl of salt, for making the tequila taste, well, salty, and
- five shot glasses, serving as ritual vessels.

It was a talking spell, and if I may say so myself, it worked spectacularly.

Truth was not a cure but it was a damn good start. Something fundamental had been broken, collapsing the fine webbing of secrets and denial that had caught us all like flies. But walls could be rebuilt and truth was something you constantly had to work at. Luckily, as I kept pointing out just in case no one noticed, I was really, really into the truth. I meant to be a pest about it.

That evening, over the tequila, we told our parents everything that had happened since last summer. They, in turn, told us about the ill-fated night ten years ago when they had formed their own *enakelgh* with Aurelian Guillory to try and bring Iona back from the dead.

To do so, they had shipped us off to cousins up north for a few days, a trip I vaguely remembered, and then together with Aurelian and Miranda, Esther and Gwydion had set out on a windy night to the shepherd's cabin on the moors with Iona's murderer, unbeknownst to them, in their midst.

For whatever reasons, their *enakelgh* hadn't been as strong as ours. They managed to conjure Iona, but they quickly realised that whatever she was, she wasn't Iona. She knew secrets about each of them that no one could know. She tried her hardest to get them all to . . . do things. When I asked what kind of things, Esther would not be pressed.

'Bad things,' she said shortly.

I thought of Angus Morton, Ella Drummond and all the others Wolf's trickster had managed to get its claws into . . . I could imagine what kind of bad things.

Aurelian in particular spent almost all his time by the magical construct's bedside, listening as it whispered into his ear. He was so under its spell that the other three, frightened, made a plan to eliminate it before it could make him do some real damage.

Given what happened with Fenrin, the trickster was likely trying to persuade Aurelian to let it in so it could survive inside him – but he would have needed the rest of his *enakelgh* for that, and the others didn't want to keep a reflection of their basest desires alive as a constant reminder of their capacity for cruelty and selfishness.

Our family had turned away from Aurelian. Ostracised him. Their desire to resurrect Iona might have brought their *enakelgh* together, but it had also torn it apart.

I wasn't going to let the same thing happen to mine.

During the course of our truth-telling evening, the phone rang in the hallway. Gwydion answered it and returned shortly afterwards with the news that Aurelian's body had been positively identified among the burnt remains of his town house. He had died the same way as Iona in the end.

I wondered if Gwydion saw it as poetic justice, but then again it was hard to find any poetry in death by fire. Maybe for him it was simply justice.

To the surprise of no one, Wolf's body was not found. I remembered it liquefying into seawater and soaking into the concrete ground. There was no body to find because he had never come back in the first place.

Gwydion had suggested we spare Wolf's parents the pain of losing him all over again by attempting some kind of spell that might help them forget the last few months. I understood that he was trying to be kind, that perhaps this was his way of trying to forge a new connection with us somehow – but we had refused.

We could no longer hide the mistakes we had made. They knew everything we had done. It was their choice to forgive us or not. I hoped they could, but we would figure out how to live with it either way.

Ignoring my squabbling siblings, I walked over to Esther with a mug of fresh ginger-and-honey tea.

'Tell me honestly,' I said. 'How much are you regretting saying yes to tonight?'

Esther sighed. 'I'm staying out of it. I promised that, and I keep my promises.'

The truest thing she had ever said. The woman had a stubborn streak as wide as the world in which we lived, which was one more thing I was grateful for inheriting from her.

I became aware of her gaze on me.

'You look different,' she said.

'Different how?' I asked cautiously.

Esther shook her head. 'Older, I suppose.'

The irritated ribbons threading through Thalia's voice drew our attention for a moment. She was telling Marcus and Fenrin about the exact ratio of fairy lights that needed to be strung in the branches of the grove trees ahead of tonight, and neither of them was paying her the slightest bit of attention.

Esther's voice was quiet underneath the kitchen chatter. 'Your brother seems to be coping better.'

I regarded her. 'You knew about Fen and Wolf all along, didn't you?'

'You must think we're completely clueless. Of course we knew.'

'Why push Wolf and Thalia together, then?' I dared to ask.

'You know why. The promise between Wolf and Thalia was a very old ritual to join two like-minded families together, and it's safer for you to be with someone you don't love. Love invites the curse.'

'I think that's bullshit,' I said calmly. 'The curse never existed, did it? Not really.' I turned thoughtful. 'See, I've been wondering about this for a while. We're witches. Our desires are our power. We want more than others, and such strong want can so easily turn into obsession. We aren't cursed, we're just dangerous – to others and to one another. Someone back in the day made up the curse, didn't they? Oh, maybe it came from a good place, maybe they were just trying to protect us – and other people from us – but now it's become this hideous self-fulfilling prophecy. Magic is belief as well as desire. We believe in the curse, so we keep it alive.'

Esther was silent so long that I began to think she wouldn't answer me.

'I get such a déjà vu feeling with you, sometimes,' she said eventually. 'You remind me of your aunt Miranda. She has this propensity for digging up family secrets. They always did nothing but hurt.'

'If the secrets would hurt us,' I said, 'then we have a right to know about them.'

'Spoken like a true air witch. Summer, you

don't want ...' She stopped. She was struggling – struggling for the right words, struggling not to misstep. I felt a pang of guilt, chased by empathy. You had to be careful with words – they held so much power. Words transmitted ideas, and ideas could do everything from changing one life to changing the course of history.

Words are one of the world's strongest magics.

'Let's just say,' Esther pronounced carefully, 'that I always believed in *some* kind of curse. In this family, there's not much of a tradition of marrying for love precisely because it so often seems to turn to tragedy. Is it really so bad to want to be safe? What has being in love brought for Fenrin so far? Nothing but pain.'

'And what has the absence of love got anyone in the history of humanity?' I countered. 'Nothing but pain.'

'So your argument is that either way it's all pointless.' Esther smiled humourlessly.

'My argument is that is you risk pain either way, so you might as well choose what will also give you joy,' I offered.

'You'll choose what you want to do,' she said. 'You've made that quite clear, and that's your right. But before you get to adulthood, it's my job to keep you safe. I brought you up the only way I knew how,

382

by protecting you from the truth. If it was the wrong way, I'm sorry. But it was my way.'

Being an adult didn't mean being right. That was what was so terrible about it. You spent your childhood waiting to become an adult; you waited for that moment when everything suddenly made sense, when you fitted like a key into a lock and the doors of the world opened up before you.

But eventually, you looked around and realised that the becoming was a lie. Everyone simply stumbled blindly into adulthood the same way they stumbled blindly through childhood. No one became. That feeling did not exist, and the lie of it got you this far but it could get you no further. This was the revelation waiting for you at the end of that feeling: maybe adults could see further than you ... but they could not see better.

Your mistakes and your choices were yours to make, and yours alone.

I had one question left to ask Esther, but I no longer knew if I should ask it:

Do you love my father?

Maybe the truth was that she didn't let herself love him, for fear of losing him. And in the end, maybe that truth was not mine to have. It belonged to them and I was glad to leave it alone.

I had begun to realise that our parents had whole hidden valleys inside them dedicated entirely to their own selves, apart from their children, apart from their family, even apart from each other. They didn't know everything that there was to know – they could not know our futures because they were busy living their own. My life was mine to shape.

Esther watched the trio at the kitchen table, arguing, downing coffee, spreading toast crumbs everywhere.

'You are all such incredible children,' she said. 'Impossible, rebellious and incredible. I would do it again, despite the mistakes I made.'

Her eyes were clear and bright.

'Everyone makes mistakes,' I offered. 'I'm really good at them. I'm thinking of trying out for the Olympics.'

'Then we're a family of champions,' Esther replied drily. 'I'm not an easy person to like, Summer, I know that. I've never cared about being that. But I need you to believe that everything I do is for you, not against you.' She lifted her chin to the room. 'This house – haven't you ever noticed how it keeps us contained? Why do you think I don't like you leaving it? It's not just us that gets hurt, is it? It's other people. Outsiders.'

That was why the trickster had gone wandering as often as it could – it had wanted to get out of the house. Inside, it had been limited. Outside, with access to the whole town ... I felt ill to picture it wandering through the streets looking for the vulnerabilities in people, which it could use to light a spark and bring their darkest, most poisonous feelings bubbling out.

'You and Thalia and Fenrin are my life,' I heard my mother murmur. 'I can't lose you.'

'You won't,' I said earnestly. 'But there's a chance for it to be different with us. A lot of people want to know us, not hate us, but we don't let them close. They're smart, and curious, and hungry. This whole town is full of witches, people who'd have power at least as strong as ours if only we'd let them use it. There's even someone I'm willing to bet understands magic better than anyone in our whole family.'

Esther frowned. 'Who?'

I inclined my head meaningfully towards Marcus, who was now dipping his crusts into his rapidly cooling mug of coffee and sucking the ends.

'I see,' said Esther.

I struggled to hide a grin. 'Well ... he's more impressive when you get him talking.'

'I'm sure he is.' She gave my hair a stroke and

then disappeared from the doorway, leaving us to our chaos.

Human beings all sucked in various ways – that was a given. Marcus had his complications, but didn't we all? He was also thoughtful, determined, selfless and unbelievably smart, and he had put his life on the line for us. He had become our protector, and he had done it without expectation that we would ever let him in again.

He had his reasons for that – actually it was just the one reason, and the reason was entitled Thalia in big, flashing neon letters. Thalia wasn't as sure as I was about ignoring the curse, but she still ached to risk. Each time she looked at Marcus, the rest of us could feel her complicated emotions rising in her like birds unfurling to take wing.

There were some serious downsides to this whole *enakelgh* thing.

What made one person a witch and one person not?

It was a question that had plagued me my whole life. What did the word *outsider* even mean any more? I had been taught to use it as shorthand for anyone who wasn't like us, but the truth was there were plenty like us, and we were plenty like them. We had come to believe that our troubles began with outsiders, that they were the catalyst for our pain – but this just wasn't true.

No one could tell a witch what to do. We made our own pain.

'Summer,' Thalia called. 'Have you finished breakfast? We have to get started.'

I peeled regretfully away from the doorway.

'Don't let her snappy behaviour fool you,' Fenrin informed the room. 'She's party planning. She's having the time of her *life*.'

Two days ago, Ella Drummond had caught me putting up a small poster outside our form room.

Marcus and I had been doing it all lunchtime, sneaking around and stealth taping in communal areas. You were supposed to ask permission if you wanted to put up any kind of signage in school, and party invitations were always an automatic no, but we figured enough people would see these before they were taken down.

The posters were illustrated with red-and-gold artwork copied from my memory of the backs of the divination cards that had been lost in the fire at Aurelian's house. Within the artwork's circle was a message:

A GATHERING FOR THE CURIOUS

Theme: empowerment

Dress code: the unseen world

When and where: the Grace house, Saturday, 8pm till late

Ella had peered curiously at the poster. Her wheat-gold hair was pulled back into its usual mid-ponytail, and it swung heavily around her shoulders. Her clothes were prim and neat and entirely sexless. She looked no different than before, but I knew her better now.

'How's your mother?' I asked.

She nodded. 'Better. It's not as bad as they thought. Treatable. I guess we'll see.'

'I'm very, very glad.'

She glanced at me, surprised.

'So are you free Saturday night?' I asked, my eyebrows rising suggestively.

Her gaze went back to the poster. 'Is it an invitation to some kind of demonic ritual?'

'Think of it more like a semi-debauched bacchanal.'

Ella shook her head. 'This does not sound like my thing.'

'That's a joke.'

She seemed unconvinced.

'Come anyway,' I teased. 'Know thy enemy.'

Ella just looked at me and drifted off without replying.

Well, I had tried.

The poster boasted the kind of ambiguous wording that might make some people in this town despise us even more. That was okay. One of the greatest strengths of the human race was its diversity. The world did not have to be made up of people who were anything like me or wanted the same things as I did.

Still, I hoped at least a few of them might show, but maybe the damage was done. Well, so what if it was? We would keep on trying to hammer that last nail in the coffins of our curses. Trying and failing made life worth living. Doing nothing did not.

In the meantime, we could still party.

CHAPTER 31

As the evening of the party arrived and the shadows lengthened, a gothic angel sat in front of a tousle-haired demon, finishing off his makeup.

Tonight I had chosen to be all in white, with a classic Summer twist – black jewellery dripped down my chest and black tears of makeup streaked my cheeks. An increasingly demonic Fenrin sat patiently on my desk chair while I traced the curve of his cheekbone with the face-paint pen, sharpening the planes of his face into devastating sweeps, giving him ruby skin and black shadowed eye sockets.

'Handsomest demon there ever was,' I said to him.

He smiled and tapped a curl of hair that I had lacquered into place on my forehead.

'I love you,' he said simply.

I studied him.

You sap, I wanted to say. *I'm very lovable. Stands to reason.*

But instead I said, 'And I love you.'

'Siblings,' whistled a voice outside my door, and Thalia came skating inward.

She was a Frankenstein of costumes, with netting and satin and layers of mismatched fabric, her hair backcombed to threatening levels and twined with delicate vines. One eye was ringed in white, one in green. She looked like a demented forest succubus. She looked fabulous. Complicated and dangerous.

'It's time,' she said. 'We've got two hours before guests start arriving.'

'Three, at least,' Fenrin corrected. 'As if anyone with an ounce of cool ever turns up on time to a party.'

'I happen to believe that punctuality is an admirable quality,' Thalia said.

'I rest my case.'

'Please,' my sister sniffed. 'Like you're cooler than me.'

'Desist,' I cut in. 'This ritual is supposed to be about harmony. Is everything ready?'

Thalia nodded. 'It's all laid out. We just need to collect Marcus and go down.'

'Has the wind dropped?' Fenrin asked. 'It was a bit, shall we say, *tempestuous* earlier on.'

'Like you?' I teased.

He snapped his jaws closed near my fingers with an audible click.

Just after breakfast Fenrin had insisted on going down to the cove by himself. He wouldn't say why but he didn't have to. We knew why he wanted to be there alone.

It was to say goodbye.

I sometimes wondered if our *enakelgh* was still unfolding, still growing, because there were moments when I thought I could feel not only the truth of our present but snatches of our future. Over the months and years, I saw each of us regularly visiting the cove for the same reason. First by ourselves, then in twos, in threes, and then, eventually, all together. We'd go there to talk, to drink, to be silent, and to laugh. We'd go there to celebrate, to work up charms, and just to hang out. We'd go there to live.

Living was the way we would honour him.

This evening, we would go for the first time as one.

We put the finishing touches to our outfits and made our way down to the cove.

It was wild tonight, the sea turned to churning

froth by the winds, but inside the cave, the outside world fell away into calm. The cave was a hairline, a delicate slit in the cliff face that reared up on our side of the Dragon's Teeth. It was nothing much from the outside, but inside it widened to a dry, protected area big enough for a small group of people.

We worked candles into the sand, candles of every colour, of every feeling and thought. They were arranged in two rough circles. One fenced the outside of the group, and the smaller one circled the objects that were placed on a red cloth in the middle of our cross-legged gathering: Thalia's athame – a ritual knife with a pretty mother-of-pearl handle – and an unopened bottle of wine from our cellar, together with a delicate glass cup.

My eyes fell on Marcus, his eyes huge and glassy in the warm light. Thalia had streaked his hair back for the party tonight, spraying it with a sea-storm indigo dye, and the effect pointed his delicate features into razor-sharp arrows to give him a predatory air. It was startling and pleasing.

I picked my way carefully over the candle rings and sat to Thalia's left, with Marcus taking my left. A moment later, Fenrin and River came up from the shoreline together and entered the cave. I saw the briefest touch of their fingers before they parted, as if taking reassurance from each other. River settled to Thalia's right, and Fenrin settled in between River and Marcus.

The five of us aligned with the points on a pentagram. On a human being. On a star. It was Aurelian's cellar pentacle that had given us the idea. Who said there had to be only four elements within *enakelgh*? Rules were made to be broken, especially by witches.

It seemed to me that if an *enakelgh* could be inadvertently created by a traumatic event, as ours was, it could also be purposefully created for better, less selfish reasons. If we set out with good intentions, the chances of us creating anything like another trickster would be so much lower. Not quite gone, never quite gone, because the human heart is a passionate, unpredictable thing. You can never rule out selfishness, not completely.

The trick is simply to try.

Silence settled over us. In the background the sea crashed, a comforting, never-ending sound.

'Okay,' said Thalia, her voice echoing over the cave walls. 'Let's start. Marcus?'

He looked up, startled. 'Yes?'

'You designed the ritual,' she coaxed gently. 'Take us through it?'

He cast around, cleared his throat.

'We start with earth, the grounded point, the beginning and the ending of life. Earth opens up the bottle and pours the wine into the cup. Then each of us around the pentagram cuts their forefinger and holds it over the cup until it catches a drop. Then we state our position and pledge. Then we drink.'

As he talked he grew visibly calmer, going through the details in his head. The ritual helped to focus, like working through an instruction manual. Method cleared the mind of all else.

'This,' said Fenrin, 'could really be gross.'

'The athame has been fully sterilised, none of us are diseased, and you're not going to taste a few drops of blood,' Thalia said, serene in the face of her twin's unrelenting personality.

We faced one another. Glances were shared and swapped. Something was growing in the space between us – something like belief and something like determination – connecting us up as it went.

Thalia closed her eyes. Marcus closed his. Fenrin, with a glance around the group, did the same. I thought I caught River's gaze flickering on me once like a nervous bird before she closed hers.

I was the last.

The landscape around us crept into the rest of my

senses. I heard the soft roar and drag of the sea first, like a long, slow heartbeat.

Crescendo and crest.

Crescendo and crest.

The cry of a gull far overhead. The rifling of dune grass in the wind, a sigh from the land. A rabbit scratching at the sandy earth. And closer, now, closer in. The soft sizzling of the burning candle wicks. The breathing of the group, which began to swell in my ear and block out everything else, until all I could feel was them.

I waited for that perfect moment, that feeling I now realised I chased in different ways but always with the same goal, a feeling of losing myself, like I sat inside a moment that never ended. Like I was drunk on life and made of stars.

I opened my eyes.

With careful, sure movements, Thalia leaned in, picked up the athame in our centre and used its edge to cut through the wax seal on the wine bottle's glass neck. She peeled off the wax in strips until the cork head was exposed, then she gave it a sharp twist, spiralling with her grip until it came free. Next she poured until the glass cup was mostly full.

Her hands were our focus, the centre of our

current world, hands that belonged to all of us in that moment, hands that felt like ours as well as hers, hands that took up the athame and dug the point into her forefinger. She didn't flinch. She pinched her finger gently over the cup until a drop gathered into fatness and fell into the wine. Then she pulled the cup back and swirled it, her wrist circling.

Then Thalia spoke, the little cave ringing with her voice, the only one of us who had said anything for what felt like hours, a lifetime of sorts.

'I'll be earth,' she said. 'Earth and protection.'

Thalia the earth witch.

The athame was offered handle-first to me. I took it, feeling its weight.

It was just a knife.

But when it was given purpose, it became something more. It could be as the wielder saw fit. A tool for cutting, an act of destruction – or freedom. This was magic. The will of the witch, applied for good or bad. As simple and as powerful as that.

I brought my hands together and pushed the tip of the athame into the pad of my right forefinger. Thalia leaned forward and held the cup underneath until a drop of blood was caught in its depths.

'I'll be air,' I said. 'Air and truth.'

Summer the air witch.

Marcus took the athame from me. His eyes floated up to Thalia, but she gave him nothing. It was his choice. He pressed the tip into his finger. His teeth showed in a wince, quickly swallowed. He held his finger over the cup as I held it steady.

'I'll be fire,' he said. 'Fire and curiosity.'

Marcus the scholar.

He passed the athame handle-first to Fenrin and took the cup, holding it ready. Fenrin worked the knife tip into his finger until the skin split, and he shook out a drop into the cup.

'I'll be water,' he said in a low voice. 'Water and courage.'

He offered the athame handle-first to River and held the cup for her.

'I'll be spirit ...' She faltered. Her eyes dropped to the knife before her, running down the length of its blade. Its edge seemed to keep her together. Her voice hardened. 'I'll be spirit and redemption.'

The cup was passed from hand to hand, mouth to mouth, until we were all connected by it. We drank. It tasted like earth and plums and salt and thick, dark syrup. Apple and rain.

'It's done,' said Thalia.

We looked at one another, trading glances back and forth.

'What happens now?' said Marcus, his eyes wide in expectation.

Thalia hugged herself, looking suddenly unsure. 'I guess we'll find out.'

'I don't know if it'll be sudden, like last time, or gradual,' I admitted. 'I don't know how we'll tell.'

'I feel ...' River paused. 'Strange. I don't know. Exhausted.' She shivered.

'So do I,' Fenrin muttered. 'Like I've been awake for days.'

There was no need to say it – we all felt the same. The ritual's completion had scattered the energy we'd carefully built between us. Now all we had was a drained and lifeless aftermath.

'I wonder what we should do now,' I mused.

Fenrin let out a deep sigh. 'I want to be with lots of people,' he said. 'I want to get lost in them.'

So we did.

The candles were blown out and carefully stored in the wicker boxes we had brought our supplies in, along with the athame and wine. The boxes could be collected tomorrow since this was our place.

As we left the cove, talking quietly, and made our way up the slope to the dunes, I felt the old Summer leave me, a ghost on the air. Each event that happened, each action we took and feeling we felt remade us over and over, shucking off old versions of us in our wake like snake skins.

None of the Graces of last year were ever coming back.

It was a good, exciting thing.

CHAPTER 32

As we walked, River dropped back to walk beside me, leaving the others to pull away from us.

We climbed the dunes in silence, helping each other over the steepest part. River's hand was cool in mine. Always cool. My palms tended to sweat like grilling bacon.

'Do you think I'll end up like him?' she said, after a moment.

I didn't have to ask who she meant.

Aurelian was the only other spirit witch I had ever heard of. It would be strange not to compare herself to him. They had both been very good at hiding their true selves. They had both allowed their obsessions to get the best of them and cause the death of another. Aurelian had been closer to his darkness than River – he had planned a murder, after all – but not by that much.

Those similarities, though, were surface at best. They were not the things that mattered.

The choices they had made. That was what mattered.

'It's impossible,' I responded. 'For a start, you have me looking out for you, making sure you don't turn all psychotic. So if you start feeling murderous, you just let me know.'

'You'll know,' she said.

Enakelgh.

I put a hand on her arm to stop her.

'It goes both ways,' I said. 'I've had ... bad thoughts. I've done shitty things. I've wanted to do worse things than you have to other people, sometimes. And I wonder if you can ever get rid of those impulses, or whether you just have to live with them.'

'Heart versus head. Desire versus wisdom,' she said.

I gazed at her, my heart swelling.

'I'm not in love with you,' I blurted.

River stopped on the path, looking everywhere but me.

I began to babble. 'I thought I was for a while. But I do love you, as if you're my sister. I never say it to people and I need to say it more. I'm saying it now. So you know. And if you don't love me back, that's okay.'

She was shivering. I hoped it was from the wind.

'Whatever it is I feel, I only know that I feel,' she said at last, 'and that's because of you. You showed me how not to be afraid of it. You never stopped coming after me, this whole time. You're my courage.'

'And you're mine, River.'

'It's Morgan,' murmured the girl in front of me.

I studied her. 'You're sure?'

'I think I need to stop pretending. It's the name my mother gave me.'

'It's a good name.'

Morgan smiled.

I took her hand gently, and we began to walk again.

Everything had seemed so insurmountable just a few weeks ago, but now . . . now I had my *enakelgh*. I had a wall to put my back against, and it made all the difference in the world.

'Holy shit,' Thalia breathed. She was up ahead of us. 'Guys, look.'

Our house was packed to the rafters with people.

We could see the press of bodies inside through the conservatory's glass windows. Music hummed over the human buzz. It was hard to recognise anyone from the outside – the crowd was a wild menagerie of masked and painted faces. People dressed as fairies and ghosts, angels, demons, sprites, gods of love and death and desire. The masks would help to shift tonight out of the everyday. Protected by a mask or a character, you could be brave. You could become anything. You were free from yourself.

Heads turned our way like owls peering out through the windows. We had been spotted. We walked together across the paved stones of the courtyard and entered the house through the back door, making our way through the throng.

There was Gemma dressed all in white, a pair of tattered fairy wings on her back. There was Lou, her hair a violent blue and spiked into dizzying peaks. Niral, looking incredible in slick black lipstick and lenses that gave her slitted snake eyes. There was – dear lord – Jase Worthington, his face half obscured by a plastic ghost mask. Ella Drummond, ethereal in gauze and mother of pearl sequins. There were more, far more people than I'd ever dreamed would come.

Tonight was an experiment. The biggest magic we had ever attempted.

As the party thrived, the presence of this new blood, this new generation of witch, would expand throughout the house and fill up its dark spaces. Spreading, infecting, pushing cursed Grace spirits back into the walls as they went, and unfolding their own in place. It might not last forever – the spirits in this house were old and had been here a long time, long enough to grow their roots right in – but maybe it would be enough to change things for the better.

What made one person a witch and one person not? I thought I knew now: a witch is someone who cannot help but burn up with both curiosity and desire.

So many people think magic isn't real. This, I know for certain, is not true. Magic can be found everywhere and often if you go after it and don't wait for it to find you. In those kinds of moments, the universe seems to make complete and utter sense; everything is connected and alive.

They are few and far between, these magical moments that make us ache fiercely, hard to create and even harder to sustain. Each moment is finite – they have to be, since a thing that goes on forever is a thing you can no longer call special.

So happiness cannot be a constant – but then neither can pain, and though in its midst it feels like it will last forever, this is always a lie. There is no happiness without pain, no love without hate, no power without consequence. One highlights the other and makes you aware of each. They are connected, twinned forever. If you want one, you get both.

There are no do-overs, and there is never any going back. But there is always forwards because the world keeps going, always forwards, and you can go with it. If you want, if you have the courage.

You'll have scars. No getting around that. But then scars, I have decided, make you more interesting anyway. Who wants to be perfect? Perfection is complete. Perfection is closed. Perfection, then, is death. Much better to be changeable, improvable, a constant open.

We are none of us either good or bad, but curious and wild.

Joyful and unafraid.

On the night of the gathering at our house, a highly unusual proliferation of magical things happened across the entire town.

They were as follows:

- One hundred and twenty-four people said, 'I love you.'
- Four hundred and eleven people said, 'I'm sorry,' and they were forgiven.
- Fifty-six people said, 'I'm sorry,' and they were not yet forgiven, but the apology provided the release that people needed.

- Two male priests from different religions snuck away together late that evening and eloped.
- Thirteen people in thirteen separate houses stopped whatever they were doing at 11.13 p.m. precisely and broke into song. Each of them sang the lyrics to 'The Witch' by the Cult. It was not playing on any local or national radio station at that time.
- Five people left their partners when they realised they would never be loved to the same degree that they loved.
- Six people got engaged.
- Fourteen children were conceived.
- Three hundred and twenty-seven people dreamed of being at the party of their lives.
- Ninety-one people looked up at the full moon at different times and realised that the world is an extraordinary place.
- Four hundred and fifty-five people had dreams of meeting a dead loved one again and laughing with them so hard that they woke up the next morning with aching ribs.
- Finally, one entirely impromptu dance-off

happened at The Gull, the pub on the beach, between a local farmer who walked with a cane due to a twenty-year-old hunting incident and a young accountant who had come down for the weekend to visit family. The farmer was unanimously declared the winner, and after that night, he never walked with the cane again.

ACKNOWLEDGEMENTS

This book simply would not exist without the following people. My heartfelt thanks go to:

Alwyn Hamilton – for your readiness to wine/prosecco our way through life trials, plot problem-solving like a total boss, and most importantly, being an amazingly supportive and talented friend.

Katherine Webber – for your beautiful and infectious energy, your unwavering excitement, your writing day hosting skills, and most importantly, being an amazingly supportive and talented friend.

Samantha Shannon – for your wonderful and steadfast loyalty, those Costa sessions together, our shared bond over iced coffee, and most importantly, being an amazingly supportive and talented friend.

Anne Heltzel and Alice Swan – for your perseverance and faith in me. I have never doubted your commitment to have this be the best book it could possibly be.

Jeff Zentner – my musical twin. Your recs got me through some hardcore deadlines, and your friendship is very important to me.

Jay Kristoff and Sarah Lemon – not only do you both have fabulous music taste but you are fantastic humans, and I wish I could spend more time with you in person. Hopefully someday soon!

Susan Dennard – for your willingness to support a stranger. Thank you for your candidness and kindness.

Laini Taylor, Jim Di Bartolo and Clementine – for the French castle, but really for being generous, clever and joyful. You inspire me.

Ioannis – for being one of the most exceptional humans I'll ever have the privilege of knowing.

The following bands – All Them Witches, Ritual Howls, Cold Cave, Drab Majesty, A Perfect Circle and Nine Inch Nails. You're part of the fabric of this book, and of me. I'm so grateful for your music.

And finally, to the readers. Your messages always mean the world to writers, especially when the going gets tough. Never doubt the impact your support makes. Thank you!